BEST CANADIAN STORIES 2020

BEST CANADIAN STORIES

2020

EDITED BY

PAIGE COOPER

BIBLIOASIS

WINDSOR, ONTARIO

FIRST EDITION
ISBN 978-1-77196-362-6 (Trade Paper)
ISBN 978-1-77196-363-3 (eBook)

Edited by Paige Cooper
Cover and text designed by Gordon Robertson

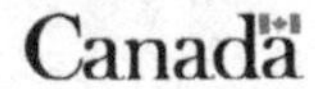

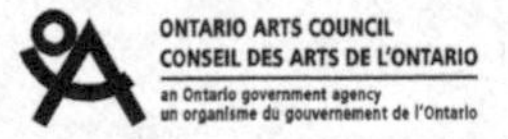

Published with the generous assistance of the Canada Council for the Arts, which last year invested $153 million to bring the arts to Canadians throughout the country, and the financial support of the Government of Canada. Biblioasis also acknowledges the support of the Ontario Arts Council (OAC), an agency of the Government of Ontario, which last year funded 1,709 individual artists and 1,078 organizations in 204 communities across Ontario, for a total of $52.1 million, and the contribution of the Government of Ontario through the Ontario Book Publishing Tax Credit and Ontario Creates.
PRINTED AND BOUND IN CANADA

CONTENTS

INTRODUCTION

Paige Cooper

Once, eight years ago, late on a breezy spring afternoon, I was in the bath reading an anthology not unlike this one. This was during the brief period in my personal history where I owed several hundred thousand dollars on a clapboard house beside a freight railyard. The house, recently renovated in a dim, pretty, heritage-adjacent sort of way, was near the city centre and had a lilac bush in its yard, but was unlivable by local standards because it lacked a garage. The bathroom was the house's sunniest room—the walls blue, the sky blue, the clawfoot tub new and plastic—and I'd tied back the curtains my mother had proudly sewn in order to better feel like I was happy.

I'd been infectious with an acute and inscrutable misery for several years, by that point, the onset traceable pretty much to the morning after signing the mortgage. "Only thirty-three more years of this," I'd promise myself, as I walked the rescue dog through the gentrifying industrial park, spritzed diluted vinegar at baseboards, vacuumed gravel out of the car. The dog ate organic meat patties and rightly preferred my partner, who tenderly prepared them for her, to me.

That afternoon in the bath—perhaps it was a weekend, or perhaps this was after I'd been laid off, and the mortgage was becoming not just oppressive but alarming—the short story I read was written in a measured, mournfully wry third person. It involved a dog, a divorce, and a relocation to an ill-lit, polar place. It was wistful, maybe a little escapist—in the way of stories, like this one, where the comforts are secure and the financial concerns are theoretical—and I proceeded gamely along until, at the very end, at the very last word, the writer of the story switched from third into a brutal, wondering second—*you*.

I splashed in my plastic tub, affronted and exposed. The story had nothing to do with me, until it did. I flipped to the note at the back of the book: it had been written during the writer's month-long residence in Riga, Latvia; a place I doubt I'd ever actively imagined until that moment. By fall, the garageless house with its sunny bath and lilac bush was someone else's, my ex-partner and ex-dog had a new place of their own, and I was alone with a rook-gutted pigeon carcass on my snowy windowsill in darkling Riga, where I belonged.

I'm not sure whether this anecdote—sterilized of certain distracting but relevant factors that I'd be likelier to include if this were fiction—is meant to horrify, annoy, caution, or inspire. But what is pertinent is that an annual short story anthology "changed my life." Not in the sense of enabling some personal seasonal foliage swap, or an acceleration of the inevitable, but in the sense that it added an entirely new constellation to the firmament, with resultant mid-course navigational chaos. Did I tell the people of my life, as I dismantled what had up to then seemed geologically scaled, that a short story was responsible for the upset? Did I tell them I'd been moved—moved thousands of miles out of a life and into a new one that would be scarier, lonelier, poorer for quite a long while—by an interesting formal choice made by a stranger? Did I give them the story to read for themselves? No. It was too strange, and I was new to strangeness, or at least to admitting it.

I tell you this because over the past few months, as I read for this volume and chose the stories included here, I approached the task with all the caution of someone who could be responsible, at least partially, for someone's imminent and irremediable personal cataclysm—for yours.

Selecting these stories I visited the usual stations: print magazines; online magazines; a public call in the form of a tweet; the occasional private solicitation. It was not a scientific or objective system, but I read as widely as I was able. Locating recent French short stories translated even more recently (the rule here being that these stories ought not to have appeared in book form in 2019) required help from several translators, writers, and publishers in Quebec, to whom I'm grateful. I am grateful as well to the editors and readers of the literary magazines I reviewed, whose labour does not generate profit for shareholders, and is therefore unquantifiably generous.

I'd also note that my approach to the definition of "Canadian" was embarrassed, given that—at least up until the borders started closing in March—I'd smugly enjoyed filing Canada's nationhood in the back stacks alongside craft beer, reality television, household firearms, the Crusades, and public yoga: a source of great comfort and catharsis to some, but needless suffering for everyone else. In the spreadsheet where I tracked my reading, I typed: *I make a shitty border guard.*

Obviously I am interested in writing about place; setting, landscape, the ultra-detailed and irreducible local. This seems more primary and difficult to me than many other abstractions, including whatever we mean when we say "character." But thoughtless, constant access to the internet means I spend a lot of time thinking in an anonymous, globalized un-place. For instance, if I spend enough time on Twitter, an unwieldy notion like "Canada" starts to look more and more like an arbitrary collection of highways, opinions, atrocities, and resource extraction companies adorned with a lumpy healthcare system and competent branding. Landscape, in this mode, falls under branding, of course;

borders fall under opinion or atrocity. But, on the other hand, this is the year the prime minister shuffled out of his isolation cottage to gaze into the camera and intone, "Canadians, it's time to come home,"—and I did, despite myself. I waited with my passport at the gate, and I eyed the jittery crowd lining up for JFK next door; instead of my usual mild envy, I pitied them. I feared what their country might do to them.

By virtue of timing, the stories in this anthology illuminate some of what writers in, or around, or peripherally tied to Canada, or the notion of Canada, were thinking about before this moment stumbled us. These stories are concerned with the opioid crisis, climate crisis, police violence, patriarchy, intolerance, family, money, sex, mortality, hypocrisy, ancestry, aesthetics, art. These concerns haven't disappeared; if anything they've been compressed and made explosive. But what remains true, as it does every year, is that what we imagined yesterday is different than what we'll imagine henceforth.

Reading through these stories on my first pass—during a series of windowless, late-night winter baths in a different cheap, plasticky tub—I thought I knew what I didn't want. I had my suspicions about taste; certainly my own seemed vain and fleeting, borderline astrological, somewhat fatal. (*Spare me the sick parent story*, I typed into my spreadsheet the day before my father called to tell me about the tumour in his throat.) But whatever my desires for content or subject—interpellate me, transport me, etc.—I honoured my gut when it came to execution. I looked, ideally, for sentences that had been starved down and built back up into golems that obey and resist their makers. I generally wanted, in terms of language, a sense of what had been excluded and suppressed: maximalism can't afford to be any less picky than minimalism. Because no matter what a story is on its surface, we are here to gander at its subconscious. (In my spreadsheet I also typed, equally prophetic and stupid: *I am so sick of knowing what's happening*.)

My primary requirement for the stories I selected was that they possess a secret capacity or consciousness—be it emotional, intellectual, political, linguistic, whatever—like when the grocer touches the back of your hand because you are weeping again, or the painting over the fireplace remains turned to face the wall for the duration of your visit. Yes, I love to be consoled or cajoled with the sound of my own name, by which I mean the pleasure of seeing my very own special self in a stranger's prose, but that capacity must be surprising enough that it stutters me to a halt, or I am unsatisfied. Defamiliarization—the Russian formalist Viktor Shklovksy's term—describes what I would want done to me, if someone were to ask: a sunny day for a pandemic; a metaphor that turns back to bite itself; a wrong aphorism; a love letter read over the phone by a messenger; a heartbreak; a hangover; jetlag; jargon.

Today, as I write to you from vernal isolation, it's not unlikely that you are reading this in one species of defamiliarization, or another. We are learning to describe a world that most realists (American, Canadian, perhaps even Socialist) would've waved off as fantastical, histrionic, *a tad genre*, a month or two ago. You line up outside the grocery store. Police officers lean into your car and ask how you're feeling. A woman gets arrested for going for a walk. A man sneers at your mask and swerves across the sidewalk to cough on you.

But it must also be evident, at this point, that defamiliarization—narrative or linguistic—was not my only selection criteria, as noble as it is. Because, as I progressed, it turned out there are too many good short story writers in this country: writers with a high tolerance for ambiguity, that not only accept gaps but revel in them, and have the generosity to let something chthonic crawl in.

So I narrowed the vise further, added a selfish requirement that interests me as a writer but might be inconsequential to many readers. I wanted stories that were difficult to write. That demonstrate what Christa Wolf called "moral courage on the part of the author—the courage to risk self-knowledge." I wanted the stories that my soul said could not have been made without exacting some toll from their maker. Labour; pain; deep thinking; Sisyphean imaginative muscle; a mothly instinct towards explicit, immolating honesty. I wanted blood to be spent; evidence of collapse, of that grating, unwilling metamorphosis that occurs when time passes in mortal lives.

As I've drafted this essay, the world has been made progressively stranger, which is another way of saying our sense of reality has been expanded. The ways in which people resist reality—using denial, or delusion; or else lovingly, humanely, with sweetness and honest rage—indicates to me that reading fiction isn't just a rarified aesthetic affectation, but an act of imaginative malleability that feeds resilience. What do I mean? That there are those of us who are frozen, holding still until the familiar carapace returns to us unchanged—waiting for our daughter to come back to us from the far end of the empty parkette—but there are also those of us who are paying careful, stunned attention to how she is never the same, moment to moment, how our daughter is and has always been a sussuration of unpredictable sparks. Of course, I am describing a false binary: we are all both waiting and watching; we are all always both invested in the surface and the core. But, since paying attention is the process whereby fiction describes reality's various layers, no matter the constrictions or unreliability of such, I am suggesting we err on the side of constant witnessing.

The more evident the expanding depth and breadth of our realities, the more rigorous the duties of our imaginations: first, we have to imagine our new reality in order to understand how to be in it, and then we have to do that for every person we know, and every person we don't know, and the nonhuman natural world, and maybe some objects and hyperobjects and systems, and then, after all that, we must also imagine the future of this new reality without, hopefully, feeding the collective's ambient anxiety. It's exhausting work, and provoking. But you, the reader of an introductory essay in an annual anthology of short fiction, have been equipped for this, somehow. I'd venture that it is possible that the defamiliarizing aspects of fiction—not the tranquilizing escapism, not the personal identification (*you*), or the didactic "humanizing," or the empathetic universality of the closely-observed detail in our daughter's sentimental playground—have given us a capacity to expand our notion of reality to include ourselves as we are, not just as we thought we were. And all this while we remember that a knowable person, like a knowable world, is the unbelievable thing.

Like meeting a stranger, much of the pleasure of a story is its unknown power. The right story, at the right time, if you happen to be open to it, if you have a need, maybe a desperate one, to be moved outside yourself, can perhaps move you so far outside of yourself that you will not consider going back to who you were thirty minutes ago, before you started following this line of narrative with its inexplicable relevance and corollary power. Because, also like meeting a stranger, a story contains the risk that you may be touched, that you may suffer or feel pleasure, that the effects might play out over the course of years, a decade, and also that, by the end (if there is one), you might have become unrecognizable to the person who read the story to begin with. This is what I mean when I say a story can be a cataclysm. And if a cataclysm is a particularly terrifying prospect, right now, have courage. Because there are other possibilities; they are nearly infinite. And sometimes when you meet a stranger all that happens is you fall in love.

BEST CANADIAN STORIES
2020

THE GAS STATION

Souvankham Thammavongsa

Mary believed there were two kinds of people in the world. There were those who were seen and those who were not. Mary considered herself the latter.

She hadn't lived in the town for long, only a few months. It was known for its beaches. It swelled with tourists during the summer and then was quickly abandoned. There was no bar or café open by summer's end. She liked the town empty.

Mary preferred her own company. She was thirty-six years old, living, with no pets, in a small house painted white. It was one of many white houses in the neighbourhood, painted that way because of the intensity of the sun. The one she lived in had a flat roof. It wasn't a place that needed to deal with snow. Or cold. She didn't know they still made houses this small. She didn't know who owned it. She wrote her cheques to a corporation that was just a bunch of numbers. Her wardrobe was two black pencil skirts, one black jacket, and two black blouses, one short-sleeved and one long-sleeved. The house had one of everything. One bedroom, one bathroom and one kitchen. Each room had one window in it, all of which looked out onto the same pine tree. It was not a pleasant sight.

What was a pleasant sight was the man who worked at the gas station. She saw him there, but they never talked. He had a terrible reputation. Something about him taking in women and leaving them, always, wailing in the street below his window, begging. Mary wondered what he did to make them lose themselves that way. And whether it would happen to her.

Mary worked from home. She was an independent accountant. During the tax season she often found work at a clinic or some pop-up arrangement, or sometimes clients came to her. She had many types of clients. They all surprised her with their needs and problems, but her favourites were the ones who had to explain what had happened to the person they filed with the previous year. Their husband, their ex, their other person. In this way, she saw every stage of love. The giddiness at having found each other, the boredom of having been together, the anguish of separation. This was how you lived a full and human life. It was like a play acted out in front of her. She spent her days listening to people describe how things had fallen apart. Did they see it coming?

One client Mary never forgot. She worked for the government. She was a redhead with large blue eyes. She booked and rebooked her appointment on the phone and then finally arrived. Her ex wanted to claim the childcare expenses, but she was the one who paid them. Mary looked at her papers laid out on the table and advised her that since they were not together, and the child lived with her, it was her right to claim the expenses.

The other woman's eyes welled with tears and they began to fall one right after the other. Mary started with the 1040. She made sure to leave blank the box that asked for $3 to go to the presidential election campaign. She filled in exemptions, calculated total income, then adjusted gross income. This went on for quite some time. Mary filling in the lines, and the woman and her tears. The woman apologized. "I've been with incredible men," she said. "Men who really loved me and cared for me. And appreciated me. But he, he was the only one." It sounded like a cheap old country song. "I had been told I couldn't have a baby. Given my age. I didn't give it much thought. So when I got together with him, I wasn't thinking. And then suddenly I'm pregnant. After all the tests, the pills. He's the father of my child." Mary did not say anything. She was filling out the forms.

*

The gas station was on the edge of town, before you hit the interstate. It was bright green like a tennis ball. Easily spotted from miles away. This was where he worked. The gas station man. He came out to pump the gas. He was not beautiful, but she liked looking at him. *Grotesque* seemed right to describe him. It was not yet spring. The white sand in the town still glimmered. The ocean still swelled, wave after wave crashed into shore. There was a chill in the air, but he was shirtless. He had hair all over his chest. Like pubic hair. Messy and wet and shining. It was inappropriate to walk around like that.

From inside the car, Mary pushed the button that unlocked the door to the gas tank. She watched him in the mirror where there was a note of warning that said objects in mirror were closer than they appeared. He knew what to do. He came over and pushed aside the door, reached his hand in, and twisted the lid. Mary knew it opened to a little hole. He turned, pressed a few buttons on the machine, brought over the pump, and pushed the nozzle in. Mary could hear the oil, how it rushed in, eager and desperate. It took a while to fill that voluminous tank. He came over to the driver's side and she opened the window just a slit. She ironed out the wrinkles on a bill with the warmth of her palms. She pressed on the side with that old man's face, and pressed again on the reverse on the image of a white building. All the money was green. It was easy to give away the wrong denomination. She checked all four corners for the number fifty, to be sure. The bill came out of the window like a tongue and he grabbed an edge. Mary drove away before he could give her back her change.

*

The town did not encourage much walking around. There were no sidewalks, only grassy ditches along the road. Most people drove pickup trucks, and at interstate speed. Every bank had a drive-through window. The tax deadline was approaching and Mary relied on being noticed. It would take some time before anyone did. She had to set up her office in a public place early this year, get a head start, especially in a town like this. Besides, she could use the money. She worked out a deal with the manager of the community centre to let her set up her office there, in front of the library. She brought in a foldable desk and put out her sandwich-board sign. She looked around and thought it was the perfect place. There was a lot of foot traffic. There was a pool and a gym, too.

She saw the gas station man. His whole body was covered up. The only flesh she could see was his hands and his head. She wondered who was at the gas station now that he was here. He was checking out a book from the library. She saw it from the back but couldn't tell what book it was. He noticed her sitting at her desk and came over and said, "Hey, can I ask you some questions?" He had on large black-framed glasses. They looked too big for him. His eyes were grey or blue. It was hard to tell. There was glass in the way. And while she was trying to determine their colour, he was seeing all of her. Most people stared at a detail of her face or at the wall behind her. To be in someone's gaze was something more.

Even before she answered his question, she did not like how he used that first word. *Hey*. As though she were some hole in the wall you could just stick your questions into.

"You have to make an appointment!" she yelled. There was fury in her voice. She pulled down her skirt, which had been creeping up, showing too many details of her legs. The ankles and their bony joints, the muscled curve of her back legs, the rough patches of her knees, and the area above that did not tan. He laughed.

"Okay then. Can I do that?"

When she turned to look at her schedule, he had taken the seat in front of her. He continued with his questions. "There's no one here." He looked around. It was true, but she was a professional. He couldn't just walk up to her and take up her time as though it were free.

"I am a professional, sir," she said. "Professionals take appointments."

He seemed amused. "I never met anyone like you."

She did not know whether that statement was a compliment. She decided it was an observation. An observation of a fact. Well, working at the gas station, how could you? she thought.

"Oh. I get it. Dressed in black. Death and taxes," he said.

She ignored his comment. She handed him her business card and said, "How is nine o'clock tomorrow morning?"

"But I'm here now."

"That's correct, sir."

"What's the problem then?"

"No problem. As I said, you don't have an appointment."

He kept pushing.

"We're done here," Mary said, making a small circle in front of her with a finger, a boundary that needed to be drawn.

He put his hands up, as if preparing for an arrest, and said, "Ma'am. I like you. Sharp. Real tough. I'll see you tomorrow." And he walked out.

Mary drove home that night, glad she didn't have to go by the gas station. On purpose, she drove over three bumps in the road. She made sure she went slowly, so she could feel the rise and rise, rise and fall, of the car. The bounce was more pronounced at a slower speed. Her eyes looking up at the ceiling, her jaw loose and open. At high speeds you couldn't feel anything at all.

She didn't make anything to eat. She wasn't hungry. She took a shower, washed her hair, and polished her only pair of shoes. She read a book that had belonged to her as a little girl. It was about a monster. It wasn't scary at all. She had played both parts. The beauty and the beast. Mary loved being the beast. She could roar and pound at her chest and no one ever said that was not how a little girl should be. She could be ugly and uglier and even more ugly. She threw the book across the room. It left a dark mark on the wall, like a bruise. To be a monster, a beast of some kind. Watching everything shudder, down to the most useless blade of grass.

*

The next morning, Mary smoothed out her black hair, put on makeup, dabbed some lipstick onto two fingers and patted them on her cheeks. She spread this same colour on her lips. She wore black. One of her black pencil skirts and the long-sleeved blouse.

It was 8:15 when she arrived. The sky was a long unbearable lump of grey and there was rain all over everything. When she walked up to the community centre, the sliding doors parted. It made her feel like some god parting the ocean. Sometimes, when she thought no one was looking, she spread her arms dramatically out to the sides.

Instead of going to her desk, she went to the bathroom. It was clean and bright with lots of room. You could smell the bleach. She sat down on the counter next to the sink and pulled her skirt up to her thighs, spread her legs apart, and arched her back. She closed her eyes. She brought a finger to her mouth and her teeth clutched it there, muffling a moan of pleasure. The fluorescent lights were unflattering.

She went to take her seat and opened her laptop, looking at her list of appointments. The gas station man had an ordinary name. If you looked him up in a phone book, his name would take up several pages. Everyone knew at least one person who had that name.

A brown suit came into view, something definitely from a second-hand store. The lapels were wide. It belonged in a different time and to a different person. It was sad.

"I have an appointment," he said.

"Take a seat." Mary rested her elbows on the desk and interlaced her fingers. He asked his questions and was gone.

That afternoon, she stepped out into the rain and tried to look for something familiar, to steady herself. Everything was wet and muggy. She stepped back underneath the awning and noticed a little mound of dirt. Ants. At the centre of that mound was an entrance and an exit, efficient. Everything in one place. She hated that it was closed off to her peering. That world of work, their little secrets of living together and lifting things greater than themselves. She imagined the networks below her feet. How they went on forever. She lifted a foot and wiped away the mound. As if nothing had ever been there. They would build it back eventually. That was the magic they had, together.

*

Mary got to his apartment and pressed the button in the elevator to go up to the fifth floor. It was not the speed she liked. It crept up too slowly, moved in jitters and jitters and then jolts. She could have walked up the stairs. It would have been faster. She would have liked to feel her legs pound each step.

When the elevator arrived, there was a ding, like a microwave. Her black shoes clicked on the floor and when they stopped, the door to his apartment opened. He served dinner. He explained everything to her. How it would all unfold. He said it was going to be sweet and tender and loving. Then, at every opportunity, he'd tell her he didn't love her. It'll be a lie, he said. "I don't like feelings." She was going to go home, but he sat there on the bed looking lonely and sad. It was the thing she loved most in the world. The one no one saw, the one no one wanted. So she stayed.

It turned out the gas station man was an artist. He pained only with black. He had very large canvases leaned against the wall. They all looked the same to Mary. There didn't seem to be any difference, until she got closer to each one. The thing about these paintings was their strokes. Each one was particular, original. She angled one until the light hit it and saw where the strokes had been slapped on, where they changed, where they thickened, where they swirled.

*

It was just as he said it would be. It was tender and sweet and loving. When he was around, all Mary could ever see was the black at the centre of his eye. The world and its little towns fell away. What time it was, what day or hour, where the sun was in the sky, Mary never noticed. All she saw was him. "I want to stay in," he said. He kept himself inside her, attached, his body forming an appendage that grew out of her centre. After a while, he said, "I don't love you." Mary did not say anything back. She was listening to his breathing, feeling. She saw now that his eyes were grey. And she was not there anymore. She said nothing about love, asked nothing about it, or how he felt. "You're lying," she said. "Like you said you would." He said, "Don't be ridiculous." What was the difference between someone who lied about love and someone who didn't love you? Nothing.

Mary packed her bags and left all her furniture. She knew if he called her, she would go back right away. But she didn't want to go back. She wanted to go and stay gone. She was free. Free, she drove to the gas station and pumped gas into the car herself. He watched her from his tiny glass box. When she was done, she threw the pump down on the gravel and didn't pay. She twisted the lid to the gas tank, and when it was tight to her satisfaction, she drove away. She took the one road out of that town, picked up speed, flying over the potholes, not feeling any bumps. She knew she would reach the city. Its bright lights sprinkled across the sky like broken glass. She would become one of those bits, in a few hours' time.

And as for him. He'd still be there, in that town. Nothing would change there, but she imagined a few years from now the gas station would be shut down. Its bright tennis-ball green faded. No one would be able to see it from the interstate. The glass box broken on one side. Weeds growing through the concrete cracks. No one would be paying him to be there anymore, but there he would be, not even knowing why. Probably the hair on his head would fall out and would not come back. His face round and heavy and drooping. Two front teeth missing. The glasses he wore still there on his face, but behind one lens the eyelid remained closed. It didn't matter what happened there anymore. She knew what she never was, a void that was not immense.

COMMON WHIPPING

Naben Ruthnum

"You've been here how long?"

"Two years ago. Christmas, '71. Quit my course in Scotland, came over. My family still doesn't know."

"You never talk to them?"

"My old flatmate, Brian, he forwards me mum's mail. He even sends replies back for me. I put five or six letters in a big package, ship that to him, he takes them to the postbox once a week." Brian had been Renga's first real lover, a resident in the psychology program who now lived with a fake girlfriend (herself a lesbian, a psychiatric nurse who was especially skilled in electroshock therapy treatments, as Renga himself had witnessed on a ward visit he'd made with an identification badge nicked from the Sikh resident who shared their Citroën).

"Two years."

"Yes. And I still haven't played on a single track. I've written a lot, though."

"Your Italian?"

"Mostly decent, but I run into trouble when I'm describing something a little abstract," Renga tried to say in Italian. He could tell from the mingled confusion, pity and disdain on Massimo Troisi's face that he was butchering both language and accent. Renga crossed his legs to hide the dark stain he'd just seen near the left knee of his pants, and the movement smoothed his transition back into English. "It's not good enough, is what I'm saying. Apparently not good enough."

"Why didn't you go to India? Plenty going on there. You would have had more luck." Massimo leaned back to allow the waiter to set down a platter of transparently thin cured meats. Renga took and gnawed, swishing liquor between his teeth to dislodge studs of pig gristle.

"No Morricone out there. And I don't speak Hindi."

"So you're as useless there as you are here. And for money?"

Renga grinned and looked away. The waiter mistook his sidewards glance for another drink order, which was not a problem. Another glass of Fernet Branca arrived, bobbing with miniature semi-spheres of ice that would melt in seconds.

"I didn't think I was your only one. Just glad you're doing well," said Massimo. This time he was the one to cross his legs, perhaps to cover a stirring under the expensive cream trousers. No one would have been able to see it. Like most of the cafés and bars Renga's clients favoured, Rubinetto was dark, underground. The stone walls were old, and the cement holding them together was no longer distinguishable from rock, the whole room tinted by decades of liquor stains and smoke.

Massimo poked Renga's knee with the tip of his shoe, something he'd been doing since they'd sat down. The origin of the stain. Massimo's constant touching was proprietary, his attempt at a physical claim on something he'd never encountered before. Renga was a rarity in the city, a place where most sexual options were anything but. Slender, more-or-less Indian, accommodating, with a pleasing accent. Passage-to-India rough trade.

"You enjoy this? Not with me, I mean. The job in general," Massimo asked.

"I like the hours and some of the sex," said Renga. "Even some of the bad fucks you learn from. And anyone I go with is someone I know, or knows someone I know. Like you.""

"Right," Massimo said. He didn't ask Renga which category of fuck he fell into.

"You like Cipriani? Stelvio?"

"Of course I do." *Anonimo Veneziano* was currently the third-most rotated LP in Renga's collection.

"He just cancelled on a project. That's what the director says, but I think it was probably that he hoped Stelvio would do it and never got an agreement. They've got to get some kind of music on there. You got anything you can show the director? Mirazappa, a new guy."

"I have a record." He did. A pressing of one hundred vinyl discs, each with a cover that he'd screenprinted himself in a cheap shop in Mauritius, a red circle on a dark blue background.

"Is it classical sounding?"

"There's a variety of different sounds."

"Hm. You might want to make something new, bring it in on tape. Mirazappa was very specific, says he wants something classical, chamber-sounding. Says Bach a lot, but I think Bach is the only composer he knows."

"I can do that." Renga would need to pay for six hours of studio time and a cellist, an engineer as well. And write something new, but that was never the problem.

"Why d'you like Morricone so much? I know why I like him, but you?"

"I hate voices, what they do in popular music. It's why I couldn't stand to go to India. You write for the movies there, you're a slave to the playback singer, the stupid melody they want. Morricone, he makes voices behave. Forces them to be music. There's a line, structure, something written on piano, a theme the flute will pick up when the voice can't reach. Either that or he just makes them yelp in the recording booth, at the right pitch, the right time. That I like. It's how voices should be used."

"Right. For me it's the whistling. You know he laughs in all the wrong places if he's around when they edit? Really threw Sergio off the one time I was there, for *Buono Bruto*. Ennio's in his own world, takes a few things from the script, from discussions, then goes and does his themes." Massimo gazed off as he said this, watching condensation form in one particular depression in the ceiling, which the waiter had already walked over to poke dry with a mop once that evening. Renga too was feigning an experienced carelessness, which worked well when he was selling his cock and mouth, and seemed to be effective currency in the movie world as well. Being present as Ennio saw his score matched to film for the first time was swoon-material, as the linen-draped manipulator across from him knew. The story was almost definitely a lie, or something Massimo had stolen at a party.

"I've heard that, yes. So when can I meet Mirazappa?"

"You meet him after you give me the music. I'll pay for half the recording and the musicians. We'll call it a little gamble. Fifteen percent if Mirazappa likes it, and you give me a few free nights if he doesn't. He won't want to see you if he doesn't like the music. And he really prefers working with Italians. Didn't want to cast any Americans or Brits, but he did because he had to. You he doesn't have to use. So we have to make him want you. Got an Italian name for the credits?"

"Reinaldo Pazone."

"You serious?"

"No," said Renga, too happy to defend his carefully-arrived-at pseudonym. He gave Massimo his real address, something he rarely did with a client, and left the bar after promising to meet back there the next day—unless Massimo wanted him for another hour that night?

"I'm fifty-two," Massimo said. "I'd just fall asleep."

Massimo watched the departing boy, who'd reached for his wallet when the bill came with something approaching genuine grace. He walked that way as well, with the elegance of the unwatched. Renga didn't act like a whore. At least not like one who charged his extremely reasonable rates.

The need to shower overtook Renga as soon as he turned away from Massimo and headed up the stone steps into the afternoon. Under his light, stained shirt and cotton pants, Renga's flesh felt tacky, and the heat would soon turn this into viscous stickiness. It was an unpleasant, tactile part of a job he mostly enjoyed.

The apartment he occupied, on Via Prospera Santacroce, was in cruel proximity to Titania a Roma, the studio he was supposed to be recording in by now—passing out charts of themes and careful indications, cueing violinists and guitarists, getting ready to scream at anyone who bucked his instructions. Aside from his keyboards, the flat was a couch, a mattress, two heaps of clothes, and thirty-seven unwashed teacups. There was a slight form on the mattress, a normal-sized head on the pillow and a narrow comma under the sheet: Enzo, who had a key and often napped here after a night with a client. Renga didn't wake him, heading straight to the shower to wash Massimo's skin and fluids away.

He'd wake Enzo up by testing a theme that had occurred to him a few weeks ago, one that might fit Mirazappa's film. A massively heavy Fender Rhodes organ and a Roland Piano occupied the never-cooked-in kitchen, which was above the building's boiler room and the only place in the apartment where he could make sufficient noise to properly feel out his ideas. He'd even made some baffling walls out of egg cartons and Styrofoam, shutting the keyboards into a soft room-within-a-room that was tropically hot on summer days like this.

Renga enclosed himself and took his place at the bench. He turned the Rhodes on, pressing the keys as the tubes warmed up. Enzo moaned from the other room, probably in pain from another night of feeding his body to sadists. Enzo only made sounds when he turned over in his sleep, which meant that he was facedown now. On his back, a river-map of junior lash-marks intercrossed with a few raised maroon scars that had been very expensive indeed for the man who had put them there.

The name 'Enzo' was arbitrary, a career pseudonym that had overtaken his birth name, 'Magnus'. A Swedish–Turkish mix, he was used to discussing his racial origins in the terms of a dog's pedigree, leaning toward purity and legacy for some clients, muddying his blood for others, even telling one client, a Catalan, that he was Renga's half-brother. This was the one who had left the marks.

Enzo had looked young that night, extremely young. All sorts of plays on fascist dominance had been acted out on the flesh that coated his bones like frost on grass. Many of his clients came straight from the old guard; Mussolini's closeted friends, former Futurists and politicians who had eventually washed up in the business and film worlds of Rome, either making regulations or doing their best to break them. The role Enzo had come up with, literal whipping boy to a fallen elite and its acolytes, justified the emaciated body he'd created long before he took on his name and career.

Renga wouldn't have been able to name Enzo's disorder even if he'd recognized it as sickness. The skinniness looked like a business strategy to his fellow hustlers, a committed shaping of his most essential resource to provide an experience that was unique in the city, and therefore highly valued. He could sew, too, and had effectively modified a number of formal jackets and surplus army garments into a variously-sized Nazi and Blackshirt collection. He kept these in a dedicated wardrobe that stood locked in his own apartment, while his own costumes—rags, licked with blood in distressing areas—were stuffed into a suitcase under the living room couch. When

Renga and Enzo went out together with clients, something they did often with new ones, to create a certain level of security, Enzo ate off Renga's plate. A few cherry tomatoes at the end of the meal usually sustained his friend and trainer.

Clients, including the Catalan, liked talking about general topics over meals, perhaps trying to make it seem as though they were taking out some foreign junior partners or courting actors for a production. Enzo had a different character at the table, wise, witty, presumably the opposite of the cowering pant-pisser he played in the client's room. More educated than Renga, as he was constantly reminding his colleague, he called this the geisha part of the job.

"Most physical beauty is an accident, but maintaining it is as hard as keeping two cars in perpetual collision," he said, talking to Renga at their dinner with the Catalan. Another dark room, this one oddly empty, as though the Catalan had paid for several tables to be kept clear around them.

"That sounds wise and stupid at the same time," Renga answered, deferring his conversational place to the third man at the table. Their tall North African waiter, idle since they'd been served their last bottle, had started to circle the edges of the room. He was using a long spoon to snuff every second candle, drawing the walls closer in.

"And how do you maintain your beauty?" asked the Catalan, who carried his own salt cellar and sprinkled each slice of steak before he ate it. The affectation made Renga quietly angry, distracting him from the taste of his own fish every time he saw the man drop a pinch from the engraved wooden box. He was about forty, but unhealthy, with skin the colour of an old rope in a gymnasium. The heartbreaking falseness of his wig made it clear that even great wealth couldn't cover everything.

"I maintain it the same way I developed it. I had to start the accident. My parents' shabby cells couldn't do the job. For my nose to make sense, for my cheekbones to counterbalance my jaw, I had to impose reductions elsewhere."

Enzo took a photo wrapped in paper out of his wallet. He removed the picture from its folded sheath and pushed it over to the Catalan, who owned three garment factories.

The Catalan, who had lied and told them his name was Umbrosi, stared at the photo. The subject, a teenage boy, wasn't fat, but he was anonymous, a background actor who would never be called forward to deliver a line. Enzo described the process of unearthing himself from that accidental body.

Renga picked up the paper the photo had been folded in; it was a prescription, a few years old, for glasses. The doctor's name was Nordic-sounding.

"Is this your father's handwriting?" Renga asked. Enzo picked up the photo and the prescription and returned them to their folded clasp.

"No, he charged too much. I only go to doctors I can fuck for the bill." Saying this in front of a client ran counter to Enzo's first tenet of the job: Never act like a whore. Whether he'd said it impulsively or with calculation, it worked. The Catalan laughed.

"Let's go to the house," the Catalan said. It was eight miles from the restaurant, and they made the trip by cab. The Catalan never used his own car on nights when he was seeing a boy, Enzo said. His driver was an old friend, a scholarshipped classmate from secondary school who'd ruined his former career with drugs, and now clung to Catholicism and the job he'd been given. Umbrosi didn't like to make him uncomfortable by having him chauffeur Roman street meat.

Their cab took Grande Raccorde, a dull but effective route, circling towards the part of town where they needed to be before penetrating back through the concentric slices of the city. The house had all of its lights on: Umbrosi's theft deterrent and a way of keeping his dogs comfortable.

They fell on Renga and Enzo when Umbrosi opened the door. Enormous, friendly, poorly-trained Irish wolfhounds, alien-bodied and unreal beasts that Renga had recognized from the inclusion of the breed in Powell and Pressburger's *I Know Where I'm Going*. They moved like new fawns in the constricted hallway entrance, their legs sturdy but their bodies large enough to destabilize the tiny space they crowded into.

"They only live six, seven years. So I let them have their fun," Umbrosi said. The larger of the two hounds had its paws on Enzo's shoulders and bore him back into the door, which closed beneath the boy's feathery weight. Umbrosi finally called the dogs when Enzo's knees started to wobble. They corralled themselves, backing single-file toward a pile of small Persian rugs in front of an empty fireplace.

Their heads bobbed as the immense curving backs receded, wheeling and trotting out of sight. Renga's former terror of dogs had been alleviated by the endless sequence of lap-bound near-invertebrates he'd encountered in clients' homes, small creatures with misaligned jaws and flat muzzles that had no function or ability to threaten. Quite a few had bitten him, their soft teeth denting his skin and leaving sulky trails of mucous. Soon he was able to see kindness, deference, or indifference in the eyes of larger domestics. The scavenging wild dogs of Rome were quite easy to avoid, and were constantly being impounded or secretly executed by angry homeowners wielding guns left over from the war. The wolfhounds in this house had fewer aggressive instincts than their owner, who was watching his night's hire with a particularly charged lust that Renga didn't think he himself could ever feel or inspire.

Enzo straightened and brushed dog-hair epaulets off his blazer, which he then took off and hung from a hook by the door. His lucent thinness was exposed by his pearl-white shirt. The pants were narrow and tapered to pencil-width at the ankles, and a red leather belt was shelved on his hipbones.

Renga eyebrowed his friend. Enzo had told him that the Catalan's sessions always started with the dogs, but thankfully they weren't involved in any of the later portions of his evening's entertainment.

"Do you want to stay down in this room, Renga?" The name came out as Wray-Gah when Umbrosi said it, as though he were addressing some foe of Godzilla's. "I can set you up in the screening room, if you'd like."

"No, I'll stay here. The dogs are fine with me?"

"They're fine with everyone. I've never seen them hungry, perhaps that would change things." Umbrosi was looking up the stairs, barely glancing at Renga as he spoke, touching himself through his right pocket. He'd prepared things for Enzo before meeting the boys for dinner, alluding to the "scene being set" at least four times at the table. He wasn't like most clients, who kept their stuff in the basement.

"Most of these fetish dungeons they take me to, they're totally historically incoherent," Enzo had once said after an appointment on Via Frattina. "It's medieval as well as fascistic. Thomas More used to have people who read the Bible in English instead of Latin tortured, you know that? Maybe executed, I can't remember, but surely tortured first. This fat client today, takes tongs just to find his cock, he collects old implements. Devices. A flat piece of iron he paid thousands of lire for, with a handle at the back—he says he has its lineage, stolen from some museum when the Allies came. It's an abacinator. They'd heat it up white, hold it in front of your eyes, melt them right out. You cry them out, the sockets are left empty, the optic nerve seals up and shrivels. Terrible. I always worried he'd use it on me, get too worked up, but he's just a sweet dentist. And I never let him tie me up."

Enzo had been silent since they'd come into the house, sinking into passivity, acting his way into the Catalan's fantasy. Renga watched them walk up the stairs to a second floor that had been imposed on the original structure, rooms slotted between the roof and the stone first floor, supported by grim, immense beams, which had likely been salvaged from some ancient barn. The wood throughout the house was the same greyed-brown as the hounds, a colour that Renga identified with Flemish paintings. Peasants copulating in the dirt by collapsing buildings.

Umbrosi needled Enzo in the back with a finger as they mounted the top stair. The boy stopped and let Umbrosi walk around him to open the bedroom door, which was just visible to Renga. The Catalan liked going through his sexual paces in his proper bedroom, the place where he slept and wanked and sometimes brought models and actresses for a night of puzzled slumber while he leaked a more salacious story by phone to a collection of trusted gossip columnists.

Renga took a post on the couch behind the curled enormity of the canines, with a copy of the only novel in English he could find on Umbrosi's shelves, *Double Indemnity*. The cushion next to him was stacked with copies of *L'Unita*, the communist paper. Umbrosi probably read it for research on the unions that he fought against to keep the shirts he made, but never wore, as cheap as possible.

Renga fell asleep a little after the dogs did, waking only when the negotiations upstairs passed from lash to bullwhip, and the yelps turned into three real screams, sounds that Renga had never heard from his friend, which rose and pitched into an androgynous then animal screech. One of the dogs moved its legs, dream running somewhere, following or fleeing a phantasmagoric parallel of the screams upstairs.

The theme that occurred to Renga as he was on that couch, starting with the screamed G that followed the first crack of the whip, was a fairly plain nine-note run with an unexpected diminished seventh as the penultimate strike, a recurring pattern that would overlap successive bars to abolish any sense of certainty.

Enzo was driven to the home of a veterinarian after Umbrosi had finished ejaculating and started panicking. The Catholic chauffeur had been summoned from the coach house, an explanation involving a fall on a stray rake left on the lawn conjured, and Enzo was carted off, facedown, to be stitched up as well as possible. Umberto had left Renga with a huge roll of lire bound by an elastic band, the bounty for Enzo's flesh.

Renga forced that night's theme to return as he sat in his own kitchen two months later, with Enzo sleeping on his mattress in the next room. He struck it out on the Rhodes, playing it repeatedly, altering timing and emphasizing different notes while staring at the matte black plastic cover that concealed the strings and pickups. Eventually his eyes stopped working, filtering out the dull blackness, as a smell vanishes to a nose before it vanishes in a room. He corrected the theme, perfected it, then continued to play as a contrapuntal harmony line for xylophone unfurled in his mind. He placed the sound somewhere behind his right eyebrow, and auditioned a theremin accent behind his cheekbone before dismissing it. Cellos came in, and he put these behind his mandibles, two behind each back molar, keeping the arrangement sparse, manageable, bonding each note physically with a chew or a twitch, staring down into the keys and repeating until it was assembled. There was a counterpoint that almost had its shape, but kept shifting, like the features of a character in an amateur's novel, changing based on what they were doing, how they were acting.

"It's boring until it keeps happening. Then it's not exactly interesting, but you want it to continue, you know?" Enzo had swiveled open one of the soundproofing walls of Renga's practice chamber. He had his Wise Critical Judgment face on, which made it annoying to agree with him.

"That's about as good a description of a theme for variations as I could get to, I guess," he said. Enzo pulled the practice room open all the way, signaling to Renga that it was time to pay attention to him, and walked over to the fridge. Slices of things, mostly: meat, cheese. Discs, tubes. Strings of uncooked pasta that would soon go bad; all brought by a client of Renga's. Bottles of sparkling water, which both boys preferred to still, and which had become nearly the only thing Enzo consumed.

As he drank the knot in his throat bobbed and wriggled like a caught fish, and the scars on his back moved when he turned. There was a light fuzz on the boy's skin that hadn't been there when Renga had first met him, the night they'd decided never to fuck just because they were supposed to.

"I got a project," Renga said. "An assignment." He described Massimo Troisi's proposition to Enzo, who set the bottle down and drew his mouth over to one side.

"Do it right," said Enzo, "even if the john doesn't pay you enough. I'll give you anything extra you need. Don't give them some scratchy piano recording. Give them the whole thing, so they can't say no."

"They can say no to anything. They've been saying no for years."

"To you, not what you make. If you make that—" Enzo pointed to the air above the keyboard—"they'll take it."

"It's the Catalan, I think. The director of the movie is new, a beginner. I think it's him."

"You think?"

"Massimo used his name. His real name."

"That's a good clue," said Enzo, stretching there in the kitchen, distracting his hands so they wouldn't reach for the scars on his back. His ribs expanded and the concavity of his stomach deepened, the brittle spine making a dusty cracking sound as he leaned backwards.

Two weeks later, Renga met with Massimo and the director on an enormous outdoor patio. It was the Catalan—false Umbrosi, real Mirazappa—and he stood and blanched when he saw Renga, the source of the music on the tape that he'd already decided to use. Renga had passed the chauffeur on his way to the terrazza, accepting and returning a nod.

"You understand my film without having seen it. I see it when—the, the violin strain, that's my heroine, the glove on her throat as she grips it and slips away, taking with her the leather but not his hand."

"And the tension notes," Renga said, leaning slightly across the table, ignoring Massimo's inquisitive brows and watching the Catalan. "Those are the whips. From the title, you know."

"Yes."

Enzo didn't turn up for the premiere of *La frusta e il calice*, which came out stunningly fast, a month after the sound was finalized. He didn't reply to phone calls beforehand or afterwards. Renga thought he might find him at his own home, perhaps finally ready to have sex, now that only one of them was in the business of it. Enzo wasn't there, so Renga let himself into his flat an hour after the party had wrapped, walking over ankle-twisting cobblestones through a pre-dawn crowd of bakers, newspaper vendors and the drunken young.

Enzo's books, his fascist trousseau for clients, and his own clothes were still in the apartment. His wallet, with its paper-wrapped photo of the boy that might have been him, was gone. That, at least, suggested that he had left with some purpose. Renga looked for more missing objects in the apartment as the sun lay lengthening beams of heat across its uncurtained rooms, but found everything else his friend owned intact, present, abandoned.

YOUR RANDOM SPIRIT GUIDE

Eden Robinson

My Haisla and Heiltsuk ancestors would never come to you in a dream. They have super stressful afterlives watching over their great-grandchildren as they make unfortunate dating choices at the All-Native Basketball Tournament or decide to put their lustrous, black hair in un-Indian man buns.

If you want to talk to my ancestors, you need to burn their favourite food and drink. Put it on plates and in cups; real ones, not disposable. Don't throw it in the fire. Say their names as you place the dishes and drinks near the flames. Otherwise other ghosts will try to steal their food.

They're not going to emerge from the clouds like angels or the Lion King. They'll be a flicker in the corner of your eye. Your keys showing up on the coffee table when you're sure you left them on the kitchen counter. A song that repeats endlessly in your mind, usually their favourite, a song with sentimental meaning. They're not going to whisper their stories in your ear as you sit at your laptop, no matter how much you feed them. A ghost doesn't have that kind of energy. Our worlds are separate and difficult to transcend.

Or you might be listening to a liar. Human ghosts aren't the sole inhabitants of the other world. The thing that's whispering to you can say it's my ancestor, but I doubt it and so should you. Know the names. Trust, but verify.

HAZEL & CHRISTOPHER

Casey Plett

1

When Hazel grew up and moved out of the prairies, she would learn from movies and the news that small towns were supposed to be poor and dying. But Hazel never thought of her unhappy childhood as horrific, and Christopher's family was not only happy but rich. They lived in a cul-de-sac next to a canola field with a wide yard surrounded by poplars; they were always renovating their basement. If you had pressed Hazel as a child, she maybe could've admitted she was jealous. In a glossily submerged way, maybe. Mostly, at that age, she just loved being Christopher's best friend.

When they first touched each other they were eight, sleeping in an old inner room without windows in the basement. They were hyper and laughing hard and then her eyes were close to the freckles on his shoulders.

They talked about gay-ness exactly once, just after Hazel and her mom moved across the province. They were on the phone and about to start high school. Hazel was in a stage of proto-transness, a stage in which she was terrified of herself and had no idea why.

She brought it up this way: "What do you think about gay people? Are they OK or should they be killed? I don't know."

"They should probably be killed," Christopher said.

"OK."

They talked on the phone a lot after Hazel moved away. She'd always wondered if Christopher remembered that. It would've been unusual for two boys. ("Boys.") Mom let her call him for twenty minutes on the weekend. Long distance. Hazel'd say, "But you talk to your boyfriend every night for hours!" And Hazel's mom, forever calm, just said, "This'll make more sense to you as an adult."

It did make sense to Hazel now, if not in the way her mother probably imagined.

Christopher was always happy to talk. He didn't have the same emotional needs back then and even as a young teenager, Hazel recognized that. But he always made time for her. He did.

Hazel last saw Christopher when she was twenty. Home from out west, knowing her boy-days were numbered and so were the reasons to come back to this part of the world. She and her mom were at her aunt's for Christmas and Hazel walked from the other end of town in the snow, the creak of her boots the only sound in the pale afternoon sunset.

She walked in the door of Christopher's house and no one was on the first floor. She went down to the basement, noticed a bedroom off to the side with power tools everywhere and half-installed hardwood floors. In the rec room, Christopher and a couple other guys were watching *The Departed* with a two-four of Bud. (There was a particular kind of American, Hazel had learned since, who was bummed to know that Canadians drank Bud.) One of the guys said he wanted more beer, but hated the girl who worked at the vendor.

Hazel had felt herself teetering on an edge then, between a fear of how volatile it might be to continue knowing these boys, and a distant sadness in the knowledge she might never see these stupid fuckers again.

Crazily enough, there *had* been a trans guy in town, her age, who'd come out around a year prior. He'd announced himself, then right away skipped off to the city. Hazel brought up his name like a test, like hazarding an exhibition round.

"So you guys hear about...?"

"Oh god the *dyke*!"

And everyone laughed.

"I have no problem with gay people," Christopher said. "But gender reassignment...." A visible shiver came over him, something real and revulsive. He shook his head like he'd stomped on something crawly and was trying to forget about it.

When the two-four ran out, they all went to a party where they did shots, then played a drinking game, then drank rum out of Solo cups, then shotgunned beers in the garage with their coats on, and when Hazel stumbled into a wall the boys laughed and said incredulously: "Are you *drunk*?!" It was 7 p.m. and the moon was shining behind a cloud of blankets and after that they went to the bar.

The main takeaway for her: How did Christopher Penner, in Pilot Mound, Manitoba, years before Chaz Bono would ever grace a magazine, know about the term *gender reassignment*? Weeks later, Hazel got on a plane and flew back west, and weeks later she transitioned, then dropped out of school, then fell away from all she'd ever known. And as the following decade churned, in tiny rooms in roiling bright cities, the thought of Christopher would flit down onto her, like a moonbeam startling her awake.

*

Ten years later Hazel crash-landed back home—untriumphantly, the prairie winter beginning its months-long descent into lightlessness. And among other things, she began to search for him.

She didn't have any friends left in Pilot Mound. Her aunt wouldn't talk to her, her mother didn't know anything, having moved to the city years ago. And Hazel couldn't even fucking find anything on social media. Last she'd heard of Christopher, years ago, he'd moved to the city, too. Even his parents she couldn't track down.

Idly and with pleasure, she set up parameters for him on OkCupid, boys of a certain age and height range. She looked for boys with red hair and dustings of freckles around their collarbones. She checked this every week or so. When she heard of anyone with the name Chris, she would ask, "No chance you mean Christopher Penner, do you?"

Hazel really didn't expect anything to come of any of this. Her searches were like periodically buying a lottery ticket: a nice, dependable, dopamine-filled surge where the come-up of hope somehow always eclipsed the comedown of disappointment.

She wasn't doing much with her days besides going to AA and volunteering with a nascent sex workers' rights organization, of whose members Hazel was somehow the only one who'd ever touched boy parts for money. The nights she was home, she made dinner for her mom, but usually Hazel's mom was at her boyfriend's place or at work, and usually that suited Hazel just fine.

She had no idea what to do with her life, if she had a future, or if she wanted one. In the absence of the alcohol she'd flooded herself with for half her life, her tired, newly sober body handed her a sense of alertness she hadn't felt since she was a teenager. At the same time, she also felt herself turning into a slug as that body barely moved. Many days she never left the house. She slept and watched Netflix and cooked.

Hazel figured sooner or later one of three things would happen:

1) Welfare would dump her
2) She'd fall off the wagon
3) Her mom would move in with her boyfriend, who, no matter how much he got along with Hazel, would be unlikely to in tandem take in a 30-year-old transsexual ex-hooker in recovery

Or maybe all of those things would happen at once. Regardless, she didn't imagine this quiet un-life would last forever.

In the meantime, she hoarded her cash, went to AA and the nascent sex workers' rights organization and shut off her brain. And one of few bright spots in imagining her future was when she indulged this loving spot of her past and scanned the internet in search of Christopher.

*

Well, Hazel did do one other unusual thing in this period. She went on a date.

Marina from the nascent sex workers' rights organization—Marina who was not a sex worker, but who was a grad student—introduced the two of them. Marina knew the guy through lefty something or other. Hazel had seen him around at a couple things. He was cute. Tall, blonde hair, glasses. Good politics, ungregarious. Hazel was into all of this.

"You're getting dressed up like that?" asked her mom that evening.

Hazel was in the bathroom with the door open, in a flowery blue dress, applying eyeliner.

"I'm going on a date," said Hazel.

"A date," said her mom slowly. "Where?"

"Baked Expectations."

"No shit," said her mom. "Your dad and I went there once. Long time ago."

"I haven't been on a date in years. A real date, anyway. I don't remember the last time that happened." Hazel said this awkwardly, still re-learning how to talk to her mother as an adult, a woman, a person commiserating.

Her mother softened at this. "No, huh?"

"Nope."

"It'd be nice if you met someone," her mom said quietly.

Hazel turned to look at her. *What a normal conversation,* she thought. *What a normal conversation for a daughter and a mother to be having.* Her mother shut the door behind her, and Hazel stared at the towel hanging on a hook, her feet shifting in the fluff of the rug.

The guy had a steaming tea in front of him when she sat down and he invited her to get a coffee or something.

That was the most disappointing part. *Not even dinner?* she thought.

He didn't get her, but he was smart, turned out to run an after-school arts program, and by the end of the night she'd started to like him. "I did a workshop in the country," he said. "Seventh-day Adventists, right? And they asked me if I was an atheist, and I said yes. And then they had this look of shock on their faces. And they said to me—I swear—they said: 'Do you live in Osborne Village?'" Hazel laughed.

It was eleven o'clock when he revealed he had a wife. And a kid at home. They were opening up their relationship after thirteen years. "She's cool with us being here," he stressed, as if this would soothe her. When he drove her home, he joked about making out in the car and she got out the second he parked.

Then a Facebook message half an hour later: *I wish I had kissed you. I just wasn't sure if you wanted to. I'm not always totally sensitive to*—blah blah blah blah blah blah blah blah blah blah blah blah blah blah blah blah blah blah blah blah blah blah blah blah blah blah blah blah blah blah blah blah blah blah blah blah blah blah blah blah blah blah blah blah blah blah blah

blah blah blah blah blah blah blah blah blah blah blah blah blah blah blah blah blah blah blah blah blah blah blah blah blah blah blah blah blah blah blah blah blah.

"How was your date?!" her mom asked the next evening.

Hazel savoured the excited look on her mother's face, letting its image settle and take root in her mind. "He had a wife and kids."

"Ew!" her mom said instantly.

"I know."

"Ugh! I. Well. You deserve better, I suppose that's all I'll say. You deserve better then someone expecting you to—slink around."

Hazel didn't tell her she wouldn't have had to slink around, that that was the thing that pissed her off, the burning phrase in her head: "She's cool with us being here." *I don't care how goddamn cool your wife is.* Was that progress, that the wife now gave the other woman her blessing? Why wouldn't Marina have mentioned this? (Would she have done so with a cis girl?) Was it really so weird she wanted to see what Christopher was up to these days?

*

Months later, after the new year, she was restless. Her mom was spending more time at her boyfriend's. She'd filed some job applications for real, but her heart wasn't in it. Plus, having firmly committed herself to alcoholism and sex work for much of her twenties didn't do much for her resume.

The nascent sex workers' rights organization was plugging along, though. It had grown to ten members and consisted of two factions: white academics/camgirls and twinky Métis social workers. The latter were starting to get their way after a disastrous public event led by the former.

Hazel was cheered by this, though she didn't say much in the meetings. When she'd joined she'd hoped to just do boring legwork, but once it became clear the group was in infancy—and the others discovered her to not only be the sole transsexual but also the sole person who'd sucked dick for money—suddenly everyone wanted her *opinion* on things, and a decade of Facebook and queer culture had made Hazel very tired of needing to have opinions.

So when Festival du Voyageur came along, Hazel went and she went alone. She wanted to be in a crowd and watch people get stupid. She put on her old faux-fur coat and vamped up with thick makeup and a purple toque and caught the 29 up Route 70 and then the 10 over to St. Boniface and began to feel alive and did not want to drink, not one iota. Hazel felt good about it. Those two things had been connected for a long time.

Drinking socially was never her problem anyway. Passing the LC after dark, being alone and sleepless ten blocks from the late-night vendor—that was hard. But now? Going to watch idiots instead of being the idiot? That sounded fun.

She had her last thirty dollars for the month in her pocket and paid fifteen to go in and watch Radio Radio thrill a crowd in a tent. Wandering outside in a cold chill of French and English and pretty young people in spacesuit coats, she saw a stand advertising "Giant Perogy Poutine with Bacon—$10" and barked: "Ha!" to no one. *Throw in some bannock to soak up the gravy and you'd have the peak Manitoba food*, she thought. Then she bought one. Twenty minutes later she was walking back from vomiting in the Porta-Potties, but even that didn't feel horrible—who knew the last time she'd thrown up from something besides drinking? It felt innocent in its own way.

It was while drinking water in front of the main tent that she spotted red hair in a circle of snowsuits, and right then Hazel knew.

She lingered on the periphery of their circle. An alpha type with a ballcap who looked so much like Christopher's old buddy Matthew was talking. The whole circle, actually, looked like those guys from years ago.

Christopher glanced at her with a second's blankness, then went back to listening to the ballcap.

Hazel thought: *He still looks so young. He looks so unbelievably young.*

Tall—a couple inches taller than Hazel. She'd forgotten. Freckles all over his face. His mother's Irish red hair grown just over his ears. Thick, loose black jeans, blue mitts, and a grey toque sticking up like a chef's hat. And blue eyes with a ring of gold inside them. She was that close to him.

And he'd looked through her at first, as if she was any other girl. A specific kind of joy came to her in that, a joy she would always treasure in not being noticed.

The boys left to go back inside, and she said: "Christopher?"

He stopped, confused. "Yeah?"

"It's Hazel," she said.

"Hazel?"

At first he didn't get it, and she waited for him to at best laugh or go lifeless—but then it was beautiful, old Hollywood in the finest way, and Hazel would never forget this scene for as long as she lived. A dawn of recognition traveled across Christopher's body. She said, "Hazel Cameron," and took off her toque and shook out her hair, letting it spill down her fake-fur coat, and added: "From Pilot Mound."

His face spread and cracked, like sunlight coming out of an egg.

"We used to know each other," she said, smiling. "A long time ago."

"HOLY SHIT! HAZEL!" And without another word (they came later: "You look amazing!" "I've thought about you for years!"), he hugged her. He hugged her and lifted her off the ground, her boots kicking and her nose buried in the back of his hair. It all really happened exactly like this.

*

On the first call (he *called*), she made it clear: "Do you want to go have dinner with me?"

"Yes," he said immediately. "Yes, I do."

"Like a date," Hazel said, unwilling to entertain any maybe-fantasies anymore. "You realize this, right, what I'm asking you is to go on a date?"

I sound like I'm his boss, she thought, leaning against the kitchen cabinets while her mom's dinner burned.

"Yes," he said again. "Yes. I want to go on a date with you, too."

They went to Paradise, that Italian place by Gordon Bell with the tinted windows. It was almost empty, with a sweet, apologetic, middle-aged waiter and menus with two-word items and no descriptions and prices that, if Christopher didn't offer to pay, were just low enough for Hazel to still make it to the next month. "Well, fuck, I dunno, you were in Toronto then?" he said to her. Christopher was wearing a hoodie and blank T-shirt, and Hazel wore a tank top and a pencil skirt.

"Montreal," she said. "Though I did live in Toronto a couple years. And Vancouver before that."

"I went with my parents to Montreal once," he remarked. "In high school. For a fencing competition."

"The fuck," she said with a laugh. "A fencing competition?"

"I was on the fencing team in high school!" he said, grinning. "I did it all four years. I"—he paused with a sense of grandeur—"was internationally competitive."

"Internationally competitive?"

"We went to Fargo once," he said.

"Wow."

"Montreal was better."

"Yeah."

"You still play hockey?" she said. (Chris was always into sports, Hazel tagging along to his games. What kind of fucking boy in grade school goes to watch his friend's hockey games?) "No," he said. "No, I haven't played anything since high school." He tugged at his hoodie. "I don't mind."

"No?"

"It gets—stupider as you get older," he said, frowning. "Competition is more fun when you're a kid. It's literally the entire world but like it still gets to be pointless."

He took a huge bite of his food. He ate by slowly gathering a large forkful on his plate, lowering his head, then quickly and decisively stabbing the food into his mouth, like domination. "It gets ridiculous when adults make it mean something," he said. "You know?"

"I think so," said Hazel.

"I go to Jets game with my dad sometimes."

"I hate the Jets."

"Aw, c'mon, really?" He bit into a piece of garlic bread and Hazel followed suit, sawing into it with her knife like an animal.

"I fucking hate hockey," she said, scooping up butter.

"Nobody's perfect," he returned, unfazed. "How's your mom doing?"

"Fine. I live with her. She's fucking some guy who owns an art gallery."

"Good for her," he said. "She still—aw, shit. What does your mom do again? I can't believe I don't remember this."

"Hospital tech. Sanitizes instruments. They ever cut you open at Health Sciences in the last five years, good chance my mom cleaned that scalpel."

"Well, good for her, eh?"

"She does OK. And the guy has family money, so. What about your folks?"

"Um. My mom's dead."

"*What?*" Hazel said. Christopher's parents had been very kind, and always seemed so in love. There'd been a short period, as a kid, where Hazel'd prayed seriously and nightly for her mother to have what they had.

Hazel reflected, in a nanosecond, that without realizing it she had always considered this a bulwark against death. As if there had been an x = x equation of happy straight marriages with long lives.

"Yeah," Christopher said. "She killed herself, actually."

"I'm so sorry." She broke the last piece of bread. "When was this?"

"Like two years ago."

Before she could stop herself, Hazel asked, "How's your dad?"

"Never been the same." Christopher delivered this information like he was in a meeting. It was calm as space outside, cars half-covered from vision by the snowdrifts. Hazel could make out antennas, the tops of SUVs.

"I'm sorry," said Hazel. "I've lost a couple friends that way. I'm sorry."

"Yeah, well," he said, showing the first signs of discomfort. "Not exactly nice dinner conversation, I guess."

An old guy with a Michelin Man jacket walked in and shuffled over to a table.

"My mom's here now," Hazel said, offering this, knowing the difference between sympathy and self-concern. "In the city."

"So you don't have any connection to Pilot Mound anymore?" said Christopher. The guy in the Michelin jacket slowly lowered himself into a seat, putting his hands on the table and closing his eyes. The waiter sauntered over, now with a lazy smile.

"None. No reason to visit anymore. Ever."

"Me either," Christopher said, sounding scared and unsure. "Damn, I guess I really don't. My dad moved here last year, too. Which is good. It's good he's near me."

They ate in silence, then Hazel went to the bathroom, where an ad for a dating show stood next to the sink, a colourful list that said, "DOS AND DON'TS ON FIRST DATES." Her eyes rested on a DO:

Offer to go Dutch.
(Welcome to the 21st Century.)

She straightened her ponytail, smoothed her skirt, and went back downstairs.

The old man had a half-carafe of wine and a basket of bread, staring ahead, inserting the food into his mouth. "So what were you doing in Montreal?" asked Christopher.

"Becoming a girl and a drunk. I came back to quit at least one of those. Got any advice?" She'd planned this line out, to say at some point during the night, to gauge his reaction—and it sounded so stupid coming out of her mouth, but Christopher laughed a true, un-self-conscious laugh, and Hazel started to like him for real.

*

When he kissed her, hours later, on her doorstep, after paying for both of their meals, Hazel started to cry. She went up into her mom's bathroom but instead of peeing, she sat on the lid and cried. And then Hazel's mom heard her crying. She entered without knocking and Hazel told her there was a boy. She said, *You remember Christopher Penner, right?* and her mom laughed a delirious, beautiful laugh, and got down on her knees and hugged Hazel where she was sitting. *You two always did like each other so much.* Hazel put her face in her mom's coat and let her mother touch her as she sat there, the carpet of the toilet seat rustling against her skirt.

*

After they fucked for the first time, Hazel thought Christopher might cry. He had that look boys get after they come when the sex has really meant something to them. Something grateful unlocked from within his body, with Hazel's legs wrapped around him like a spider. So many boys thought they were warriors after they had an orgasm. That, or they got sad. Or gave off waves of dissociation and then weeks later admitted they were girls. (This had happened to Hazel not once nor twice, but *three times*.) But Christopher didn't cry—his eyes closed briefly, like he was with God, and it made Hazel feel beautiful.

2

Can I even begin to phrase how hard I began to re-believe in my life? How his bedroom is forever preserved in my memory as a centre of peace? Christopher had a big studio on Corydon with purple curtains and gentle traffic sounds and a neighbour who watched cable news that came through the walls as a burbling lull 24/7. For many months, when I stayed over at Christopher's house, he would get up, make coffee, and kiss me, still sleeping in the bed, before he went to work. I lived between that apartment and my mother's house, doing nothing. He didn't seem to mind (something I would later realize I took for granted). It sounds chaste saying it now, though it wasn't. We fucked against buildings, and I went with him to parties. God, he liked to drink, almost as much as I had in the old days, but that part wasn't even hard. Once everybody knew I was sober and wasn't trying to get me to drink, parties got fun! It was a kick to be around drunks and see so clearly now what was happening to them.

And sober sex. Do you know that had never happened before, either? It was in fucking Christopher that I felt my body flower and come back to me. I felt my skin as a real part of the world. It was weird. Sex became not something that I tolerated, or even assented to, but a thing I *wanted* and *liked*. It felt like the same restless and tingling part of me that stayed up late as a kid. A ghostly hand touching my insides, bringing something back to me about desire.

*

"You know, I only ever dated one other girl in my life," he said one night, after we'd made love. The moon was out and tinged his red hair a pale blue. A car's shadow from the street washed over the room.

"Really," I said.

"We dated for four years," he said, staring straight up from his pillow. "She had a kid, a little daughter."

I propped myself up on my elbow. "Why'd you break up?" I didn't mind hearing this stuff, and it wasn't unprecedented. We liked filling each other in on the vast blankness of what had happened during the past half of our lives.

"She fell out of love with me," he said.

"That's cold."

"No, it's fine," Christopher said. "I mean, it was awful, and it dragged out too long. But she didn't have the guts to leave me. And I wanted to believe she still loved me. It happens all the time."

"I see."

"Not that I'd know, I guess," he added. "The sample size is n=1, as they say."

"Dating blows. You didn't miss much. How'd you meet?"

He hesitated. "Speed dating."

"*What?* That still exists?"

"It was in Fort Garry," he laughed. "It wasn't even at a bar or anything, it was so awkward. But we ended up liking each other. They give you a little piece of paper and they call you up if you marked each other as a match. We went on one date afterward and then it was just normal."

"No shit."

"Did you ever date girls, too?" he asked. "I mean, after you—after you—"

It never fails to amaze me, in a fond, quiet way, how boys can touch and fuck a transsexual body then stammer their way through any implication of how that body got there. I don't know why I have a soft spot for that, but I do. "I've never dated a woman," I said. "Except in high school, once. I hooked up with girls a few times and it was fun. I never really dated men, either, to be honest. I didn't have many relationships as an adult, period." *Any relationships*, I didn't say.

We lay there in the moonlight. I'd never felt so calm. I felt like the first thirty years of my life were slipping into place and closing. We were very quiet for a while, but he wasn't sleeping.

"What I can tell you," I said, "is the first time I slept with a man. It was right after I moved east. This was in Toronto. I wasn't in a good place. I worked with this boy and I lived in a shithole just east of downtown. Even today it's a rough corner. Anyway. This boy, Will, he asked if I wanted to hang out. Twice I went over to his house and we watched TV, got drunk. We talked long into the night. Both times I expected—like, I thought: *He's hitting on me, right? This is how this works, this is how it ends up, right?* But then around 1:00, 2:00 a.m. he'd say all abrupt that he had to get to sleep, had to get up early for work, see ya. I was like, *I work at the same place, bitch!* But whatever. The third time I go over again. Will says he's gonna make tacos and he's got a two-six of whiskey. I brought a six-pack. And right away, he says he broke up with his girlfriend the weekend before, so he's all emotional. I was like, *Ah, OK, here we go*. He put bacon in the tacos. I told him to eat some of the spare bacon and take a shot of whiskey. We called them bacon chasers. I have a picture of me, still, that he took that night. I've got a flip phone and I'm wearing this stupid scarf. I look mad for some reason. But I was really happy.

"Anyway. Eventually the whiskey and the beer go and we are *fucked up*. And then I kiss him and he's surprised! I don't know. But he's into it, and we have sex, and let me tell you, baby, it was bad, like it was *nooooot* good. I'll spare the unsavoury details but like, we were both too drunk to stand. And we were scared, and we didn't know what we were doing with each other's bodies."

Christopher sat up and put his arms around his knees, watching me talk to him.

"We blacked out and woke up the next day feeling terrible," I said. "He had to work, but it was my day off. I walked him to the subway and said, *Kiss me*. He did, then he left, and almost right away I had a Facebook message saying he just wanted to be friends."

"Motherfucker!" said Christopher.

"No, the sadness of that hadn't kicked in yet," I said. "I walked home, even though it took over an hour. And I felt so clearly that I had finally lost my virginity. It seems silly, right? It wasn't the first time I'd had sex as a woman. It wasn't the first time a lover had stuck something up me, either. It wasn't even the first time I'd touched boy penis. But fucking him and sleeping in his bed felt special, like something I would read about. And I guess maybe part of that feeling was heterosexist patriarchal whatever. But it occurred to me, as I was walking, hungover in the wind, feeling so in my body—that virginity is not the lie. *Singular* virginity, that's the lie. It made me think: Maybe virginity *is* real, and it can be lost, but it can also be given. Maybe there's something beautiful in the concept, and not just . . . ruinous. Maybe the truth is just that virginities are malleable, personal, and there are lots of them. And maybe you can even do them over again if you don't get it right the first time."

Christopher was quiet. I'd like to say he eventually said or murmured something before we fell asleep, but I just don't remember.

*

Once, when Christopher was drunk, he hit me in the balls. Well, he tapped me in the balls. It was supposed to be a joke, I guess. There was a split second where I didn't understand where the pain was coming from.

"*Haaaa*," he said. "You remember that? You remember that?"

I clocked him back before I even realized what was I was doing and then he was on the floor. He sobbed once, not from pain, I don't think. He said he was sorry. He said he was drunk, and stupid, and that he was a bad and evil man he was bad he was bad he was bad he was evil.

Usually, when he was in blackout mode, I'd just guide him around like a cat. I remembered how pliable I used to be, at least the shadowy mental cross-stitch I could summon from pinpricks of memories and what my friends told me later.

But this time I told him that he was good, that I loved him, and that I'd never leave him. I said, "You're a good man" over and over. I hoped it would sink in even if he didn't remember. In grade school I used to hit him in the nuts all the time, unprompted, for fun, and he would go down just like that. Sometimes he'd get mad. Sometimes he'd laugh. No one thought it was weird. Boys. When I said I was an unhappy child, I meant that I was also an angry child.

*

Later that summer, a job offer came in for him in Kingston. They offered him a lot of money. For me it wasn't a question at all. "I'm thinking of taking it," he said.

"If you wanted me to come with you, I'd come with you," I said.

He was silent.

Then he changed the conversation.

A couple hours passed that night where I said goodbye to him in my head. I thought: *Okay*. I thought: *Never mind*. I thought: *This strange boy from my past sewed my heart back together. I will mourn, I will hold him until he leaves, and then I will move on.*

As we were getting ready for bed, he turned to me with screaming eyes: "Are you coming with me? Are we doing this? Are we really doing this?" He was shaking as I kissed him.

*

So we left the city and I moved east, again. We settled into the second floor of an old house with a balcony, a house with no screaming outside, no one beating on doors, no sounds of male rage through the walls. Ontario Works got me a job in a rental management office and I closed my eyes the one time they evicted two hookers.

We lived there for a year. I'm thankful for all of this. If your early thirties can be a rebirth, after rebirth had, supposedly, already been part of your life (I bought into the transition-as-second puberty stuff hard), then any period of your life can bring renewal. Can't it? I believe in that.

One day, I had this clear feeling: We went to this diner that had just opened. They used all local ingredients, claimed we really didn't have to tip, said that they were proud to pay their workers an actual living wage. I had a sandwich with soft thick bread, a kind of cheese I'd never heard of, fresh greens, and coffee that was somehow so fucking good I didn't even put cream in it. I'd paid for meals that nice before, but this was the first time without any regret or anxiety. That was the special thing. And we drove home (he drove home) and I thought, *I made it.*

3

And so then. The morning when it happened. You and I had been together eighteen months. We woke up in terrible heat; the A/C had broken during the night. You went to open the windows and the air outside was wavy. Our room was shimmering in the light. Kids outside were running through the back lane, burning in the sun.

I put my head in your neck when you laid back down. "Hazel," you said.

"Christopher." I folded my legs over yours. Your phone rang. I saw it was your dad. You said you didn't want to speak with him.

I only found out later that you told me second. I was always grateful for that. I was grateful you didn't tell me first.

*

When you did, I hated you instantly. Because I knew my hurt would need sealing immediately. That I would need to fold my pain, stow it somewhere to shrivel and grow pale. This is the order these things go. Someday, a girl might do the same thing to you.

You told me how you knew from when we were little, how you admired me from afar, how you thought, when we got together, that maybe you didn't want to be a girl, that maybe just being with a trans girl would soothe this part of your mind. Do you know what it's like to so completely understand the force about to blow up your life?—well. I barely remember what you said after that. You were vacating your guts and I was listening and nodding but I could only think, *I don't want you to transition. I don't want you to be a girl. You were the sweetest boy to me, and I loved you, and I still love you but now I have to help you. I have to guide you through clothes and bras and every way of dealing with hair and I have to watch your eyes grow heavy and frightened when you step outside the way I've seen countless girls like you. I have to listen to it all, over and over, again. To see you grow out your hair—oh God, you're going to dye it, aren't you? Of course you are. You'll dye it something besides that pretty, pretty red. That pretty red hair.*

*

It only took me two weeks to break up with you. Isn't that awful? I couldn't—I don't know. I couldn't do it. You didn't know what was coming and I did. I know you wanted to try, but I promise you, we wouldn't have made it.

For the first couple months I'd get off work and I'd feel it in my body. I mean a heavy shroud would emerge from my arms and vibrate through my skin. I mean it was a physical feeling. If I hadn't known that feeling, been able to name it, known exactly why it was happening and that eventually it would end, I probably would have ended up dead. You probably don't want to hear that. But, well, I'm not dead.

I stayed sober for three weeks after I left you. I knew that was only a matter of time, too. I don't feel awful that I started drinking again. I was sober for long enough, and if alcoholics are always alcoholics, then can't that logic apply to sobriety too? I can feel sobriety still there, those years of clarity and re-sprung desire still alive and sleeping in my bones. Like a patient lover forgiving me more than she should, waiting to come back when I'm ready.

I've seen your pictures. You look beautiful now. I guess you always were—well, I mean. You know what I mean, don't you?

You're applying for arts grants somewhere out east, I think. Like, east-east. From what I heard, you're living in an abandoned factory by the sea that's been turned into beautiful apartments. Your career has turned into the good-paying part of the gig economy and your girlfriend's name is Mauve. How can I honestly start to tell you how happy I am for you, and how much I want him back? Do you know I would never admit this to anyone? Do you know what it means to be turned into the kind of person you hate against your will? I'm writing this down in private. God forgive me, God please give me the strength, the kindness, the wisdom to cover this in my soul and keep it there. I would never tell you or another breathing creature how resentful I really feel.

JIKJI*

Jeff Noh

"Tout personne est titulaire d'un patrimoine."
— art. 2, Code civil du Québec

Dust blows from the Sahara and travels, through the prevailing winds, to the Republic of K. White masks purchased from small pharmacies in the capital provide a layer of protection against this dust, the condensation of breath gathering inside white cotton, humidifying it to make the barrier permeable. Such imperfections of division were, in essence, what the Bibliothèque Nationale had been referencing when it claimed that the French libraries were better suited to protect the *Jikji*, this proof of the *universal heritage of humanity* that deserved the protection of French climate control technology; French library protocol; the perfectly darkened enclosures

* The anthology of Buddhist teachings known as *Jikji* was printed in Heungdeoksa Temple in present-day South Korea in the Koryo dynasty. A notably early example of a text produced on metal movable-type, *Jikji* preceded Gutenberg's forty-two-line Bible by seventy-eight years. The last copy of Baegun's anthology survives in partial form in the Manuscrits Orientaux division of the Bibliothèque nationale de France.

of France. Because I had an aunt who lived in the Republic of K. who undoubtedly sold such masks in her pharmacy, this patrimonial disagreement pertained not only to the still recent memories I had of O. and her aspiration toward French culture—an aspiration that I had begun conceiving, however unfairly or inaccurately, shaped by my idiosyncratic understanding of pain, in terms of the broader project underway in Quebec to maintain its connections to France, the ceaseless maintenance of white infrastructure that took place in our favourite neighbourhoods of Montreal—but also, more improbably, that part of my life that I had imagined was uncontaminated by my memories of O., the interconnected fragments of family history that I tried to recombine with the scraps of free time that remained at the end of each day. It didn't add up to much. The translation of the article on the *patrimoine* for which I was employed at the Centre de Recherche was now long overdue. The messages that I received from the director had grown, in recent weeks, terse and impatient, but I justified the office hours that I allotted to the reconstruction project on the secondary benefits it might accord to my translation efforts. How could a translator properly work, I rehearsed asking the director, with a tone of indignation, without a full understanding of his relationship to the languages? I had not heard from O. in almost a year, but the humanizing discourses of the French librarians helped me understand the euphemisms she had employed to describe the reasons she *did not foresee things continuing into the future*. (In addition to *future* and *things*, she also spoke of *momentum*, problems of *space* and *time*; she spoke of *missing pieces*.) I wished to forget these memories and realize that version of the future from which she had deleted herself. My research into the *Jikji* would thus help my translation of the *patrimoine*. These scraps of history would reconstitute my knowledge of the French, a language that was first recorded inside my blood, the prestigious cadences lapsed and imperfectly transmitted by the French soldiers arriving at the shores of Gwanghwado, mouths closing over mouths, the proof of my *universal heritage of humanity.*

From the bay windows of the Victorian building that housed the research offices, one could enjoy a partial view of the side of Mont-Royal, and an implied view, in one's mind, of the iron cross that overlooked the city, whose steel base resembled that of the Tour Eiffel. I occasionally looked up from the outdated computer station at the Centre de Recherche, trying to find a perfect line of sight between the two gaps of my past and beyond the obfuscations of other intersecting lines—that period of lost time in my family's history from 1950 to 1953 and the gap in the historical record, between 1866 and 1886, when the *Jikji* might have first entered French possession. A few years after American state representatives consulted back issues of the *National Geographic* to draw the 38th parallel, dividing my family history into two clearly demarcated regions of the future, the printed characters of the *Jikji* would have, I thought, passed under the gloved hands of the librarians at the Bibliothèque Nationale as they catalogued the Henri Véver estate. If the division of my extended family attests to the transformative powers of representational drawing—the straight line at the 38th parallel becoming analogous to other such lines that appear in Soviet and American painting in the mid-twentieth century—then the printed characters of the *Jikji*, I believed, also possessed the ability to decode the incomprehensible chronology of my life. Victor Collin de Plancy had sold the *Jikji* to Henri Véver, the collector, in 1911 in exchange of 180 francs; the Bibliothèque Nationale had received it from the Véver estate in 1950, as part of his testament. Perhaps as a rehearsal of those problems of *time* and *space*, I attempted to reconstruct the twenty years from the French *punitive campaign* to Collin de Plancy's instatement as the French minister to the Republic of K. During those years, the *Jikji* remained in the climate-controlled archives of the Bibliothèque Nationale in Paris, the city that so many of my colleagues yearned to visit. To hear it from them, the *universal heritage of humanity* lies not only in the document held in the Manuscrits Orientaux division, but is ensconced in every aspect of the city, from its architecture to the passing gestures of its denizens, the smallest details of the kind of life that is possible only there. I have heard argued that the leisurely attitude of the French regarding the relationship between life and work has an inescapable Frenchness (the extended lunch hours of Parisian bureaucrats described in novels that I began reading but could not finish) and that the liberated attitude toward politics one perceives there also has a specific Frenchness, particularly when compared to North America and those places that are neither North American nor European; I have heard similar theories about the inescapable Europeanness of other European places, as when someone who has recently returned from Sweden commends the Nordic attitude toward child-rearing (they single-handedly invented the Babybjörn, for God's sake), the physical beauty of Nordic people and their beautiful socialism, their wide adoption of cycling culture revealing a sense of stewardship and care of the environment, conjuring up the smoke, dust, and pollution that waft over the Oriental continent, held off by the invisible borders of a unified Europe.

The French diplomat had arrived on the Peninsula in his capacity as a foreign minister in 1884, envisioning a railway between Seoul and Uiju using French railway technology from Fives-Lille. Of course, no French railway has ever connected the cities of Seoul and Uiju; yet, the idea of the application of French technology through French diplomacy existed somewhere in the *Jikji*'s history, as an alternative vision of the past that included my grandparents' hometowns in the French empire, a hypothetical example of the European interconnectedness that is so venerated by the tourists who travel the continent. On their return from Europe, these tourists often express astonishment about the ease with which one passes through the borders between countries (Germany, France, Switzerland), a fluidity made possible by the technology of the Fives-Lille corporation, which, in this alternative Peninsula of Victor Collin de Plancy's colonial vision, would have connected those place-names that were now lost on one side of my family to the European continent. Although I felt a certain disgust at these celebrations of interconnectedness, I could not help but wish to be a part of it. A tourist who rides a train through this version of the French countryside might, if she were to fall asleep or consciously attenuate her indifference to that part of the world, wake up to find the train arriving in the town in which my grandparents had met, before the division of the Peninsula. Because of their unknown status, the towns that were never connected by the French rail technology enjoyed in my mind the simple geometry of farm landscapes that are made familiar to us by certain canonical paintings, although logic and history suggest that people lived and continue to live there. These lines intersected across acres of a land I could not imagine, an abstract shape constructed of shaded regions and one-way mirrors that contained, inside of its impervious structure, the hundreds of thousands of people who continued in their ordinary lives since my grandparents might have last seen them in the 1950s, their daily habits conducted not in their capacity as relatives to me, or, as implied by the questions my colleagues asked, people living under a particular political regime, but in a dailiness that existed merely as a form of dailiness, their invisible faces that looked like mine as it might in a half-reflected window of the train.

The uncertainty of the twenty years between the French *punitive campaign* and Victor Collin de Plancy's arrival reminded me of the photographs taken from outer space of the Peninsula, which showed the yellow glow of the Republic of K., the network of highway, city, and information, against the constructed darkness of the D.P.R.K. When I saw such maps in childhood, the darkened area reminded me of a cushion separating the Republic of K. into an island, framed on one side by that darkness and what my colleagues today called the *Sea of Japan* on the other. Previously, the diplomat's career had fallen into question—could you remind me of your *real name*?—when it was discovered that the diplomat's father, a person whose work continues to cast a shadow over events today, had appended the title *de Plancy* to the family name against the rules of French aristocracy, referring to Plancy-l'Abbaye (a minor region of France which nevertheless would invoke, in the minds of my colleagues, the charms of the French countryside to which they were eager to ingratiate themselves). Following the diplomat's career, the *Jikji* would pass, through the robust rules of the transmission of property under the Napoleonic Code (the name that is passed down without change, and which, to the historic individual who is alive today, presents a rope connected to some darkened region in the past), passing to the jeweler and art collector of the Orient, Henri Véver, who, in his own will and testament, would transmit his possessions to the Bibliothèque Nationale in 1950, on the eve of the war that would separate the Peninsula into two parallel realities. This much I could easily ascertain from the Centre de Recherche in Quebec, another node of the French symbolic empire.

What I couldn't discern was the connection between the *Jikji* and my own history—a connection that, I thought, against better judgment, would prove the *universal heritage of humanity* within me if it could only be described accurately enough. The *modernizing efforts* of Collin de Plancy were, undoubtedly, a continuation of the Hungarian and French Catholic missions of the nineteenth century, and the efforts to design a railway merely one current in a general flow that included the English lessons that my father had taken in the army and the English lessons that I had taken as a boy during my brief time in the Republic of K.—could you remind me of your *real name*, I imagined Victor Collin de Plancy being asked at the École des langues orientales vivantes—the

English teacher who had, like the French diplomat, been on the Peninsula on some mission that was now lost, the window looking out onto the lights of nighttime Seoul, a city that, among the people I knew now, remained a symbol of historical division (as if the demilitarized zone were a landmark one could visit on a tour of postwar architecture or en route to a party around the Ringbahn) or simply a layover to another destination that was more frequently visited, Vietnam or Japan. I, too, have visited that country, I have heard *world travelers* say about the Republic of K., referring to extended layovers that were scheduled in Gimpo in the past and now in Incheon. I landed in Gimpo the way there and came from Incheon on the way back, these travelers might say, as if they had entered a room in a house by mistake, I experienced the history of the Peninsula in its entirety, from the roots of the old airport's existence as Keijo New Airfield under Japanese occupation, built with the boulders that were carried over by manual labourers from neighbouring mountains and fields, to its fully modernized airport in Incheon, voted one of the best airports in the world. Having devoted a polite amount of time on the topic of the country that I came from, the traveler would then extricate himself from our conversation about airports to direct, across the circle, to someone who originally comes from Finland, questions about that country's geography and culture. Was it a Nordic country, he might ask, as if he were suddenly relieved of a burden, or a Scandinavian country? These were places that, for reasons that were inscrutable to me, inspired a vigorous line of questioning, not to the *political situation* of a place but pertaining to the people, language, and food there, the half-remembered traditions of snatching puffins out of the sky and biting into their heads and baking Nordic breads whose recipes precede the global trade of sugar, that concentrated version of sweetness naturally found in berries indigenous to that region of the world, the berries' tartness whose sugary enzymes would linger on the tongue as a faint aftertaste in their smiling bites. From the point of view of the tourist who visits the Republic of K. on a layover to somewhere else, landing for a few hours in the old airport that I still remembered, and, on the complicated route back, stopping over at the new airport made of glass, the country might have seemed to modernize between the three weeks that made up a trip to Vietnam or Japan, providing a glimpse of that wonderfully titillating experience of disorientation that my colleagues in the faculty celebrated in their discussions of *global citizenship*.

Improbably, even this limited vision of the Republic of K.—reduced to the old airport and the new airport and the transposed rocks that are around those air fields—seemed to contain my entire life, as those hours waiting in the respective air fields contains the view of the mountains that separate the halves of the Peninsula (the seasoned travelers in the faculty preferred to *stay in one city* over a week rather than string together multiple short visits, changing hotel rooms each night). In this way, it was as if the six months that a colleague spent in the Villa della Torre, studying sixteenth-century food and architecture (it was pure arrogance, this colleague said, describing his travels, to imagine that one can learn the ins and outs of Italian culture—a culture that spanned thousands of continuous years—in a week-long visit to that country, as so many visitors do, for it took a lifetime of dedicated eating, touring, and fornicating within a single small village simply to begin understanding its depth of culture), were telescoped into the three hours between airplanes experienced in the old airport and the new airport in the Republic of K., two places that seemed endpoints of my family history. Space itself seemed to transform according to the imagination of my colleagues. The airports that exist in the Orient behaved, in their minds, and therefore in my own, like ballrooms and apartments, places where coincidences are free to happen, where one might run into a friend or a neighbour unexpectedly, as in the story that I had once heard in my childhood, after my family had emigrated from the Republic of K., about a classmate who ran into the family of another classmate in the terminals of Narita International, the families approaching each other in the long concourse of the Japanese airport, and, unable to believe it, collapsing into laughter as the smiling women in kimono next to the *duty free shops* turned their painted faces to the family, the white neighbours laughing, shaking hands and hugging in astonishment at the coincidence, as in those passages of the *Divina Commedia* in which the poet looks down and recognizes distant cousins and old teachers in the preliminary stages of hell. This was the only part of the three-week tour of Japan the classmate seemed to remember, recounting his *summer travel* in front of the room at the teacher's invitation (I pretended as if I had not visited the Republic of K. with my mother and my brother to visit my father, making up the story of an uneventful summer). By contrast, airports like Charles de Gaulle and Heathrow are rarely discussed other than as places of passing misery. They are not experienced as destinations intrinsically, but as pathways to somewhere else, a well-designed corridor exists to be forgotten, while the airports of the Orient can determine the traveler's entire experience of a country.

I could imagine each of my colleagues passing through the airport in the Republic of K. as temporary visitors who would eventually make their way to somewhere else, conveyed from arrival to departure, the glass partitions of empty concourses, escalators that will continue to run into the middle of future nights. On the day that both sides of my extended family gathered at the airport tables, a temporary visitor to that country might have looked down from the continually moving steps as he was transported into a higher dimension of the structure and witnessed a scene that is remembered by no one else in my family who is alive, and which will be deleted through my work at the Centre de Recherche. In the scene, my grandmother from one side of the family asks my grandfather on the other side of the family, the author of our plans to leave the Republic of K., *why he decided to disturb our lives*. I don't remember the particulars of his answer, though it involved some aspect of the collapsing economy, the freedom afforded by education, *erziehung zur freiheit*—even, improbably, the International Monetary Fund. What I could recover from this forgotten scene was not my grandfather's answer but the question that incited the answer, I mean the timing of the question that incited the answer, delayed until the last moment. Minutes later, my parents, brother and I slipped behind the paper screen that blocked the view into the international security area, as a printed character disappears when a page is lifted and turned, bleached fibers tearing against the motion of the hand, the vaulting lines of steel that would remind someone, under different circumstances, of those great cathedrals of Europe, burned and rebuilt with international capital, as my brother and I take off our sneakers to board the airplane that will disappear into the atmosphere.

With a hand on the elastic railing of the rising escalator, the visitor looks down into the food court. He sees, through the layers of glass, the entirety of my life in that moment. The years are ground up in the unseen gears of the escalator and recombined into a passing impression that barely registers in his memory (I've been to the old airport and the new airport, the new airport is nice…). Outside the window he sees the edges of Gwanghado, where the French had arrived to the Peninsula on their *punitive campaign*, the pillaged documents attesting to my *universal human heritage* conveyed, through a pathway as unattractively tangled as my own, to the Bibliothèque Nationale, where the secular values of the Republic remain stored. In their peculiar practice of politics, my colleagues spoke of their *split identities* between the French and the English languages, a split that ran through the foundations of the faculty of law, which spoke to us in long flowing emails that would lurch suddenly into the French language partway through a paragraph or even a single sentence, tracing the airflow behind a jet's passing wake or the air-conditioned chambers preserving the *Jikji* in the Manuscrits Orientaux division, a relatively unpopular section of the Bibliothèque Nationale which by that very fact was all the more essential, setting the stage for the discovery of the document by a librarian who was a foreigner in Paris the same way I was a foreigner in Montreal. In 1989, the French president had promised the return of the *universal human heritage* on the condition that French rail technology be sent to the Republic of K. in a second chance at transforming the infrastructure of the Peninsula in Victor Collin de Plancy's vision (the portico installed at the Saint Antoine entrance of the metro Square-Victoria was, like O.'s distorted perception of me, a gift that originated in Paris). There never was a French railway in the Republic of K., but the *universal human heritage* remains in the archive, preserving the Frenchness that O. saw everywhere except for the places associated with me. The railway, she once said to me, *remains an obsession of mine*, recalling the journeys by train that she had taken across Europe, her national identity card proving European status and the steel interconnections below expanding the world in which I did not exist to more distant zones of the continent: fields of lavender blurring into olive groves and crumbling sections of Roman masonry, the lost cargo of the Mediterranean sea.

DRAGO

Michael Melgaard

I got a job at a used bookstore on Yonge. It was one of the last ones in town that had a back-room porn section. The front of the shop sold old paperbacks, the till was at the back in front of a shelf that separated the porn room from the rest of the store. The porn section just sold DVDs and took up twice the space as the books. It wasn't much of a bookstore.

Greg ran the shop. When I'd dropped off a resume, he told me his guy had just quit and asked me if I was comfortable selling porn. When I guessed I was, he had me start a trial shift right then. He showed me how to use the till, how the porn DVDs were filed—the cases in the back were all empty, the discs kept behind the till in numbered binders—and what to pay for used books (a dollar for paperbacks, two if they were any good). When I asked what I should do if someone brought in a rare first edition, Greg said, "You're not going to have to worry about that."

He watched me ring through a couple of customers and buy a bag of paperbacks before he said, "OK, you got the job. I'm going to get some food and catch a movie. I'll come back at the end of the shift and show you how to cash out."

On his way out, he added, "Oh, and there's this guy who comes in named Drago. Big guy with an accent. He's a friend of the owners. He gets 75 percent off whatever he buys." I nodded. "And do what he says, okay?" I was still thinking about what I should do if someone brought in a first edition of *The Great Gatsby*, so that didn't register as a strange thing for Greg to have said.

Drago didn't show up until a few shifts later. I was filing porn discs into the binders when a big guy in track pants and a long, soft leather jacket came in. He said, "You're new?"

I told him I was.

He said, "I'm Drago. I get a deal." He leaned over the counter and looked behind me. I leaned back. "The other guy knows me," he said. I thought he was maybe looking for a note behind the till that said Drago gets a deal.

I said, "He told me."

"Good. Good." He leaned back to his side of the counter and said, "I'm Drago." We shook hands. He squeezed mine hard and pulled me toward him at the same time. He looked me steadily in the eye. He said, "You."

I said, "Nice to meet you."

And he said, "You."

"Oh, I'm Matt."

He let go of my hand and nodded. He said, "Matt." and went into the back. He had to tilt his body sideways to get through the entrance.

Ten minutes later he came out with a stack of DVDs. He said, "I get a deal, the other guy knows."

"Greg told me."

I rang it up, hit the discount button, the total came up. He said, "I don't pay tax." He leaned over the counter to see my side of the register display. I couldn't figure out how to take tax off. I pressed some buttons. He said, "No, no. No tax. The other guy knows."

I voided the sale and started over. The tax got added on and Drago said, "No tax. I don't pay tax." He was right over the counter. I voided everything and put the numbers into a calculator I found under the desk. I told him the total. He pulled a roll of bills out of his jacket pocket and paid. I handed him his change and after he left I rang up the sale on the register with the tax and wrote a note that explained why the till was a few dollars short. I put the note in the till and at the end of the night taped it to the deposit bag.

The only things Greg knew about Drago were that he was from Serbia or Yugoslavia or somewhere like that and that he did the store's owner favours every now and then. I never met the owner, but Greg told me he owned a lot of property around town and ran a lot of small businesses that only seemed to break even or lose money. The bookstore was a money-loser. When I asked why he didn't just rent out the building if the bookstore lost money, Greg said, "I don't ask too many questions." I had never been asked for my SIN number or address and I paid myself cash out of the till at the end of every week. Greg said, "Drago's okay. Don't worry about him." And then he looked at me and added, "Just do what he says."

Drago came in about once a week. He'd browse for ten minutes and then buy eight or so DVDs. He always said he got a deal and leaned over the counter and paid with cash. The back room was busy and there were plenty of porn-section regulars who drew as much or more attention to themselves. One guy insisted on letting me know what fetish he was into each week, another always called his purchases "items" in a way that made me deeply uncomfortable—"Just these three . . . *items*," he'd say—and there were hagglers that wasted a lot of my time. Drago didn't stand out too much the first few months I was there.

Then, a week before Christmas, Drago came in near the end of my shift and went into the back. I heard a noise and looked into the security monitor behind the desk—by then I'd learned to check the monitor rather than run into the porn section to see what the problem was. Drago had stumbled into a wall of DVDs and knocked the cases over. He bent over to pick them up and knocked a bunch off another shelf. I left him to it. Eventually, he came around the wall and I pretended like I had been sorting porn DVDs. I realized Drago was very drunk.

He dropped the brown paper bag I handed to him and bent over to pick it up. A gun slipped out of his jacket and fell onto the floor. He picked it up and tucked it behind his belt. I handed him his change and he left.

Greg knew Drago carried a gun and told me not to worry about it, Drago wouldn't cause any trouble at the shop, "He helps out around here."

"With a gun?"

"No, no. He gets us porn from some of his old buddies in Bosnia or Yugoslavia or whatever country he's from. A lot of that really hardcore stuff is illegal here." Greg saw me react. "It's an old law. They only enforce it at the border—no one will ever come in here and give you a hard time." I didn't say anything. "Look, Drago is fine." Greg added, "Just do what he says."

There was a regular who always picked up a book on his way into the back. When he came to the till, he'd have the book on top of the DVDs to disguise his stack of porn. Every few months he sold the books back to the store. A few weeks after Drago dropped his gun and I found out he was smuggling illegal porn into the country, this regular sold me back a bag of books. One of them was *Secret War: The Break-Up of Yugoslavia and the Balkan Wars, 1991-2001.*

The book opened with a crane lifting a semi-truck trailer out of a lake somewhere near a town called Peć. The crane's chain snapped. The trailer fell onto the beach and tipped over, cracking open the back doors and spilling water and months-old decomposing bodies all over the shore. The bodies had been wrapped in tarps. Their hands were bound behind their backs where the rope or arms had not rotted away.

The next chapter jumped forward to the International Criminal Tribunal for the Former Yugoslavia. The book's author was one of the lawyers prosecuting the men responsible for putting those bodies in the truck. He began to trace the history of the case of the bodies in the truck as a means of examining the whole history of the Yugoslavian Wars, and the genocide that came of it.

I barely knew about this war. I did not know about the genocide.

The author recreated the scene of the mass killing. A paramilitary unit whose later-arrested members would argue was not part of the Yugoslav People's Army, but who were most certainly working under orders from a low-ranking officer in the Yugoslav People's Army, who was himself almost certainly working under orders from even higher up, had been sent to a small village to round up rebels. The village was predominantly Albanian; the soldiers worked under the assumption that anyone not an actual rebel was housing or abetting the rebels in some way. They rounded up everyone they could find and locked them in the city hall. The commander of the operation came into the village once it was secure. His name was Drago Mošević.

I put the book down.

I picked it back up and flipped to the index and read every page with "Mošević, Drago" on it. A few pages ahead of where I'd been reading, Drago Mošević had the town hall lit on fire and ordered his troops to shoot anyone who managed to get out. A few chapters later, he and his troops went on the run after the fall of Slobodan Milošević, and, further on, several of his troops were caught while Drago Mošević managed to escape. Toward the end of the book, it was revealed that the investigators had not yet found him. They believed he and a few others from his unit had escaped to North America.

I checked the copyright date. The book was two years old.

Drago came into the bookstore. I tucked *Secret War* under the till and pretended to be filing porn DVDs. I didn't see until he was at the till that he had a kid with him. He said, "This is Petr. Keep an eye on him a minute."

Drago went back outside and headed north up the street.

I said, "Hi."

Petr pulled out a phone and sat on a box of books. He looked maybe eight. I wanted to read my book but didn't want the kid to see what I was reading so took a stack of DVDs into the back and shelved them. When I came back Petr had grabbed the DVDs I'd left behind and was flipping through them, looking at the covers. I took them back and moved the stack under the counter. He went back to looking at his phone.

Drago came back two hours later and said, "Let's go," to Petr.

Petr didn't look up from his phone but said, "I just need to finish...."

Drago said, "Now."

And Petr said, "No, no, I need to—" Drago hit him on the side of the head.

Petr's eyes turned red and Drago said, "You going to cry like a little pussy? Come on." He pushed Petr down the aisle ahead of him and out the door.

I took the book home after my shift. A few more chapters in, I saw that Drago was a very common name in the former Yugoslavia. Aside from Drago Mošević, there was a chief investigator, a village mayor, and a forensic doctor all named Drago. I also realized it would not have made sense for Drago Mošević to move to Canada and not change his name to something other than Drago. But then, I thought, if it was a common name, another war criminal who escaped to North America could have named himself Drago and moved to Toronto.

Greg thought it was unlikely that Drago had been involved in anything like war crimes, but he did know that Drago moved to Canada in the late nineties, which lined up, time-wise, with the war. "But it's more likely he moved here to get away from that life," Greg said. "You said yourself, there was a civil war or something. Would you want to raise your kids around that type of violence?"

I said, "I saw him hit his kid."

"Well, that's a cultural thing. It's rough where he's from. I don't judge. But he doesn't strike me as the war-criminal type. Just an average, small-time porn smuggler." Greg laughed, but stopped when he looked at me. He said, "Look, you don't need to worry about Drago, he's never been anything but fine to us." I waited for him to add, "Just do what he says."

After I finished *Secret War*, I looked in the history section for more books on Yugoslavia. There weren't any; it wasn't a very good bookstore.

The shop had a theft problem. The till at the back of the store meant it was easy to walk in, grab some books from the front, and leave. Greg told me not to worry about theft; books weren't worth getting punched over. I followed that advice unless someone was being too obvious to ignore.

I had my eye on an obvious thief the next night Drago came in. It was a kid who was looking at me every time I looked at him. He had a large, open gym bag on the side of the shelf I couldn't see from the till, but which I could see in the security monitor behind the desk. I was waiting for him to actually put a book in the bag so I could tell him to leave.

Drago came out of the back and handed me some DVDs. I pulled the discs out and looked at the shoplifter. The shoplifter looked down at the shelf. I rang in the titles and hit the discount button and looked at the shoplifter, who looked down at the shelf again. Drago looked around and leaned into me. He whispered, "Trouble?"

"No, it's nothing."

Drago went over to a shelf and took a book out. He looked sideways at the shoplifter, who was still looking at me. I walked over to Drago to tell him not to worry about it. The shoplifter dropped some books into his duffle bag. I rolled my eyes and said, "Put those—"

Drago walked down the aisle and pushed the shoplifter down to the ground. He said, "You stealing, you piece of shit?" He bent down and picked up the kid, turned him around and ran him into the door, opened it, and threw him on the sidewalk. The door swung shut. Drago walked back up the aisle and picked up the duffle bag. He kicked open the door. The kid was just getting up. Drago threw the bag at him and then grabbed him by the front of the jacket and said something I couldn't make out through the door. He let go and when the kid turned around to run, Drago kicked his legs out from under him. Then picked him up and slammed him into the dollar-book cart that we kept in front of the store. He hauled the kid back to his feet and kicked his ass to get him moving, then picked up the bag and threw it after him.

Drago came back in. He was shaking. He said, "Piece of shit." He came around the counter. I moved away. He reached under and started looking around for something. He was sweating and breathing heavy. He said, "Tissue." There was a box on the shelf behind the till—I handed it to him and he pulled a wad out and put it on his hand. I hadn't noticed it was bleeding. He said, "Fuck. That fuck." He sat down on my stool. I stepped around to the customer side of the counter.

I said, "There's some water. . . ."

He grabbed the bottle and drank. He took a deep breath and said, "Piece of shit."

He got the bathroom key from where we kept it under the till and went in. I thought about calling Greg. Drago came out ten minutes later. His face was wet and his hair slicked back. He said, "I always look out for you guys."

I said, "Thank you."

"You need anything, let me know." He slapped my shoulder, said, "You look shook up. Don't worry. That guy was nothing. He wouldn't have done anything to you." He laughed. "He won't be back." He slapped my shoulder again.

I got a job at a bookstore that didn't have a porn section on the other side of town and forgot about Drago until a few years later. I was waiting for my lunch at a falafel place that had the 24-hour news channel on mute. The closed captioning lagged behind the footage, so it was a minute before I realized the man being led out of a courthouse in handcuffs had been arrested on suspicion of war crimes committed in Yugoslavia twenty-five years before. He had been living under assumed names in London, Ontario. His real name was Drago Mošević. It took me a minute to remember where I'd heard the name before: he was the man who had ordered anyone who got out of the burning town hall shot.

I looked up the story when I got home. Mošević had been living in a quiet subdivision outside of London, Ontario, under an assumed name for almost a decade. His neighbours were all surprised by his arrest—he was a quiet guy who kept to himself, but had done small favours for his neighbours over the years that made everyone say they couldn't believe it, he seemed like such a nice guy.

He'd been caught because he'd gotten into a bar fight years before. He hadn't been charged, but he had been taken into the drunk tank and fingerprinted. The prints got uploaded to an international database, where they were eventually flagged. The Yugoslavian War Crimes Commission had been alerted. Mošević had been found out years before all the agencies involved were able to coordinate an arrest.

I kept an eye on the news after that, but the only follow-up articles were in Balkan languages and Google translate only really helped me confirm the obvious: he was going to jail. As far as the Canadian news was concerned, it seemed to have just been a news-of-the-weird, war-criminal-in-our-midst story that didn't warrant a follow up. The war had happened a long time ago, in a country that didn't exist anymore. It wasn't the sort of thing people cared about.

The next time I was downtown, I stopped by the old bookstore. Greg was working. It had been long enough and staff turnover was such that it took him a minute to recognize me. He seemed happy to see me, wondered what was new. We swapped stories about some of the old regulars, and then I asked if that Drago guy still came in.

Greg said, "I haven't seen him in months." I asked when, exactly, and he said, "I don't know, maybe two months ago? He just stopped coming in."

Drago Mošević had been arrested two months before. It seemed like too much for it to be a coincidence that Drago stopped coming in at the same time as the arrest. If he was into anything more serious than porn smuggling and knew a co-conspirator had been arrested, he'd want to disappear.

I wanted to get more from Greg, but couldn't think of a way to do it that wouldn't draw attention to my questions and make me look silly; I knew Greg would just say he "didn't ask too many questions." And he had already moved on to telling me a story about an old regular who he'd had to ban for pissing himself in the back room. I let it go and, after a bit, said I had to run. It probably was just a coincidence, and, after all, didn't really matter.

VICTORY DAY

Cassidy McFadzean

I've only been in Tbilisi twenty minutes when I'm smoking hash out of a can of Borjomi mineral water that Sasha lights for me. Nara and Davit have given me a ride from Yerevan where there's two weeks remaining in the art residency, but I've brought all my luggage and haven't decided if I'll go back. Sasha sucks his lips against the can, and I tell him how our car was searched at the border, that I walked in on a guy at the squat toilet, standing naked from the waist down. Sasha asks if the guy had a bigger cock than him, and I don't answer. Instead, I tell him I feel guilty for missing the election of Nikol Pashinyan and the celebrations of the new prime minister following the Armenian revolution.

"You were there for the important part," he reassures me.

We have sex and when we come at the same time Sasha shouts, "Team sport."

The next morning, we sleep late and smoke more hash at his desk, overlooking the mountain, forest, and graveyard below. Sasha has added more transplants from his forest hikes to the ceramic planter on his windowsill. He shows me the winding succulent, thin green stalks of something that resembles clover, and deep red grasses with small spiky flowers.

I ask if my breasts have gotten smaller while in Armenia, and he tells me that he is attracted to my body, which is not the answer I am looking for. "You were so anxious there," he says, drawing his lips from the aluminum can to suck my right nipple. "My poor anxious poet, it's good you came back."

He's taking me to the sulfur baths to make up for missing my birthday and on our way to Rustaveli Street, we pass the cemetery where an old man is building a section of concrete wall.

"Is he just going to build right over that gravestone?" Sasha says, gesturing to a stone in the side of the hill. He is aghast. He tells me that the Soviets used grave markings of people they didn't like to construct new buildings.

The gravestone is etched with Georgian writing, and I make the observation that the characters of the Armenian language are angular, while Georgian is rounded. I wonder aloud whether this is reflected in the disposition of the two nations, citing the severity of the Armenians compared to the jolliness of the Georgians, or even their appearances: the skinny frames of Nara and Davit versus the fattened bellies of Sasha's Georgian friends.

"You're exoticizing again," he says, grasping an unripe green fruit from a tree. "Soon you'll be eating figs off the street."

In my absence, roses have bloomed all over Tbilisi, red, pink, and white. We walk to the sulfur baths and pass cherry trees buzzing with flies as the hot smell of yeast rises from basement bakeries. All is in a state of exaggerated growth and fermentation. I step over a dead water beetle on the sidewalk, and we dodge fly-covered dog shit, pale yellow and frothing.

We get lunch at a restaurant close to the baths, and Sasha tells me the way I eat khinkali turns him on. Afterwards, he gets a boner in the sauna, but we don't have any condoms. I'm tipsy from the beer we've brought with us and tell him I have my period so it's okay. He bends me over a stone massage bed, and spits on his hand, rubbing it on his dick. He thrusts only a few times before stopping. "I don't want to come inside you," he says, and I drink the rest of our beer. When our time in the baths is up, my hair is still wet at the nape.

We walk until it dries, and Sasha holds onto my thumb, like he's a little kid and I'm his mom. I make a squealing sound and he tells me sometimes I remind him of a wolf pup and other times of some sort of weasel.

We walk past men in yellow vests directing traffic and take the bus to an art show Sasha wants to see. A woman is passing out flyers and the girl in front of us tells her, "Shansi aris" which Sasha translates to "Not a chance." We brainstorm ways to incorporate the word into our vocabulary. We board a bus, and though there's nowhere to sit, it's less crowded than any of the buses in Yerevan and I can grip a pole without men's bodies pressing into me. Sasha pays with his transit card and hands me a ticket. The driver gestures at a pothole, announcing it with his hand like an orchestra conductor, and we laugh at his indignation.

"Shansi aris," I say to the pothole, half a block behind us. We order beers at the art gallery and Sasha introduces me to Grigol, a young photographer who is presenting his work: a limited edition book consisting of photos of his parents' youth in the Soviet Union. He discusses the project with a bashfulness I find endearing. Half the audience has opted to sit on the floor of the gallery and I watch Grigol's eyes moving up and down as he surveys the crowd. The event is well documented—at least three people are taking pictures on their phones. There are two people with DSLRs and an older grey-haired man records the entire event. When he is finished speaking, Grigol takes questions from the audience. There are many queries including but not limited to: how old he is, whether his parents gave permission for the project, whether his project has opened conversations in his family, what he imagines is the reason for silence surrounding the Soviet years. A conversation like this would never occur in Toronto, where people are too self-conscious.

One woman remarks on the ubiquitousness of cameras for our generation and says that she doesn't think such a project would be possible for the generations before Grigol's parents, who are barely older than Sasha. The grey-haired man pauses recording to argue with the woman; he himself took many such photos in his youth and therefore he disagrees that his children would have no record. That was not what the woman was saying, however. She asks the man to consider how many cameras he saw in the hands of his peers growing up, but a full fledged argument breaks out in Russian, stealing attention from Grigol. The event concludes to scattered applause, and Sasha whispers that the old man is a famous photographer.

We finish our beers quickly. I te2ll Sasha I have cramps and need to find a bathroom, but he tells me there's no public toilet. We stand outside with two women Sasha knows. They tell us about the fentanyl crisis that's erupted over the past couple of weeks. There's been more and more deaths and now government agencies are warning against using any sort of drugs.

"What about hash?" Sasha asks.

"I'm not sure," one woman says. "Just to be safe they're saying not to use anything."

"What if I've already smoked it?"

"It's definitely in MDMA," she says. She tells us about a friend of a friend who used MDMA at the club one night, and ended up in a coma. The ecstasy was laced with fentanyl.

"I have a guy who uses the stuff before he splits it with me. If there was any problem, he'd let me know."

"Just be careful," she says.

We take a taxi to an abandoned warehouse where Nara's group show is opening, and Sasha promises me there's a bathroom. When we get there, Nara is in a white satin gown and I don't feel the shame of being underdressed in jeans and Nikes because my guts are churning. She asks if I'm getting a ride back to Yerevan with them and I tell her I haven't decided.

"We're thinking of leaving tomorrow after lunch," she says. "So let us know."

"I will."

I remind Sasha about the bathroom and he asks Davit where the toilets are, but he doesn't know, and we run into Nara's boss, who Sasha stands and talks with.

Finally, we go outside the warehouse and around the side of the building. There's a dark room with a squat toilet that I use, expelling the black shit that often accompanies my period. I wipe with a napkin from my purse, and then rinse the squat toilet with a jug in the corner of the room. I feel slightly better, and Sasha insists that more alcohol will help. We go to a restaurant and split a bottle of rosé and he raises his glass, imitating the famous Georgian toasts.

"Someone's twenty-nine," he says. "Where did you think you'd be at twenty-nine, in your husband's asshole?"

"I'm not in the asshole of my husband," I say. "I'm shitting in a toilet."

We go back to his place to smoke more hash and have sex. The skin on his pelvis is bumpy from shaving and resembles a plucked chicken. He gets on his back, and spreads his legs wide open. He is a dead chicken in a grocery store. I lay beside him and he sits on my face, and I shove his balls in my mouth. I insert a black silicone butt plug into his ass, pushing and pulling back and forth until he's hard. He fucks me with the toy inside him, and when he comes, his moans are tender and feminine.

"You're my monogamous girlfriend," he whispers to me before falling asleep.

While I was in Yerevan, the smoking laws had come into effect in Tbilisi. Now we can work in all the cafes that Sasha was too allergic to enter before. We're working on our laptops at a bar, and I pick his baseball cap off the table and place it on my head.

"Do you like looking like a clown in a public place?" he says. "Do you like looking comical?"

"What?"

"That hat is way too big."

I don't want him to know he's hurt my feelings so I leave the hat on and take a selfie. My phone lights up with Nara's name, but I ignore the call. Instead, we work for another hour and then take a taxi to the apartment Sasha has arranged for me to rent and that the landlord Joni says I can take early. Joni only speaks Russian and Georgian, and so I'll have to communicate through Sasha, or the other expat tenant Chris, who Sasha says practices bass clarinet all day. The taxi drops us off beside the Terrace Hotel, and we descend the narrow cobblestone street next to the music school, where children are practicing piano scales. We reach the two-storey house and enter through a rusted green metal gate around back. Inside the courtyard is a fruit tree and a staircase to the apartments, two of which Sasha has already tried living in. They didn't work out because of his allergies to mould, particleboard, detergent, and other yet unidentified sources.

"You'll have fruit," he says. "Maybe cherries."

He carries my suitcase up the stairs, and leaves my luggage on the balcony while he goes up another flight of stairs to get Joni. They come down and Joni says, "gamarjoba" and I pay him the deposit. We take a picture of the electricity meter, and Joni translates through Sasha. There's a feather pillow and a synthetic one, and I might consider unplugging the water heater to save a few lari on the power bill. I thank Joni using one of the few Georgian words I've memorized. "Madlobt," I say. "Didi madloba." He leaves us inside the apartment, which is partially built into the side of a hill, the other half a renovated porch.

Sasha gets the Wi-Fi password from Joni's son in the neighbouring suite, and I open the kitchen cupboards. Inside, there's a vegetable peeler, one pot, a knife, four spoons of various sizes, and a fork.

"I used the pot to make tea when I stayed here," Sasha says.

There's no matches and it looks like it will take forever to boil, but I agree it's suitable. He enters the Wi-Fi password into my phone, and I open the fridge, which has been humming loudly since we arrived.

"This isn't the one that was filled with all that meat?" I ask him, remembering Sasha's anecdote of scrubbing blood out of a fridge his first week in Tbilisi.

"No, that was next door," he tells me.

It's cold in the apartment. I open the drawers in the bedroom wardrobe, and they're filled with packets of insect poison. Sasha notices a square door in the wall, and makes a joke about a dungeon. He opens it, revealing a crawlspace a few square metres in size. He clicks a switch and a red bulb illuminates brick walls.

"I think it's a good sign, this torture chamber in your apartment," he says.

Although it's cool in the apartment, he says he'll have to ask Joni for a fan; he's too allergic to stay inside even for a few hours.

"There's no towels," I tell him.

"You want me to ask Joni for towels?"

"I don't know."

"You come from a family of great artists and poor communicators," he says. He runs back upstairs. I hear him speaking to Joni in Russian, and then in a few seconds, Sasha comes down alone.

"I told him to get a kettle for you and a fan," he says.

"Thank you."

"You should open these windows," Sasha continues, unlatching the frames. "You could get some plants in here, hang them in the windows."

"I'm barely going to be here," I say.

"This place could be really nice," he says. "I should get going."

"Are we meeting later?"

"I'll message you," he says.

"Okay."

After he leaves, I unzip my suitcase on the bed and hang my jacket on the hooks by the door, but I leave the rest of my clothes packed. With Sasha gone, the imperfections of the apartment are all the more apparent: the tile flooring of the kitchen is slanted, and all of the cupboards are crooked. In the bathroom, the container of hand soap slides off the sink, which is built on an angle. I pee and flush the toilet, but it takes three tries for the toilet paper to go down. The apartment is dark, and I can hear Joni's son next door, exiting his suite and entering his bathroom, which has a separate entrance from the balcony. I close the windows Sasha opened but I still hear Joni's son shitting into the toilet, and then talking on the phone in Georgian. I read in bed but after no more than half an hour Sasha messages me, asking if I want to come over.

"Okay," I write him. "I just need to change."

I move to the doorway of the bedroom, where I can't be seen from the window, and change from shorts into jeans.

"On my way," I write him.

I leave the apartment, turning the key two times behind me, though the lock is so flimsy the action feels pointless. I descend the stairs and exit the yard, the gate clattering behind and announcing my departure. I start back up the cobblestone street, stepping on the sharp edges of the rocks to keep my balance. I climb up the staircase and follow the landmarks Sasha pointed out on our drive there: the evenly spaced bins of garbage, the brown signpost. I walk along the road at the edge of the trees, passing the tin-clad dome of the church and the line-up of taxis in front of the forest. I walk along a wooden sidewalk where there's construction, and then the sidewalk ends.

I stand in place as taxis zoom past.

"I don't know if I just feel tired but I feel like this is stupid," I text him. "Especially if you're never staying over."

"Come?"

"It's dangerous, there's no sidewalk," I write. "I feel like I don't get the point of this."

I keep walking, pressing my body against the side of buildings, paint peeling from concrete. The next time I stop it's to check directions.

"Hi," Sasha writes. "Are you on your way or not?"

"Yes, but I'm annoyed."

"Okay," he says. "Are you still in the mood to come over?"

"It just doesn't feel equal."

"I invited you," he says. "Don't come if you don't feel like it."

"It just feels dumb."

"I don't know how to make you feel better," he says. "I'm really allergic at your place. I have health issues. Maybe if we get a fan it will be better there."

I stop checking my phone, and focus on walking the strip of sidewalk not blocked by garbage bins or parked cars. I keep my head down to watch for mounds of dog shit. I step over the body of a pale white gecko turned upside down, its tail removed from its torso. I soon reach another construction site, this one completely obscuring the sidewalk.

"Can you please calm yourself down?" my phone reads. "Please?"

I march down the middle of the street, moving to the side only when I hear the cars approaching from behind. When I come to the street that leads to Sasha's apartment, the sidewalk begins again, and I climb the hill, passing the cemetery and reaching his building. I insert a ten tetri coin into the metal box in the elevator and press the number eight. The elevator jerks to his floor and soon opens to his landing. I press his doorbell and he answers, hugging me at the door.

"I'm glad you came," he says. I come inside and take off my shoes. "I just feel frustrated," I say. "I don't see the point of renting a place if I'm going to be here every night."

"You need an office," he says. "And I needed you to have your own place. It's for me to feel secure and for us to give this another try."

"So we're dating again?" I ask. "We're monogamous?"

"You're my monogamous girlfriend," he says. "I love you and no other, but I need you to have your own apartment."

"Okay," I agree.

The next morning is the Day of Victory over Fascism. "Everyone else does May 8," Sasha tells me on the taxi ride to Vake Park. "We do May 9 when the Soviets signed."

We stayed up late smoking hash and slept in, and Sasha is worried we'll miss the people in military uniforms or the nationalists picking fights with old grannies for wearing the orange and black ribbon of Saint George which commemorates Russian soldiers in WWII, symbolizes Russian patriotism, and is now illegal to wear.

We stop at the edge of the park. Sasha is disappointed by the size of the crowd, and tells me it was busier in previous years. Still, we navigate through the crowds of young people and families taking photographs in front of the fountains and head toward a group gathered at the foot of a giant stone figure with two outstretched hands, one clutching a flower. We squeeze past chairs set up in front of the military band, mostly occupied by the elderly. I comment that the band sounds like Tom Waits and Sasha seems happy that I'm getting into the spirit of things.

"There are the nationalists," Sasha says, pointing to men in black T-shirts and camo at the Memorial of the Unknown Soldier.

We watch parents pushing to the front of the memorial, where they take pictures of their children placing flowers on the stone surrounding a small burning flame. News cameras are arranged in formation, and Sasha points to the men dressed in green fatigues surrounding a photograph propped up on the feet of the stone figure. "There's the photograph of Stalin."

I realize that the men standing on either side of the memorial are in fact guarding the controversial figure. Stalin is still revered and worshipped in the region, Sasha explains, mostly by the elderly, but the men surrounding the memorial aren't exactly geriatric.

"I want to punch them in the face," he says. "Should I do it?"

He tells me about a Stalin statue that stood in Gori for fifty years, before being removed by police cordon in the middle of the night. It is illegal to put up any new Soviet symbols on buildings or signs, but old symbols can stay.

"So is that why people wear the ribbons?" I ask. "As protest?"

"Some people think things were better under the Russians," he says.

"They're idiots for wearing them, but the Georgian nationalists are no better."

We watch a group of young men harassing a group of old ladies, each wearing the ribbons. The scene at the park crystallizes. Sasha points out the police officers and politicians, the Russian sympathizers, the group of Georgian nationalists on the far end of the park carrying signs with an image of the ribbons crossed out like a no smoking sign.

"There they are," he says. "Maybe a fight will break out."

We observe the young men following the old ladies away from the memorial and toward the edge of the park. Sasha considers approaching the men, but thinks better of it. He tells me he's worried he's talking down to me and I tell him I enjoy his play-by-play. This makes him even more exuberant and he divulges something that happened the year before that he hasn't told anyone.

"I stole the portrait of Stalin and burned it in the flame," he tells me.

"It was in the evening but there were still a few people gathered. I ripped it in half and burned the pieces. And then I left the park before anyone could do anything."

He tells me he's thinking of doing it again this year, but there are too many people, and he's afraid of the nationalists.

"Am I a coward?" he asks me. "What would you do?"

I want to watch him rip the photograph and burn it in the flame, but I tell him to listen to his gut. We stand on the edge of the memorial for a few more minutes, Sasha waiting for an opportune moment to rip the photograph away from the group of middle-aged men and teenagers, but the moment passes, and I know he isn't going to act.

"People are watching us," he says. "We've been standing here too long."

I follow as he abruptly turns and heads for the fountains. We walk past teenagers posing for pictures in the ankle-deep water. Sasha points out the old men wearing military uniforms adorned with medals. "Some of them are faking it," he says. "Wearing their fathers' uniforms for the attention or praise. Most people that fought in the war are dead now.

This guy looks pretty young. I should ask him how old he is, but his medals look real."

A group of men in leather jackets pass by. "They're the Georgian nationalist bikers," Sasha says. "All they care about is ripping ribbons off old people."

We reach the edge of the park where the anti-Russian protesters are gathered, holding signs. "Georgia is an occupied state," Sasha reminds me. "They consider the Russians their colonizers."

Sasha calls out to the old man from the photography event, who's carrying his camera and photographing the various factions of people. Sasha laments the lack of activity compared to the year before and the man tells us that the opposing political party was apparently banned from entering the park.

"It's a public event," Sasha says. "That's ridiculous."

"The police must have thought they'd start trouble."

We reach the edge of the park, and we rest on a bench. "Okay, my monogamous girlfriend," Sasha says. "Do you want to get food?"

I'm tired of Georgian food, oily eggplant and heavy khinkali, so opt for his favourite buffet, which Sasha warns is going to be a madhouse.

"You take a number and everyone's salivating over the glass display case," he says. "It's usually a war zone in here. They installed the number system to add some civility, but sometimes forego it entirely."

We try a new location on the edge of Vake Park and Sasha is disappointed that it's not as chaotic as he imagined. "I guess no one's heard about this one yet," he says.

He chews with his mouth open, meat sticking to his lips, as he asks whether I'm still thinking of heading back to Yerevan to finish the residency.

"Davit and Nara have already left," I tell him.

"You could take the marshrutka."

"Then what was the point of getting the apartment early?" I say. "I thought that meant you wanted me to stay."

"I asked you to come, and I'm glad you did," he says. "But you should think about yourself. Don't you think it looks bad to leave the residency early?"

"You think I should tell them that I left? You told me it was fine."

"Well, if you're not going back you should probably email someone."

I start to cry, and Sasha tells me he's sorry for bringing it up.

"I'm only trying to look out for you," he says. "I say this because I care."

When we have sex that afternoon, Sasha asks if I'm still on my period and comments that I'm dry. He spits onto his hand and rubs it on my cunt.

"You don't seem that into it," he says.

"I am," I say. We lazily start fucking, but he asks to stop after a few minutes.

"I lost my boner," he says. "I was thinking of World War Two and the Ukrainians murdering Jews. My mom will be happy."

He gets up to use the bathroom and I scroll through the pictures of Yerevan I have saved on my phone. I've decided to pretend I'm still in Armenia, that I haven't left the revolution for the asshole of my boyfriend. I hear Sasha showering, and settle on a picture of Mount Ararat taken from the Cascades on my last clear morning, its peak a wisp of cloud floating over the last of the Soviet expansion blocks, weightless and free.

MOTHER TONGUE

Madeleine Maillet

The neighbourhood has the quietude of the muggiest summer days; cars pass on the road, air-conditioner blades turn in backyards, but there are no sounds of kids playing, no birds call. Arousal washes over me like a breeze. Since *Maman* died, desire, when it comes, has been divorced from any object. When I asked my high school boyfriend what was the weirdest thing he ever masturbated to, he said, summer vacation. Just the idea of it. Now I'm a mildly depressed forty-three-year-old woman with the sex drive of a boy. A respite from noise makes me horny. But my husband's starting the lawn mower, rupturing the quiet. He's got his shirt off. His posture has that correctness that comes from the motor's kick. In the evening sun, he looks like he belongs in a naturalistic painting, but his sweating and squinting undo the impression—it's 98 degrees Fahrenheit with the Humidex, whatever that means, probably boiling in Celsius. Claire is working on a landscape with her sidewalk chalk in the driveway. I can see her horizon: blue above, green below. She has her shirt off too, her eight-year-old shoulders starting to broaden.

My husband says it's fine—says we raised her to be uninhibited by her body. Whenever he says it, I wonder, why not *of*? Does it mean something that I think she's uninhibited *of* and not *by* her body, as if it's only an incidental part of the whole. But there are more important things than prepositions, for which there are no rules, only conventions, which means they can only *feel* wrong. I call Claire inside, say, "Daddy has to weed whack the driveway, *tu le reprends plus tard*, finish your art after." But it's that I don't want a debate: Why can Daddy take his shirt off and I can't?

I'm washing the potatoes for supper, new potatoes, the little ones. They seem lucky to me, luckier than the larger less regularly shaped potatoes, more likely to be chosen in the store. Although, there is something pleasing in the wartiness of yams. Claire is singing along to *Hey Mr. Postman* in the living room. I peek in and she's running out of breath, singing back-up and lead—*De-liver de-letter*—looking into the bay window, at her reflection and past it, trying to win herself over while shaking her finger prohibitively. *Wait! Wait a minute Mr. Postman.* She places her hand on her hip jauntily and I notice she's knotted her tee-shirt to reveal her midriff. Her voice thrills itself as it rises to a panic. She throws her head back. She's a natural.

The water is boiling. I throw the potatoes in and put the green beans in the steamer. I feel like I'm getting away with something, with both side dishes cooking in one pot. The radio is playing Earth Wind & Fire now, and I bet Claire is lip syncing. In a pan yellow bubbles of oil pale and chase each other around. Because denying this rhythm is a waste of joy, my shoulders bob along to the music. I slice a trout fillet into three pieces. Claire's little slice is first, always Claire's first, then mine, then my husband's. It pleases me to slide my knife along the cutting board, separating each piece from smallest to largest, making sure it's perfect before they go in the pan. Claire isn't lip-syncing, she's making snow angels, enjoying the friction of her limbs against the carpet. She's never bored. She gets that from me. And Earth Wind & Fire, the horns, they are very heady, too heady for children really, but the rhythm is easy. I take out three plates and three knives and three forks. I flip the pieces of trout and their colour has richened from the true red of flesh to the brown red of meat. I call to Claire, "*À table! À table!*" I am teaching her French because of *Maman*. Everyone knows you can only love your child properly in your mother tongue, or is that a French thing, *la langue maternelle, la langue du coeur.* A matter of elevating a preference to the status of a value, like frankness.

When I go into the dining room she is straddling the arm of the sofa, dragging herself forwards and back against the fabric, her hands gripping the edge, her hair a curtain. One knee is bent on the sofa, the other leg trails lazily along the floor as she masturbates. I cannot look at her. I watch the pallor of the bottom of her foot travel back and forth.

"Stop it. Stop."

She plants her foot and looks at me with resignation. I want to slap her.

"How many times, Claire? *Avec ta mine de qui, moi? T'as pas honte*?"

Sam's sweaty hand is on my shoulder, and my throat's readiness has become a tightness. He sighs and his voice is conciliatory. "You do your exercises in your room," he tells her. "You know better."

She says she's sorry, and there is trepidation in her voice. I want to send her to her room. I don't want to feed her. He is so understanding of her. Behind me, I'm sure he's smiling a reassuring smile, because she is at ease again, standing, waiting. It's like he's her mother. I give up. Go back to the kitchen. Retreat, at least, is never an over-reaction. They set the table together. She wonders what insects eat. Sam knows the answer is leaves and twigs. I put the green beans in a bowl and drain the potatoes, this oppressive moisture on my face that smells faintly of dirt, it's a release. I exhale all this hot steam very slowly. I slide the trout onto a plate and carry the food to the table. Claire is talking about butterflies, wondering what they eat. She asks, "Is it different, because they look so different? Do they get their colours from the things they eat?"

"How do you mean?" Sam asks. He balances green beans across the width of the spoon. I should've brought tongs, but I'd just be fussing if I got up now. He has beautiful hands—musician's hands. He plays viola. We live in Minneapolis. We've lived in Cleveland, Chicago, and Cincinnati. Chicago was my favourite, because they have jazz like Montreal has jazz, but the symphony here offered him the first chair, and here we are.

"Like in the fall," Claire says, "a caterpillar eats yellow leaves, red leaves, purple leaves, then it goes into its cocoon, and it's colourful; when it comes out a butterfly. But if all it eats is green leaves in summer, it'll turn into a green butterfly, and that's good! It's good camouflage!" She is so smart, my daughter. She isn't looking at us, she's staring off at green butterflies, a green too stiff in a flutter of green leaves. It's hard to hold a grudge against a person with no guile.

My husband still holds the serving spoon, beaming at her. "How many potatoes?"

"Four," she says, "They're little. They're my favourites."

"I know," I say, and it feels like a reproach, but I haven't spoken to her since I got angry, and I can't help that it sounds like that. Only talk will make talk easy again. "I've seen a butterfly being born," I say. "When they're ready the thread of their cocoon starts to unravel, and they come down slow and steady. It looks like they're in an elevator. An elevator in the air."

"I bet they get dizzy being born," she adds.

My laughter brays with the ease that is between us again. "Yes, yes, I bet."

Sam smiles at me. "Thank your mother for supper," he says with a nod to me and to her.

"*Merci, Maman*," she says.

We don't speak French at the table, for Sam's sake, but we know he loves the sound of it. Claire, reminded of her dinner, smashes her potatoes with the back of her fork, and takes her knife and scrapes up some butter, and awkwardly spreads it across the potatoes she's still smashing—striking the fork's tines. Her hands are contorted. We don't correct her. We watch her figure it out together.

I ask Sam about his rehearsal tonight. They're preparing for the Pops series. Of course, the Sunday Pops series. Last month was music from the movies, *Star Wars, The Godfather*, etc. Before that it was Sinatra.

"What is it this month?" I ask.

"We're doing The Beatles," he says. "Haven't you always wanted to hear an orchestral arrangement of Yellow Submarine?" We laugh our cultured laughter, and Claire laughs to be laughing with us, too loudly.

"There's a yellow submarine?" she asks. Her nose wrinkles; this is her incredulous look—it's my sister's too. This slightly upturned *retroussez* nose that's so expressive. Sam smiles grimly—his pitch is obviously right, he can't fake that, but his tone is a protest against the song's—nasal, thin, worse than Ringo's. I groan. Claire gets the gist immediately. Now she and Sam are a team.

"We all live in a yellow submarine!" they sing wildly.

I take my part: in a frail irate tone, I ask, "What is that infernal racket?" She guffaws at me for making fun of my own seriousness; to prove that I can take a joke, that I am a joke with my adult prudishness. Why am I trying so hard? But it's too late to sing with them.

Serious, suddenly, Claire asks, "What was the yellow submarine?"

"Oh," Sam says. "It was imaginary. An imaginary submarine."

Sam asks if my sister might come down for Christmas, *à propos* of nothing, or maybe it's that I told him she feels like she hates her husband now that he's become interested in municipal politics and talks about it all the time. I couldn't resist betraying her sadness and anger, the way a child will never fail to point at another child their own age, eternally surprised to find others moving through the world experiencing it the same way as them. Anyway, I've told him a million times, no. No one wants to come to Minneapolis—not from Montreal. And we were just there two months ago for *Maman's* funeral, so holiday travel won't be in the budget. I shrug. We'll just have a token *tourtière* again this year and he'll ask me again to tell Claire how my family stays up all night on Christmas Eve. That we wait til after midnight mass to eat, and that we eat until dawn. When we were dating he asked me what we ate for Christmas, and I told him we ate venison pies, head cheese, blood pudding—and we did, but mostly the old folks ate that. The rest of the food was what midwesterner's would have: casseroles, sweet gherkins, pickled onions, and ham. Did I feel more lonesome for my family because I'd married an anglo, or because I'd described them to him as exotically as possible? Compared to his family, mine *are* more colourful, but now I fear I've made them seem cartoonish, and worse, more unreal to me in the bargain. Last Christmas when I couldn't sleep I took some cognac to my smoking spot, the second step of the back porch. I let the snow purple my fingers, and sang the folk song about the girl who wanted to get married, but all the men were at war. *C'est la belle Françoise, qui veut se marrier, maluron, lurette....* And I cried because my voice was not *Maman's*—had none of her warmth, and you have to let yourself be maudlin. You have to give into it sometimes.

At half past six, Sam stands and says, the way he says every night he has a rehearsal, or a concert: "Ladies, I take my leave." He bows. Claire bows. They bow at each other as if she's Chaplin and he's her straight man, again and again. I love their complicity. I wish I wasn't her mother, so I could be in on it too. Stupid, childish thoughts.

Everything is quiet after he's left. Claire puts her dishes in the sink and asks, "*S'il-te-plait Maman, je veux dessiner dehors*?"

"*Je voudrais*," I say.

"*Je voudrais dessiner dehors*," she says blankly, but using the conditional as I asked. I watch her, crouched on the sidewalk like a small, malleable frog, while I do the dishes. She is totally absorbed, her arm mirrors the tree limb she's drawing like one of those movement lines in cartoons. I put the radio on again and the music isn't quite satisfying. From my collection of audiobooks, mementoes from when I was learning English, I choose *The Old Man and the Sea* and find that dark night of waiting again. Outside the only point of interest in view is Claire's rigid body. The houses are there, but all I see is myself in this street; myself and my daughter. As the sun goes down the sky gets darker and the trees get brighter, but I don't really see it. I feel a direness. It's plain this fish is killing the old man. He's long since sliced his hand. Now his good arm has gone numb. He has no sway. He only has a line. Claire's crouching on the perimeter of her drawing now, not wanting to scuff it. The Macnamaras pull into their driveway but stay in the car. I don't imagine why. I stay with myself. I swear I see a flying fish on the Macnamara's lawn, its wings, protruding from its dorsal fin, a bioluminescence of impossible green. I wring out my scouring sponge with my fist. Imagine all the bacteria caught in the drops that strike the stainless steel of the sink. If we could see germs, the very spirit of dirt made flesh, they might be that green.

*

At bedtime, Claire has her head in the crook of my elbow while I read to her. When I feel her attention ebbing, I let the book close.

"Do you love me more than Daddy?" she asks.

"*On t'aime également, sans cesse, sans mesure*," seeing her brow furrow I hold my hands out like Lady Justice and her scales.

"No."

"*Mais si*!"

"But you love me more?"

"*Quand t'es follement amoureuse—*"

"What?"

"When you fall in love, you want to make a baby. When you have a baby, you'll see, it's different."

"Why?"

"It feels different."

The heat of Claire in my arms fills me with anticipation. I imagine the rush of her thoughts and wait for her to ask why. When she doesn't, I get my arm out from under her by making a pained expression and jiggling it elaborately. She laughs. I pull the blankets up around her shoulders, and she says, "More." I pull them up around her chin, and she says, "More." I pull them up and let them fall, covering her face, and she casts it off to show me her laughing face. Her eyes are grey like mine, naturally. I bring my face to hers, and say, "*Bisous*," like I say every night. And she puts her tiny mouth on my mouth and thrusts her tongue past my teeth.

I stand. Her head is alert, but her limbs are still cast lazily away from her. I feel my molars inching towards my front teeth. Taste the soap *Maman* slid over my tongue when I was bad. Imagine forcing that horrible bitterness on Claire, the desperate pleading of her eyes as my hand clamps the soap inside.

"I want to know what it feels like," she says. She is like a woman, saying *I want* like that. My rage is a knot in my chest, and I close the door. I've never shut her up in her room before. There's no lock on it. The mute knob offers no closure. I open the door and slam it. I imagine carrying the Shaker chair from my desk up the stairs, and wedging it between the door and the doorknob. Instead, I sit in the hall. Exhale slowly to stop my heart from racing. Is this my fault? Did I make her this way? I did, when she was a baby.

I remember that I'd been dreaming, and the man with the classic torso was kissing me, more and more—and I woke up with my tongue in my daughter's ear. There was the rawness of morning in the room and the unfirm look of her skull. I shut my eyes against the fat of her cheek, the delicate cartilage of her ear. I couldn't look. *Claire, Claire, Claire*, I said, to break my own heart. *I molested my baby at eight weeks*, I said to myself, to an interlocutor, the one you explain yourself to, to yourself.

I couldn't look at her. I knew that when I opened my eyes, I would see only how much more I was—more than she was. She was just a baby, and I could hurt her. What if I opened my eyes, and I saw the tight bliss of sleep in her baby eyelids and her baby fists, and I stuck out my tongue and licked her face like a dog—like a man acting like a dog. Because I could.

She cried all the time. And my hands were fearful of her, that I would drop her, that her face would be between my breasts, one hand supporting her head, the other under her butt, that my tired hand, my right, would get sweatier and sweatier and slip from the plastic diaper, that my left hand would cup the absence of her skull as she fell.

I told Sam about my thoughts. Sam said, "A thought is just a thought. We all have stupid ugly thoughts." He held me. He always holds me when I'm overwhelmed. Sam has this way of saying trivializing things so feelingly they seem smart. I always feel better after I tell him my secrets.

Still, he was wrong, is what I'm thinking. I work my big toe into a knot in the pine floor. A thought is not just a thought. It must be followed.

"Your daughter is a nymphomaniac," I say to myself, and I hate myself for saying it. Claire is thoughtful, and smart, and has manners. "She's not a nymphomaniac. She's an eight-year-old child exploring sex. Frankly, it's normal. You can't. You shan't. . . ." When I hate myself, I'm haughty with myself. This isn't something to give into. Talking to oneself. Letting my senses disintegrate until I'm sitting in the hallway like a lame animal, and wanting Sam—wanting someone to act with purpose, so that I can act purposefully, also.

Get up, I think. As soon as I'm standing I reason with myself: "You didn't molest your daughter." Then I laugh, audibly, an insane snort that I experience spinally, like fear. I take the stairs two at a time. Feel dizzy in the foyer. The front door looms with the porch light shining behind it. I hate that yawning glow it has. I walk around the living room, dining room, and kitchen, gathering things in my arms that look out of place. Stop when I'm holding a bowl of stale popcorn, a bottle of coral nail polish in a shade called *Malicious*, and Claire's terrycloth robe, which she took off when I said bedtime and streaked up the stairs naked as if it were a prank. She knows her nakedness provokes me and she likes to provoke me. The nail polish goes in the fridge, so it'll last. Throw the popcorn in the trash on top of the supper, but my hands slip. Reach into the trash. Grab the bowl. Feel something that is slimy enough to be trout with one finger, but the other fingers feel the innocuousness of popcorn, and then the edge of the popcorn bowl. It goes in the sink. Reach up to dry my hands on the dish towel that's always draped over my shoulder in the kitchen but, no, it's Claire's robe, her little robe patterned in pink peonies *Maman* made from the same pattern she used for mine and my sister's when we were little, smeared with popcorn butter and fish grease now. I scour the stain. I am always thoughtlessly ruining the things I love. I watch the spot go bleary, on the cusp of focus where despair is normally manifest in tears. I breathe instead. Too disgusted to indulge myself. When I felt like this I could always call *Maman*, she'd say it was all my fault and that if we'd only had Claire baptized the Lord would intercede. In a way, *Maman* would've been right. I never would have asked her who she loved best. Her affection followed an ordained hierarchy: God, husband, children, and domestic animals. She suffered from it more than we did: the dogs loved us, we loved *Papa*, and he loved his work. No one loved her best. But her fractious, fearful voice always made the world seem real to me again. Her worry was as unconditional as her love was supposed to be—and wasn't it akin to love, her worry? It certainly demanded the same kind of attention. Maybe worry is what unrequited love turns into, maybe after a time, it was all she could muster. For the second time, I laugh audibly, almost theatrically, at my thoughts, and because there's no one to see me, I don't stop.

*

When Sam comes home, I feel his steps on the porch and his key in the door so keenly. Like a dog does. I grab the newspaper and open it to a random page because I can't stand to be seen lying in wait.

Sam is smiling at me, and patiently untying his shoes. Picking them up. Putting them away. I always kick mine off so aggressively. He joins me at the dining room table.

"Claire tried to make out with me."

"What?"

"She said she wanted to know what it feels like."

"That's crazy. I mean, it's an understandable impulse, but it's crazy."

"I hate that. An understandable impulse. What's understandable about the way she thrusts herself at us? It's disgusting."

"It's not disgusting."

"I'm disgusted by it."

"Those are only feelings."

"What is a person besides, like, feelings."

"Carbon?" He asks, and I scowl. "Ok. Should we take her to therapy? Is that what you want?"

"Therapy is for rich people. So they can keep thinking the world revolves around them."

"Should we take her to church then, so she can be like the rest of the lemmings."

"I hate that you think that's what I want."

"Ok. You hate that too."

His mouth is open and that is rare. He looks at me as desperately as when he asked me to be his wife; his questioning simplified by passion, but sadly. I feel the need in me and sit on his knee, and he tucks my head under his head. My face is on his shirt, which my makeup will stain. I let my tears wash the beige pigment off of my skin and into the waffle-knit cotton. His thumb nervously traces a circle on my neck. This current runs through us—this begging of lovers for love. I cry harder. I say to his chest, "Sometimes, I hate her." I close my eyes to compose myself. I feel the edges of myself, my nose, my knees, my heels dangling off the floor. I need to remember where he ends and I begin to be able to say anything at all. "Tell me all the times she said she hates me."

"She doesn't hate you."

"Every little girl tells her father she hates her mother."

"She doesn't hate you." He says, and shushes me tenderly. I dry my tears and let him put a hand on my shoulder. But what has to escape is not inside our bodies it's in my mind.

"I hated how husky she sounded when she was proud of us. I hated her laughter. I hated the way she said my name."

"Your mother?"

"I was worried I was her."

"Claire doesn't hate you."

"Don't keep her secrets from me," I say. I can feel his posture righting itself, asserting our separateness. "If you keep her secrets, you don't love me anymore."

"That's insane."

Behind him there is the night in the screen door. It's as dull as a TV turned off. I go to the threshold and it's a bit better. The back porch is lit white against the night and so are the wicker chairs, and the wicker table, and past them the white posts and the rail. The tiger lilies nod against it. Spattered orange petals flippantly fall away from their ocher stamens. These marshy flowers proliferate across the yard with a flagrant sameness that seems to proclaim that this domestic order is also nature, merely another permutation. This casual landscaping we've inherited from the former owners couldn't be more different from the prim white-painted rocks we'd placed around *Maman's* rose bushes, touching them up every spring with stinky oil paint using artist's brushes.

"I hate these flowers," I say. Outside, the smell of the lilies is grievously sweet. I struggle to find a stalk and yank. My feet falter against the slick grass. When the roots come loose, I hold up the lily. It's as tall as me. Sam is on the porch.

"What are you doing?" he asks, and when I ignore him he pleads: "It's dark. You can't garden in the dark."

My fingers slip blindly through the sharp leaves until I find a woody stalk and yank. This time watching the bloom bob above the others as I tear it from the earth. It looks so skinny against the night with its flower now above me. I toss it. I grab for another stalk, yank. Hear the screen door clatter. Sam isn't watching anymore. After the first few, I work methodically along the perimeter of the porch. Pulling, grunting, piling a waste of orange fakery in the night. I am sweaty. Without the soft fluency of flowers along the edge of it, the porch is stark.

I go into the kitchen and it beckons me to my family. The dishes in the drying rack and the photos on the fridge all clustered in the way that is ours. I take the cognac from the cabinet and the clink of the bottle in the snifter is nice. The night bites at my conscience still. On the porch step, I sip the gold in a circle of light that makes the dark darker. I can make out the neighbour's house. She's so old. We never see her. She has a clothesline she hangs no clothes on. She has a sink next to her back door. No porch. No patio. No chair. I wonder what the sink is for. She's alone but the house is bigger than ours. It's two stories, whereas ours is what's called one and a half. The hinges on the screen door screech. Claire is in the doorway. Her features are mostly mine: round eyes, round cheeks, dainty little nostrils, and a tender underbite. They're all in disarray. Her nose quivers. Her lips are pressed. Looking at her face is like considering my own in the mirror when I've let myself down.

"*Maman*."

"Oui bébé."

"Je m'excuse."

"I'm not mad anymore," I say, staring into the night. The porch slats creak as she comes over to me. She sits a hip's width away.

"Why?"

"It makes me sad to be angry at you."

"Why?"

"At other people, I can enjoy being mad, but not at you and Daddy."

"Why?"

"Because I love you, and I'm responsible for you."

"Like how, that one weekend, I was responsible for Lola."

"No. That was symbolic. I signed the form. If anything happened to that hamster, it was my fault."

"What's symbolic?"

"It's how a picture of something isn't the same as the real thing. You just had a picture of responsibility."

"What am I responsible for?"

"Nothing," I say, and Claire's face falls. "That's not true, actually, you're responsible for yourself. Me, you, and Daddy we're all responsible for you."

"But I'm not responsible for you."

"No, that's the best thing about mothers. That's why you can always be mad at your mother." I say. Claire looks a little scared, but when I start laughing she laughs too, and she scoots closer to me. That's what's wrong with Minneapolis, and all the other places before it, there's only Sam and Claire, no family, no friends, no co-workers, the only people I know are people I'm responsible for. There's no one to hate or even dislike for a moment. It's no wonder I find myself hating her or him, or both of them. But as long as I hold onto my curiosity, I'm not around the bend yet. That's what *Maman* always said when we were kids about the old ladies in the neighbourhood, that so long as they were still gossiping they were *compos mentis.*

"What are you doing out here?"

"I was gardening. Do you like it?

"It's scary. Like a swamp. I like it," Claire says, in a whisper that respects the destruction I've wrought. It reminds me of how *Maman* would stay up all night making curtains or reupholstering the furniture. I'd wake up to pee and the living room would be a mess of torn fabrics and stuffing, and she'd be as absorbed as a child at play using *Papa's* nail gun. Then a floorboard would creak underfoot, and she'd startle to see me standing there. As if she couldn't quite place me.

"What are you looking at?" Claire asks.

"Oh," I stammer. "The neighbour's house. What do you think her sink is for?"

"It has paint cans in it. Old paint cans."

"You went over there?"

"I've been to all the yards. *T'es pas fâchée*?"

I ask, "Why did you go over there?"

"I like secrets," she whispers, her eyes sparkling.

"Do you want me to tell you one?" I ask. Claire nods soberly. "My mother thought I was ugly."

"She did?" Claire asks. But in saying it, in calling her my mother, naming her formally in relation to myself, rather than *Maman,* the air is suddenly dense with the ghost-grey weight of her. Under the flood lights, the long shadows on the slats of the porch change quickly with the breeze.

"It wasn't something she said. It was this look she had." When I put my arm around Claire her shoulders collapse against my ribs. I can feel her breath in my own body. I remember the way *Maman* got thinner and thinner while her veins and the walls of her heart grew thicker and thicker until you could almost see it beating in her chest. Since she died, visions of her enfeebled body occasionally startle me, as if I've really seen her out of the corner of my eye. It hurts me that she's stuck in my mind in that condition. If she were still here she'd tell me to give my pain to the Lord. That he can do more with pain than with happiness. Maybe she was right. Or maybe she hoarded her sorrows until she was swollen with them. It wasn't her fault. There was nowhere for her to put them. Claire sticks her thumb in her mouth, regressing in a moment of stress, and I gently take it out. Normally, if I oppose her on even the smallest thing she will insist. But she simply pretends it didn't happen. With Claire's weight on me, but her eyes cast at the sky or closed, I can't tell, I can say the kind of thing that I can't under her gaze.

"Don't keep any secrets that make you feel angry or scared. Tell me, or tell daddy, we'll keep them for you," I say. Claire rights her posture and turns her face to me.

"Even if I broke the law?" Claire asks, her face is gentle like mine, pretty in an unextraordinary way, with a gaze that's sometimes too firm, like mine, to suit her soft features. Maybe, *Maman* didn't think I was ugly. Maybe it was only the terror of recognition. "Even if I stole something? Even if I hurt someone on accident, or on purpose?" She whispers, cowed by the thought but following it in the guileless way a musician follows a chord progression to its resolution.

I laugh with all the buoyancy of the cognac I've drunk, but stop when I feel Claire's gaze flick over me with worry. "You're not going to hurt someone on purpose. But tell me, *tu me le dis*, if you do."

IF YOU START BREATHING

Thea Lim

It's the day after Chuck's funeral, the first day that there's nothing to do with him, or for him. Louise's left arm and left leg are on the floor and the rest of her body is embedded in Ben. Ben has been camping out in his parents' living room since Chuck, his dad, got sick, sleeping on a leather couch with undetachable cushions the colour of bricks. When Louise stays over, there is only enough space if they get into strict cuddle formation and don't move all night.

She extracts herself bone by bone, replacing her shape with bedding so that he doesn't topple to the floor. There is a red imprint on her right thigh where the flesh got pushed the wrong way and then just had to deal with it. By the icy light coming through the curtains, she checks her old, decrepit cell phone, its screen attached by strips of duct tape that leave sticky scum on her fingers. Ben and his family are still in that period when it's socially acceptable to miss work and ignore the phone. Louise gets some slack by proximity, but she's only a new girlfriend and her phone brims with work emails and missed calls from her mother, with whom she has been having a polite argument all week. Louise's mother wanted Louise to come home this weekend. Chuck's funeral is on Saturday,

Louise told her. *Come home on Sunday*, her mother texted. *I can't just up and leave*, Louise replied, *that would be hurtful. Why do you care about these people you just met you don't even know them*, her mother said. To win the argument Louise wrote, *Of course I'll be there why wouldn't I be.*

Louise works in fundraising at Princess Margaret Hospital, where they hold memorial services in the lobby for people who died upstairs. In November, Louise was watching the bereaved light each other's candles, tipping the white tapers away from the dark of their coats, when she noticed Ben watching too. He was tall and baby-faced and wearing a pink sweater. As she turned to leave, he whispered, "Do you come here often? I sure hope not." His dad was in Palliative, on the eleventh floor.

There was something very comforting about Ben, in the way he was neither worried Louise might reject his advances, nor that his dad might soon die. The next week as he undid her buttons in the greying light of Saturday afternoon, he said, "I know we don't know each other, but we should get married. I'll never have a better meet-cute with anyone else." She has only seen him mourn once, after they removed his father's body from the ward. He knelt on the floor, laid his forehead on the cold metal of the empty bedframe, and wept.

Last night Louise and Ben watched episode after episode of *Futurama* in silence, and she monitored him carefully for signs of the need to talk, but he stayed quiet. Quiet, even when the whites of his eyes gleamed during an ad for car insurance for retirees, though no tears came. Eventually he fell asleep and when she was sure he was far enough under that the door wouldn't wake him, she gathered her things and tiptoed to the back door. But when she turned on the light she found his sister Sammy at the kitchen table, trying to shield her crying from the violence of the overhead brightness.

"Jesus Christ, what are you doing?" Sammy said. Louise squeaked apologies all the way across the linoleum, but her winter boots had elaborate laces that took a long time to do up, so she turned off the light and sat there lacing in the dark. Sammy kept sighing, too irritated to cry.

Sammy is an Olympian, a triathlete with an aerodynamic body and a gaze that seems equally efficient, with little focus to spare for Louise. Louise is twenty-eight and even though she wishes she were not the kind of woman who thought like this, Ben seems like something of a final chance. He is gentle, a rare commodity. So his sister's disdain makes Louise uneasy. It was out of pure nervousness that Louise said, "Sammy, we haven't talked much, but I wanted to tell you, that if you ever want to talk to someone, I understand what you're feeling."

"Oh yeah," Sammy said, and though Louise couldn't see her face, she could feel Sammy's cheek scrunching with scorn.

"My sister died. I've lost someone too."

"Oh yeah," Sammy said, with different intonation now.

"Yes, it was hard."

Sammy patted the flat of the tabletop with her hand. Streetlight came in through the skylight. Sammy said, "Ben said that you didn't have any siblings."

Horror seeped through Louise.

When they met, Ben asked, as people always regrettably do, if Louise had brothers or sisters, and she had said no. This wasn't a lie; she'd *had* a sister, but she didn't *have* one. She wasn't trying to be coy; death is a faux pas. When do you tell someone your sister is dead? Certainly not on a first date. You could try on the second, but what if his father is dying? You can't say you have lost someone till you have it-gets-better advice.

Louise was trying to say "Ben must have forgotten" or "I told him not to tell anyone" when Sammy said, "Why would Ben lie about you having a sister?"

"He didn't lie." She said this too loud for a house full of sleeping people. "I just haven't told Ben yet. There hasn't been time."

"Right."

"I mean I will tell him," Louise found herself saying, "I was planning to tell him tomorrow." This was true. Louise was always planning to tell Ben tomorrow. Now she would stay the night, she would tell him tomorrow.

Tomorrow was the fourth anniversary of Joanne's death.

"This is uncomfortable," Sammy said.

*

It is just after 8 a.m. Exactly four years ago, Louise's mother called to say Joanne was dead. Louise was in the kitchen with her roommate. She remembers fixing her eyes upon a tomato stain on a chair leg as her mother told her, Joanne was drinking and she must have taken some pills and it was an accident, all in her answering machine voice. Louise remembers how the white of the tomato had dried in a pattern like the spokes of a wheel, and how she'd hung on to the childish thought that tomatoes were wheels, a reference point to keep her steady as the world began to tip.

When it had been Louise's turn to tell her roommate what had happened, it had come out in the same formal voice. It had been only later that she could have an unscripted reaction, up on the roof as the sun set at 4:30, where it'd been just her and all the crooked little houses of the neighbourhood. Sharing her pain with other people meant that her pain belonged to her less, Joanne belonged to her less. Louise never got better at the etiquette of loss. If anything she got more ungracious and stingy with her feelings. Lovers left her.

*

Ben's mother is reading a newspaper at the kitchen table. Joy seems to like Louise. She has already told Louise that it was fortuitous—with stress on each separate syllable—that Ben met Louise at such a difficult time in his life.

"Tea? There's a muffin. Biscuit?" Joy says.

"I'll just have something quick. I should be on my way."

"Stay a while. No rush!"

Joy is already neatly dressed, though her clothes bear the impact of the back of a drawer. Her regular rotation clothes are dirty and no one has done laundry.

Early on Louise tried to do the housework, a way to legitimize her presence. She longed to remain in this bubble of the doing of death, the only space where you were absolved from feeling. But Winston, Sammy's husband, told her to stop. Stop fussing, he said kindly.

Louise's anxiety dims. They make cheerful small talk about Joy's medical practice. Louise stirs her coffee.

"These are nice," Louise says, straightening the placemats on the table, printed with dancing peppers.

Joy sags. "There's just so much," she says.

"Pardon?" Louise missed something.

"You always say sorry to family when a patient dies. But I had no idea how much work death involves. Chuck left so many belongings behind."

The kitchen door bangs open. Ben comes in, Sammy and Winston behind him.

"Morning," Joy cries, her heartache put away as fast as it came out.

Winston arranges cookies on a plate and talks in a Yoda voice. Everyone is weirdly jolly, the way people are when severely sleep deprived, or when every possible thing has gone wrong and there's nothing left to worry about.

Then Sammy says, "There's no more cream." She puts both hands around the spent carton that cants weakly on the counter. She gazes down into its spout. "Who finished this?" She turns to them, sharp-shouldered.

Louise covers her mug so Sammy doesn't see the honeyed tones of her own coffee, coloured by the cream. Winston rummages in the fridge, mostly mysterious Styrofoam and fogged-up Tupperware.

"There's some skim in the back there," Louise whispers to him.

"Yuck." Sammy scowls. She looks in Ben's mug. She says something in Cantonese. Ben responds in Cantonese and soon all of them are laughing, even Winston, who is Filipino.

Louise can't understand. She is inadequately Chinese, her parents only ever succeeded in teaching her the words for 'rice', 'thank you', and 'crazy'; if Sammy is telling them about Joanne, Louise has no defences.

She sneaks out. She goes into Ben's makeshift bedroom. His shirts hang from the folding shoji screen, his comic books lean on the tchotchke cabinet. She lies on the couch and listens to the voices on the other side of the wall crest, then avalanche into laughter. Her cell phone is buzzing but she lacks the strength to get it out of her pocket.

Decorations from the funeral spool across the floor: a banner, white ribbons, huge framed photos of Chuck: Chuck on a bike hike, Chuck in Barcelona, Chuck meeting Jackie Chan. Louise has the distinction of being the last person Chuck ever met. He was almost gone, he looked nothing like the photos. "Hello Louise," he said, "be brave." He could barely speak, and she had worried about what he saw in her that propelled this message; the energy he was willing to expend to deliver it. Now she thinks it was a meaningless thing to say, as if he was just carrying out some kind of death bed protocol.

The kitchen door squeaks open and shut, and if the footsteps in the hallway are Ben's, Louise will tell him now, of course she will, this is ludicrous.

"Hi," he says. He moves her legs and sits down beside her. "None of us can stand to be in this house today. We're going to the park. Can we give you a ride somewhere?" He lifts her hair and smooths it down her back, and she loves the feeling of his hand there.

Louise doesn't know how to begin the sentence about Joanne. She can't think of a good opening word.

She says, "Do you want me to come with you to the park?"

"If you want." There's a pause. "You don't have somewhere else to be?"

Is this concern for her time, or for his? She doesn't know him well enough to tell.

"I'll come if you want me to," she says.

"It's up to you."

*

Sammy is angry. There isn't enough room in the station wagon for all five of them, plus Joy's debris, and Winston has to sit in the hatch. Sammy takes Winston's arm, holding his elbow as if his limb is a delicate thing she must protect.

Louise saw Sammy do the same thing with Chuck, fingers outstretched to catch her father's arm every time it slipped from the bed, as he drifted in and out of consciousness. It was a tiny gesture that held such boundless love, that Louise felt embarrassed for having witnessed it. Seeing it resurface, over something so insignificant, irritates her.

It's a Sunday in February, and everything has been petrified by the cold. Branches and rooftops have turned pale, and the sidewalks feel harder, as if the cement molecules are shrinking together for warmth. Toronto winters are rarely sunny, but when the sun comes out it seems to be overcompensating for the gloom. On the crest above Grenadier Pond, the sunlight slams into and off the ice, and they can barely see. Groups of people cluster on the vast, snow-covered surface of the pond, amused by the novelty of walking on water. The five of them wend their way down the long trail. Little dogs in hooded jackets scurry past.

Ben's family pulls ahead of them and Louise says to Ben, "Are you all right?'

"Sure. Why wouldn't I be?"

Her phone rings. She ignores it.

"Should you get that?"

"It's just my mother."

They have reached the edge of the pond. Sammy and Winston have taken Joy onto the ice and they are marching arm-in-arm across it. Louise puts her arm though Ben's to slow him down.

"Can we talk? Over here." She does not want anyone but him to see her face. She heads for a thicket of dead shrubbery. Ben steps off the path with her, straight into a puddle of slush.

"Oh. Shit." His face screws up in disgust.

"I didn't put that puddle there. It's not my fault."

"No one's blaming you."

He mumbles curses and her phone buzzes audibly.

"You should get that. It sounds like your mother is having an emergency."

He tugs at a branch, looking for a tool to scrape his boot. His tugging turns violent. It looks like the whole shrub is going to come up at the roots.

"Careful. The bush," she says. He tries to hide it but clear as day, his eyeballs roll. She should have chosen his feelings over the shrub's.

She could wait to tell him about Joanne, next week or next month. But the worst is yet to come for him. The funeral is the easy part. In the photos from Joanne's funeral, people were laughing so hard you could see the roofs of their mouths. It's the afterwards that's impossible, the bereavement version of the first day back to work in January. And Sammy will tattle first.

"I have something to tell you," she says.

But they speak simultaneously. "If you have other places to be today, you should go. We could use some family time. Sorry. What did you say?"

It was different when she was willing to volunteer the information. Now she is on the spot and her anger comes in, sudden and hot.

"I've been getting the feeling I'm not wanted. Especially when your mom and sister insist on speaking Cantonese when they know I can't understand." She feels unhinged. Why is she saying these things?

He is quiet for a terrible moment. Then he says, "It's rude for my mother and sister to speak their language the day after we buried my dad?"

He doesn't break eye contact. He wants an answer, but there is none.

"I'm sorry. I should go. I should call my mother. I'll come and say goodbye when I get things sorted out." She is panicky and she talks too fast; it sounds as if she is saying sorry for leaving, not for causing so many problems when she meant to help.

He jams his hands in his pockets. "Sure. Sounds good." He walks away. He steps down and rocks his weight into his heels and sails across the ice.

Louise's hands are shaking but she focuses on the new texts from her mother that say, *I am making macaroni soup for you* and *If you catch the 1:43 train dad can pick you up*.

Louise still has Joanne's number in this phone. Every time she has to call someone whose name begins with a 'J', the number's there. She can't bring herself to delete it, or get rid of the phone. She has tried to be careless, hoping the phone will fall in a toilet or get lost at the mall on its own. But instead stupendous advances in mobile technology have passed her by.

Ben has caught up to his family. He runs, then stops hard, skidding until he knocks Sammy into Winston. Louise expects Sammy to turn and yell at him, but instead they all laugh. There is an acid pain in Louise's chest. They are recklessly cheerful. Most adults over the age of thirty have experienced some great loss in their lives. But you wouldn't know it, walking around on any weekday evening, watching people's vapid faces as they pay their bus fare and post their letters, as if nothing bad has ever happened to anyone.

Louise walks down to the edge of the pond. Ice crystals cluster around the dirt. Even if there wasn't a treacherous mass of water below, it still seems counter-intuitive to walk on an unpredictable, bone-breaking surface. She can't bring herself to make the necessary great leap. She tries bending her knees experimentally.

She has to go and say goodbye. She could just leave, but that would draw attention and require explanation. It will look as if she's mad. She has tried so hard to be inconspicuous. She thought she'd been doing a good job of it, even when it was trying, but she now she sees she was wrong. When she had hoped to be supportive she'd made things worse.

The day Chuck died, Ben asked her to come to the hospital to bring home Chuck's things: scarves and table cloths that Joy used to cover every light and every surface, sweaters tenderised by time and wear, a book of *Far Side* comics, a copy of *Gitanjali*, mugs. But the nurses were off schedule and when Louise got there, Chuck's body was still there. It was plainly inappropriate for her to be in the room, so she went to the visitors' lounge. But something in Louise was twisting. A parade of distant relatives had come through in the past week to cry for Chuck and his family. But there was nothing tragic about dying at sixty-five, in a palliative care ward with prize-winning decor and free ice cream and special chairs for visitors, swaddled in love. That was just nature. What happened to Joanne was not. Louise left the visitors' lounge and walked in the corridor until she had a view into Chuck's room, and she continued to feel enraged until she saw the nurses tie Chuck's hands and feet together before they put him in the body bag. Something about that upset her severely; either the fact that he was tied up or the fact he had no idea he was tied up. She cried but she held her breath so no one would hear her. She went back into the visitors' lounge and faced away from the room, towards the blizzard exploding in white powder against the windows.

With a stern step Louise gets one foot down on the ice, then quickly brings the other to join in. As soon as she steps down, it's like there's cotton wool in her ears. The snow on ice absorbs the sounds of everything around her: the philosophy students on the bench talking Hegel, the mothers cajoling their resistant children, the squirrels who opted against hibernation, jibbering in the snow. A memory comes to her like it's been conducted through the ice. Her five-year-old ankles in her skates were ugly and turned in, the opposite of Joanne's perfect ankles. You just need to tighten your laces, Joanne said, and Louise wanted Joanne to do it.

Stupidness, nonsense. Louise keeps moving her stiff feet, one two, away from the memory, closer and closer to where Ben stands with Joy and Sammy and Winston. The coated ice muffles her footfalls and they can't hear her approach, even when she is right behind them. But she can hear what they are saying, their voices strangely filtered by the wind.

"No no," Sammy is saying. "Of course she's nice. Just . . . odd."

"Be more specific," Ben says.

"Well last night—you told me she doesn't have any siblings? But last night she told me that she had a sister, a sister *who died*. I think she was trying to make me feel better . . . but is she, like, does she tell stories about her life that aren't true?"

If Louise tells people about Joanne, she loses control. She will not be able to control when other people speak of Joanne, and they will speak of her without warning, thoughtless, profane.

Sammy laughs. Something bursts out of Louise and she is powerless to stop it. Her arms shoot up in front of her, and she grabs the back of Sammy's jacket, and shoves as violently as she can.

But Sammy has Olympic reflexes. She jerks hard to the side and Louise watches as her own arms go wide, she has too much momentum to stop, and now she is flailing forward, desperately trying to twist away from the ground, the ice one long stretch of colourlessness.

She can't see anything but the blank of the sky. For a moment, she's the only person in the world. And then the throbbing in her side and her ankle bring her back.

Louise puts both hands over her face. Someone tugs gently at her elbows. The tugging becomes more and more insistent but Louise rolls away from it, powdering herself in snow.

She crawls to her feet. They are lined up in a row, staring at her with their matching cheeks and warm faces, with the exact same look of hurt confusion that asks, how could anyone possibly behave so badly, how could there possibly be any excuse?

Louise shouts at them. She screams.

"There should be a city by-law! There should be a law! How can they let people walk on the ice? It's just so incredibly, irresponsibly unsafe!"

She makes for the bank.

*

Louise hears Ben calling her name but she doesn't turn back. When she reaches the knoll she'd like to keep going, but the pain in her ankle is intense and she collapses. Her phone buzzes again. She pulls it out of her pocket and throws it in the snow. She drags herself up onto the bank and sits in the muck. She picks up the phone and puts it back in her pocket. She gets to her feet. Her gait is demented and she stumbles off the path and starts to walk the perimeter of the pond, inside the bald shrubbery, hiding from view like a child. Snow splatters on the non-waterproof uppers of her boots. She has a five in her pocket. She could get the streetcar home. She left her funeral clothes and some make-up at Ben's but she will just have to forfeit them. Her butt is all wet and when she finally gets to where the pond meets the highway, she can't decide if she should get on the streetcar or wait until her pants dry. She doesn't know if her seat will dry in this weather. Are clothes slower to dry in humid or dry air? She just stands there, making sure to stay concealed by the rim of bushes, watching the cars go by, trying to think what to do. She shudders from cold.

Joanne will always be dead. Nothing is changed by Louise thinking about her. Thought fragments break through anyway. Against her will they struggle to trace just how Joanne's body gave up. They never come in response to cues Louise can predict and steel herself for—like an Erykah Badu song or a TV show Joanne liked. Instead they come when she's on a phone conference at work explaining best practices; when she's trying to navigate a cranky rush-hour intersection on a bike. Yesterday, in the awful basement crematorium of a big church on Parliament Street, Ben's family, his family friends, his family friends' cousins, and Louise crushed together and waited for Joy to flip the incinerator switch. It was supposed to have been just Ben, Joy and Sammy, but no one was up to the uncomfortable task of turning the rabble away. The room was a cacophony of tiny sounds, throat clearing, nose-blowing, wiping tears on sleeves. Louise stood behind a pillar and tried to focus on the floor tiles. But instead her mind went to a Joanne she had tried to forget. She pictured Joanne alone in her horrible apartment with yellowed stucco and the dirty carpet, knowing she was dying and that she'd never have children, knowing she was dying and it wasn't a sunny day, knowing she was dying and she couldn't reach the phone. Louise's mother has put away all the photos of Joanne, save for one: Joanne is a baby with a bow taped to her sparse hair, full of gummy joy, before everything.

Louise hears Ben say her name. She can make him out, twenty feet away, only slivers of his back through the snarl of branches. She has to stare for a moment to be sure it's really him. Louise, she hears him say. He says it a second time, not like a curse but like a question. She imagines herself bursting out of the bushes, her hair wild with twigs, big enough to speak.

The Saturday that Ben undid her buttons, they met for lunch at a pho restaurant, and he'd had to take his glasses off to eat his noodles so the steam didn't fog up his vision. There was something intimate about his face without them, and she'd had to work not to reach for his cheek. After the server took their plates, Ben removed the bottles of sauce and seasoning from the middle of the table one by one, lining them up against the edge. She worried this meant he was the compulsive type, but then he reached across the space he'd made, and took her hands in his.

He is such a nice man, and all she has done is sap his grief. He recedes through the park.

She watches him go.

Her phone is ringing. This time, she picks it up.

"I made chicken wings," Louise's mother says. She starts to cry. Joanne and Louise's mother is a very composed person, the kind who wears a bra even when she's home alone. Through her tears she tells Louise she's found a new marinade recipe.

"It is just perfect," she sobs.

Across the highway, Louise sees the red of the streetcar. If she catches it, she can make the 1:43. There is a break in the traffic and she staggers for it. She clanks up the steps and uses her five-dollar bill to pay almost twice the fare, not making eye contact with anyone, on account of the wetness of her pants. The window by her is open, though it is so cold, and as the streetcar pulls out of the stop, the trees thin and she sees Ben and the others far away, across the highway and that giant floe, four dots together.

They are doing t'ai chi in a row, standing with their faces to the sun. They know the sequence off by heart, always sure of which curled arm, which gliding foot, which steady hand comes next. Like a gym class on ice, they follow each other's movements in snail-paced unison.

Louise sticks her arm out the window and cranes her neck to watch them, until they disappear behind the trees. Her phone is still in her hand and though the wind blisters her fingers as the streetcar gains speed, she doesn't pull her arm back in. She feels the freezing air rush into those spaces between her phone and palm, and she imagines what it would feel like to let it go.

PHOENIX

Alex Leslie

We sit in this office by the front entrance, Dom and I, and a nurse goes in and out restless with the need to be useful. Dom's the front desk guy and he never takes a day off. I'm the support worker, which means I'm jack-of-all-trades for the endless minutiae of needs of the people who live in this hotel. A spreadsheet pinned to the wall shows the list of the residents in Dom's shaky hand-drawn lines. In careful columns: who's woken up in the past eight hours; for how long; who's passed the eighteen-hour mark of continuous sleep, in which case they need to be roused with the bell Dom keeps hanging on the hook above his desk. I often wonder where he got that bell—a fat battered thing like a ship captain's bell. I go with Dom to the doors of the red-flagged sleepers and he clangs that goddamn bell until the person in the room rolls over twice. The nurse crouches and checks for breaths, fingers held to the side of the neck.

I can't figure Dom out. He's worked at the hotel since forever, since before this was just another place for sleepers, since before the public health emergency was declared, before the poster campaigns on all the busses, before I took the support worker job here because catering got unbearable, walking around conference halls holding spoons of cold turmeric-yellow soup like a metaphor for opulent uselessness. Now I can't make myself quit, because when a sleeper wakes up and looks me right in the eyes, I see a world orbiting in their pupils, and for a moment I feel what it would be to never panic again. When our first sleeper died—a sweet Dutch guy who used to run a bike repair shop before he got ALS—Dom shrugged and said, "Water runs downhill," and I watched him, waiting for the rebound smirk that never came. Sometimes he's just like that, blunt and inscrutable. His black hair is gelled and combed straight back, and his eyes are hooped in purple like a flower in bloom on the Adriatic at twilight. I can't tell how old he is. "I know why they don't want to wake back up," he's said to me a few times, and I just nodded. I dodge invitations to his backstory. I think that he protects the sleepers because he wishes he could be one.

I work in one of those hotels full of the sleepers over on Clark Street. Not one of the nicer private ones, just one of those places where the people are curled on mats or hospital beds in rooms like stacked shoeboxes. We watch them on the tiny monitor in the office—every now and then they raise their heads and look around. We see their eyes in the static, the half-darkness of a failing celestial connection. In our daily afternoon meetings, we discuss the sleepers in batches, triaged according to acuity. The nurse speaks bluntly of a young woman who told her yesterday that she wished she could just fall asleep forever. "Suicidal ideation," the nurse intones. "Evolving acute sleep disorder." I nod. I've accepted that these terms are her way of dealing with the sleepers, their remote limbs, unreachable minds. The nurse won't come apart and she can't give up quite yet, so she hovers in clinical language like a wasp hovering over the deathly sweetness in a bottle. "Monitor for signs of progression," she says. "Blood pressure, temperature. Blood samples for iron deficiency if she's agreeable. Regular bed checks."

Dom's eyes glaze. "I'll talk to her," he says.

The nurse nods. She knows she cannot rescue, only maintain.

Next, we discuss the heat.

In the summertime, the hotel stifles, a grimy hand pressed to my mouth. There's routine housekeeping, sort of, but it's like dirty water is being dumped on top of the dirty floors and just sort of being sloshed around and it's impossible to tell what colour the floor is supposed to be. The inside of this place is the colour of exhaustion, the plate at the bottom of the sink left there for years.

Dom tells the nurse that he's heard from higher-ups that there might be funding for some industrial fans.

The nurse asks if there's a timeline on that and Dom says, "Medium range expectations."

I'm always surprised by Dom's dismissiveness of the hierarchy and his contradictory loyalty, the way he widens his eyes into a smile and makes pronouncements like "Medium range expectations" as if he has just swallowed a master-key to the infrastructure, or like he's making fun of us all, walking on the ceiling of our abjection. He spent a few years on the street before this job, before he "figured it all out," he told me.

Since the sleeper crisis rocketed and families have started doing newspaper interviews about sleepers in their homes and the slow exile to hotels like this one (and for those who can afford it, private buildings with more nursing staff), the government has started to put some money into the hotels. Once in a while, one of our sleepers leaves for a treatment facility—this is rare, not just because there are only a handful facilities in the country, but because the seduction of the sleep is so strong. Very rarely, someone goes into remission.

We tell them: please don't visit. Not this place. You need to be out there, in the world of eye contact and rainstorms and birds firing radar pulses through the sky.

Hans, a guy in his fifties on the fourth floor, has a gorgeous set of false teeth. "I got a mouth full of re-birth stones," he told me when I started working here. He tried to explain the sleep to me once, back when I thought it was helpful to ask clarifying questions. I was like a cross between Siri and your most memorable seventh grade teacher.

Hans asked me three questions: if I'd ever shot up, if I'd ever been in a car accident, if I'd ever been in love. No, no, no, I answered, his directness tearing strips off my ability to think on my feet.

Then he roared in my face: "This is like trying to explain fucking to a virgin." Then he took pity on me. "OK, kiddo, OK. Tell me about a time you felt totally ... aaaaaahh ... just *free* ... you know ... just out there ... like nobody could ever find you."

I shook my head, whitebread and useless.

"The best you can do is be harmless," Hans said to me, and walked off, swinging his dog Ulysses's sparkly purple leash in his hand.

I stood there, an imposter beside a door that said EAT PUSSY DIE YOUNG. I went back to the office, like I always did in those days, to hide.

*

When a sleeper goes, the paramedics come and perform their ballet, bag the sleeper like a fresh peach. I like the paramedics—their driven efficiency so united and cordial, footsteps as coordinated as thieves. Their starched uniforms and wide-eyed regard: "Are you the one who called?" They give dose after dose of the medicine that revives some sleepers, most of the time, after the third or fourth dose, but sometimes it takes seven or eight. The medicine is administered in a mist pressed down through a funnel placed over the mouth and nose. It was developed and released six months into the crisis; thousands had already died. Whether the person returns to consciousness is all in the timing, the course of the sleep, and little flickering coin-flips in the bloodstream, how cells gape their throats or do not, how a person's lizard-brain lurches for the surface or does not and I sit in the office at the front entrance and I sort the mail and press my feet to the floor and feel the floating-away knowledge that another one of our residents fell asleep forever today like so many others who have been lost to the sleep this year, and that there will be many more, and I feel that we are in the midst of a tide with no visible limits. A vast surge and keening.

I had lied to Hans. Yes, I'd been in love. A woman in my senior anthropology seminar, like a truck swerving toward me out of morning river-fog. I did nothing about it.

Hans's three questions had been a challenge issued to me: If you could write a catalogue of moments of weightlessness in our life, what would they be? How precious were they to you, and what would you do to make that feeling continue?

*

The public health emergency was declared over a year ago now.

When a sleeper goes, it's usually at night. We've lost so many that the shock of losing a sleeper lessens each time. The numbness is burnt off by the steady noise of emails, notes, the chorus of residents' voices, the minor hum of the engine of countless small demands. The tinny music of dailiness and conversation with Dom keeps my brain going.

Months pass. The nurses quit, replace each other. Sporty nurses wearing stethoscopes and sneaker; palliative nurses who scan their iPhones during meetings; tiny-emperor nurses citing safety protocols; student nurses who linger at doors, knocking hopefully, treading tentatively as astronauts. I know they have never seen a place like this. Most people keep their doors closed, but it's an ongoing debate: keep sleepers' doors closed to reduce theft, or leave doors open to increase the chance of being revived? The nurses carry glass balls of the medicine; government-issued kits hang from their belts. Dom and I stay in the front room alone a lot, in a wordless workplace bear-hug of solidarity or tacit professional suicide pact. My other company in the office is Ulysses. Dom sorts the mail and puts it in residents' boxes. I answer the phones. For my first season here, I worried about contagion.

The family members are the hardest calls. I hear the voice shake—"Hi I'm Shania's mom" or "Hi I'm Rocket Star's son"—and I brace myself. I know all the sleepers at our hotel, but there are 120 rooms, so sometimes I need remind myself with the master spreadsheet where I scrawl notes beside names—purple board shorts, yellow budgie, fisherman's hat, tattoo of green rose, Irish accent, pink slippers, black guitar, jumping jacks, knock-knock jokes, scoopy limp. My fingertip on the name—*oh yeah the shy guy on the fourth floor with the Rocky 2 poster and the fur coat*—and I tell the grateful loved one on the other end of the line, "Yes they're still awake." It isn't my job to give prognoses. It isn't my job to inform next of kin about deaths either—that's the hospital's job, after the ambulance collects the body—but our hotel is a magnet for the bereaved anyway. Dom and I are always so busy that it takes us a day or two to get to cleaning out a room when someone goes.

When a lover or mother turns up at the entrance, I buzz them in. I take the master key and Ulysses and lead the way up the stairs. The elevator is always broken. The elevator is a running joke. It strains and tugs, a spirit in an iron lung. The stairs are narrow, yellow, dank, up and down in claustrophobic geometry, and if someone comes rushing down at me, I have to press my body to the wall because the residents here, when they're not sleeping, are always in a rush. They awaken briefly and insist to me about tasks relating to their tax deadline, storage locker, sick aunt on the island. I make way for the driven and the blind. I'm on this side of life, moving further and further away from them, the sleeping and the nearly-breathing. I hold their voices, fulfill their requests, scribble down their thoughts, micro-manage the dwindling dailiness of it all, but when I turn on the car radio every day at 5:37 p.m. there's the report of the number of people who fell asleep today, the reports of the globes of medicine set over their mouths in increasingly potent doses, the public health experts and doctors calmly reiterating, "This is not enough, people will continue to die." Many workers like me are quitting. There are reports that people are beginning to fall asleep in public too, found slumped at their desks with the signs: blued skin, white lips, shallow breathing—at the till in Starbucks, behind the wheel of the bus, in a leather jacket factory.

Dom stopped me in a hallway one morning last week and leaned very close to my face: "How are you doing?" I almost giggled at the honey note of concern.

I smiled at him, tilted my head to the side: "How can I support you today, Dom?" I cooed.

He punched my shoulder. "You're good shit, kid," he said, and walked away. I don't know much about Dom, but I know he'll last here longer than I will.

Anyway, when a family member of a recently-dead sleeper turns up, I lead them to their door and unlock it. Ulysses roams and stress-whines about the ghost-funk vibe, and I watch the visitor circulate, brush fingers on the mat, the windowsill, the walls. I used to feel shame about the filthy state of the hotel but not anymore—this is one of the only places for sleepers to come. Sleepers are brought here in ambulances called by their landlords or family members. Sometimes the visitor asks me questions about my job, which I'm skilled at deflecting. I understand I'm a screen for their disbelief, a repository for their guilt.

I learn to stand at the door while they walk around. I never go inside. I keep the master-key pressed to the always-tender spot in the centre of my palm, a toothy reminder that I can leave any time I want.

*

Before this job—before I clicked "Apply" on that online ad for "community support worker"—I had an anthropology degree, a bunch of ESL teaching experience, and a Serving It Right certificate for catering work on the side. I was planning to apply for a Masters or go to Japan or Korea to teach ESL, because after the recession set in there was no point going into debt I'd never be able to repay. I believed in the minutiae of my sister's and friends' life-admin problems; I listened to international news sitting in the centre of my own personal pink salt lamp; I knew my life would play out normally but had never really thought it through; I had never been in a relationship serious enough to make a hole in me (when my sister had fallen in love and married, I'd observed with surprise that felt callous); I thought the social safety net existed; I thought hospitals fixed things; I imagined people died with dignity; and I had never walked around a person's room the day after their death, my skull frail and hot as a halogen bulb, knowing they were just one of many. Hurry to get the room ready for the next move-in.

I never wondered why the people around me chose to continue to breathe.

I do now.

*

Today on my commute I listen to a doctor, a politician and a journalist duke it out over the cause of the sleeper crisis. The doctor insists on environmental causes—generations eating meat ripe with hormones, vegetables in a permanent greenhouse afterlife, water spiked with disinfectants.

"You're saying thousands of people are dying because of . . . *weed killer*?" the politician says. She goes on about mental health coverage—the over-crowded hospitals, psychiatrist shortage, lack of research about the cause of the sleep, experimental treatments, alternative medications. "We have no etiology of the acute sleep disorder," she says.

Then it's the journalist's turn and he begins, his rage a blizzard assaulting the microphone: "This is why so many died from AIDS—they were killed by indifference."

"We know the people at highest risk have . . . difficult histories. We know this impacts our most vulnerable populations with the most complex presentations." I remember the first time I heard a nurse refer to a person's "presentation," meaning the clinician's impression. I thought of the sleeper's face projected outside of himself onto the air, a slideshow organized into (1) Ignoble Birth; (2) Traumatic Childhood; (3) Shit Happens (4) Inevitable Descent Into Depravity; (5) Untimely Death.

I pilot my tiny hatchback through the rivering smog of commuter traffic and listen numbly, eyelids stiff with exhaustion. Yesterday, the paramedics had to be called to our hotel nine times to revive sleepers whose heartbeats had begun to stroll away into a warm retreating tide. They were all revived. Dom and I ate McNuggets, waiting for the ambulance to leave so we could.

The doctor continues. "We need consider carefully as a society—what do we mean when we say people are palliative? People who are electing to be . . . inactive . . . are these people *palliative*? Are we just *waiting for them to die*?"

Sometimes, lately, the thought has nudged itself uninvited against the interior shell of my ear: *let them go*. If they want to sleep forever, just let them sleep. Sing lullabies, dim the lights, hand out pyjamas.

The radio program ends; they didn't interview anyone struggling with the sleep; they didn't interview any workers like me. They call us "front-line workers." I've always hated the military language.

When I get to the hotel, Hans is there chatting with Dom about the radio program. They listened to it together in the office (Hans has a way of always inserting himself into things, like honorary staff). Hans crosses his arms and says, "My big problem with research is that no professor knocks on my door in this slum and tells me my friend croaked." He points at me. "Kid, you know how many people I know who've fallen asleep?" I shrug. I don't want to be pinned by the facts of Hans's life. "Guess," he says.

"I don't know," I say.

"Ill-advised!" Dom shouts.

"Guess!"

"No!"

"Come at me, kid." He's sprightly, razory, this morning. He's been sleeping for a few days, in full oxygen rebound, pupils lapping up my sweltering hesitation.

"Ten?" I say. Safer to guess wrong than to try for tragedy.

"Ha! Ten! Ten!" He points at me. "I won't tell you the real number, kid. It'll just fuck you up." On his way out, he hugs me. His body is rock-hard and smells like rubber tires and garlic powder.

*

At the centre of an epidemic it is silent, it is still, there is the open mouth of the paramedic as he approaches, the cupped hands of the family, there is the empty space on the spreadsheet wiped of the name, there is the room after it is cleared and cleaned, there is the helpless gaze of the helper, there is the blank bullet at the centre of the eye again, the nearly imperceptible whistle of the dreamer and the dreamed.

*

It's through no fault of their own that they're sleepers. There have been so many editorials in the paper speculating about the cause for the sleep. Are these people more sensitive, more susceptible somehow than the rest of us? Can the sleep be transmitted? How does it spread? My older sister, an accountant, has called me up many times to tell me she worries about me. I started working at the hotel just before the sleepers started to edge their way into the news—and then the slow and then rapid build. When I hear the radio reports, I see faces and hear voices of our residents. When I read the newspaper, I see the doors and feel the sticky stairs on the bottoms of my shoes, that suck of neglect. The sour air fills my mouth. How do they end up here? When a person can't hold down a job, the basic structures of life fall away quickly. A few months and the savings are gone; the unemployment insurance gets cut off; and then if they don't have family, they're in one of the hotels that will accept the government's shelter allotment in exchange for a few nurses and mats and sandwiches. I try to remember that they all had different lives before—many had normal lives, lives with neither distinction, nor scandal. And then this—some stress valve embedded deep in them, virus or magic spell, and here we are, on different sides of the glass, and I watch today's nurse mark times of waking beside their surnames, and I stand beside Dom as he clangs his bell and eyes rush open—*I'm up I'm up I'm up.* If the eyes stay shut, we call the nurse to administer the medicine, or we just call the paramedics ourselves when the lips are blue, which is often enough for my hands to shake by 10 a.m.

Their eyes, when they do open, hold worlds. I stay for this, for those who awaken.

Their irises of variegated fern green, opal iridescent with tidal wash, impenetrable forest browns. Pupils tunnel to another place.

I stay for the few who leave this hotel. Groggy, aching from the first deep weeks or months of little movement, wasted limbs, always with family. It will take months of rehabilitation to live normally again. Most fall back.

They've told me the sleep is dreamless, without memories, a profound break, just so nice.

One afternoon, I ask Hans, "What can I do to help?"

And he answers, "Can you bring people back from the dead?"

That sure shut me up for a while.

Another time I ask him, "Why is this happening?"

He answers: "You know what none of you people ever talks about? How amazing the sleep is. How fucking *amazing* it feels. If something's that good—why should I stop? Because I might not wake up? We all go. We all go sometime."

"Wait—*can* a person stop?" I ask, suddenly desperate, my mind clear as a dead person's wide-open porch at sunrise.

He doesn't answer me, though. I'm useful for things like phone calls and food stamps but I'm not witness to the mysteries that happen beneath eyelids, in skulls adjacent to consciousness.

"Every day I wake up is a good day," Hans says.

*

When I was a kid, I used to sleepwalk, and now I dream every night about the people in the hotel. I know I care about them way too much. I dream about Hans, smoking out the window with one hand, dangling a shoe for Ulysses to snap at with the other. I dream of our youngest resident, Nomi, who drifted off permanently two months ago, she's sitting cross-legged on the roof of the hotel and I am sitting across from her and she's instructing me in the basics of meditation. *Just let your mind go blank and try to observe your thoughts without attachments,* she says. I dream about Lucifer, who always screamed at me on the stairs about the non-present elevator, and in the dream we meet in an afterlife boardroom aglow with fir and glass, and he has typed up all his complaints- *three washing machines for over a hundred people and half the time all three are broken; five distinguishable breeds of cockroaches*—and he moves his hand back and forth through the air like a small-town DJ. I dream about the living and the dead and, in between, I work in a building that belongs to neither and both.

*

I'm at the daily meeting with Dom and the nurses. There are three day nurses now; and one overnight nurse who leave notes in hieroglyphics interspersed with the phrase *continue to monitor* like a poem about breathing or an instruction manual for maintaining the spiritual lives of robots.

The nurse who's been here the longest, maybe five months, Shay, says she has a safety concern. One of the first things she did when she arrived at the hotel was decommission Dom's bell and put in a requisition for alarms, which are now installed in every room beside the cameras. Her eyes fixed on her notepad, she says this is *a difficult subject* and *nobody likes to make accusations*. But she walked in on Dom sleeping in a stairwell last Thursday at four-oh-seven p.m. and she feels that not bringing it up would be *unfair to the people we serve here*. I can tell she's starting to burn out. I can see it in the unnatural rigidity of her late-twenties body, the hardness in her eyes, like her grief has sprouted cataracts.

"Oh you want to be fair," Dom says.

"Yes."

"And objective too."

A brand-new nurse who sips a smoothie through every meeting glances between them and says, "Shouldn't this be managed privately?"

"No," Shay says. "This is a safety issue that affects us all."

"I have submitted my version of the event to the appropriate channels," Dom says. I have no idea what he's talking about—we have ever-shifting management and zero day-to-day oversight. There are fifty hotels like this one now, just in this city. Dom likes to say, proudly, that we were the first.

"You're the door guy," she says, and in that moment she loses control of the conversation, because Dom is the veteran of this place, the only one of us who belongs. "What qualifications do you have?"

"I watched a lot of Dr Phil and now I play with people's lives for the government," he says and smiles, showing white and gorgeous silver teeth.

Shay turns to me. "You've been here the longest, besides Dom," she says to me. "Like, four years, right? What do you think?"

"I didn't see Dom sleep," I say.

"What?"

"I didn't see Dom sleep."

"I didn't ask you that," she says, and I force my eyes blank, to match hers. "I asked you what you think of my report. I'm *concerned*."

What do I think? I think I've seen hundreds of people sleep here and lots of them have died but I haven't seen Dom sleep. Here we are. This is it.

"I heard—I heard on CBC last night that six thousand people have fallen asleep in this city since January and you're—you're worried about fucking *Dom*? He's *nothing*. Do you know that this is a *public health emergency* with no new medicine, no plan, no cure, no nothing? Nothing. Do you know? You're *fiddling* while Rome burns. Fiddling while Rome *burns*."

"Thanks kid," Dom says, sips his coffee.

And then, because there are no more items on the agenda, the meeting ends.

Dom and I sit around in the office, write up a few notes, shoot the shit, watch the sleepers on the monitors. A few stir. The psychiatrist who's interviewing sleepers for a research project comes by. He's a nice guy in his sixties, relaxed in his casual blazer, and always takes the time to ask us how we are, how things at the hotel are these days, but it always feels staged, like we're part of what he's researching. I want to interview everyone who lives at this hotel, but I would ask different questions. I would ask them: where were you the first time you woke up from the sleep, when you allowed yourself to surrender? I would ask: how has the sleep made the edges of your life more beautiful, or bearable? I would ask: are we awake together right now? Why can't I go where you go?

The way a body goes.
Signs of premature drowning.
Drowsiness in the core.
Heart slugging, dropped electric threads.

Electric surge and wander.
Water creep around the eyesockets, lips.
Blue sweet giveover.
Limbs tremble distant.
Doors thump closed one by one through the whole house.
Edge of mind, cooler.
Lungs go cloud.
The brain is the last refuge, hums dark computer.
For a long time, neural whisper.
Cells kick the current.
But who really knows.
I'm not in there.
Neither are you.

*

One morning I pull up to the hotel and a crowd of people is on the sidewalk.

I jump out, find Dom as fast as I can. "Fire?" The worst case scenario—the sleepers trapped, drugged by smoke as the papery old building wicks in a purple haze with a voiceover by a local anchor about another dark curiosity for the public collection.

Dom shakes his head. "Gas leak. Nurse smelled it."

"Where?"

"Fourth floor."

Residents I haven't seen on their feet in weeks blink at the sky, birds waving their shining arms down at us. Our people mill around like a small sidewalk convention of serene monks, off-kilter with fragility and wonder.

The gas safety people roar up in their van and charge inside.

"How BOUT a SONG," Hans bellows.

There he is—standing on top of a newspaper box.

He leads us in an arrhythmic version of "Kumbaya," then "Country Roads," then "This Little Light of Mine."

Dom joins in and a few minutes later is bellowing like a devout choirboy.

Hans conducts, arms raised in the pure May light, his khaki coat lit from behind, drawing out notes and stomping flourishes on the newspaper box, which groans the emphasis of a subwoofer speaker.

Paramedics carry out a few sleepers who couldn't get up and lay them on the curb.

The gas guys come back out of the building and roar off.

They didn't find any gas.

We all go inside and the day goes on as if none of this happened.

People crawl back onto their mats and leave the world.

Later in the day, a nurse tells us that it was a durian. That huge stinky fruit. A sleeper had stored one in their room, forgotten about it. Smells just like gas.

*

When I catch Dom napping—once in a stairwell, curled up like a chubby cobra in his sweatpants and leather jacket; once on the floor under our shared desk, cap balanced on his face; once in a dead resident's room, on their mat, when I thought he was cleaning up—I wake him gently, ask him how long he's been out, give him a few blasts of the medicine, and walk him to the bathroom to splash water on his face, rinse the wrinkled towel on his brain. I need him. The nurse who ratted him out quit soon after that meeting and Dom and I toasted her departure with mason jars of rum and coke in the office. "Ding dong the bitch is dead!" we chanted, laughed. We were the survivors.

After Dom rouses himself and slurps ginger ale he keeps in the minifridge in the office—*goddamn the sleep is dehydrating*, he laments—we sit together and say nothing for a long time. I won't report Dom. Having someone is better than having no one.

One day I get this weird feeling while I'm checking Twitter on my phone in the lobby and I run down the hall and he's grey-lipped in the bathroom. I administer seven doses of medicine, my hands sweating and slipping on the glass. I pour cups and cups of water down his throat until he gargles and hacks and water sprays on my chest. I pour water on his shirt and back and hair and knock his head gently against the wall, make sure his airway is clear, and for the first time since my childhood, I pray. Wake up.

His eyes open and he hisses, "You're too young for this shit."

"I'm not quitting."

"Oh kid. Don't stay for my sake. I'm the burnout phoenix."

I want to persuade him to apply to one of the treatment centres but I don't because I know from my years at the hotel that's not how it works, it's not about what or me or nextness.

"Figure it out, kid. You gotta figure it out."

"Let's go to my car," I say. I help him walk out through the back door, down the alley, and sit with him in the back seat of my car for an hour or so, and then we go back to work.

*

The day Hans goes to sleep for the last time, I'm running up the steps and a dice is sitting on the step at eye level with me and I capture it in my palm as I pass. I pocket it. I'm always finding little things like this all over the hotel and know I'm the only one who'll pick them up.

The ambulance comes for Hans's body and leaves. I take the dice out and set it on the computer monitor. I pack my bag and go to Hans's room. I put Ulysses on his leash and take him to my car. I tell him he's mine now. Hans had told me how many times Ulysses had saved his life—*no doctor can smell when the sleep's too heavy but that dog can.* As I turn the ignition and the car's engine gives me its reliable vibrational bear-hug, I squeeze my eyes tight shut. I hotbox the car with my tears. I spread fingers over my face and shutter myself into this place. "Fucking idiot," I say over and over and over. The pain floats in jagged pieces in my sternum. Somewhere in this, I think, how perfect, how fucking appropriate, that I will die in this little pod of my car in this underground parkade just as the people in the hotel die in their pods, lined up one after the other. They're just sitting ducks for the sleep. Oh, the spaces between the swells of pain are widening and sagging like rotting floorboards where there used to be ribs. It isn't Hans—it's all of them. All the dead ones I've known in the years since a chunk of the population started to slip into unending unexplained slumber—not enough people to interfere with the grind of life, but more than those lost to cancer, more than heart disease, more than car accidents. Many of the sleepers never die. They are subclinical.

Hans had teased me—*like trying to explain fucking to a virgin*. I hadn't known. My not knowing had changed me. My innocence had been a clear space for something else to grow. Like love for this world and also like horror against this world. The two doubled together within me, wrestling for control. I bend over and vomit, reach down to mop it up with my sleeve. I take off my shirt and toss it in a stinking ball into the back seat. I think, Hans is gone and everyone will go and then I feel scraped empty, and oddly weightless, my arms loose as they return to their original positions, the same and dislodged. I had worried about Hans's judgement of me—he had seen I had no clue and let it slide—and now he was gone and what was the purpose of any care that I had put into our conversations, my management of his impressions of me, the story he told himself? Any expectations of me he'd had were irrelevant now. Not worthless, just stale-dated. I don't believe in ghosts. That's what I've learned from the sleep hotel. The body is the only real thing. The sugar in the blood, our only proof. The radio doesn't play yesterday's death toll twice. Somehow, I have fallen into this work with the continuously-dying and this is its nature: I am in competition with time. My car stinks of what's inside me. I start the car and roll down the windows. I drink water and spit it out. I'm all acid and tendon, taut bone and fluttering nerves and names. I drive myself out of the carpark into the night.

THE LAST BIG DANCE

Conor Kerr

We ran out of hooch at that last big barn dance. It was good timing because the mounties showed up right afterwards and busted up the party. They came roaring in, with their usual big fuss and grandeur, pretending they were real tough guys, and not just a bunch of hooligans looking for booze and drunk ladies. Granny hated when they showed up. She didn't want anyone in a uniform drinking the hooch she made, and she didn't want anyone interrupting her fiddle music, least of all the mounties. Granny hates mounties. She's got good reason too, they're always showing up at her place looking for the stills, taking all the canned meat and vegetables from the cold cellar, busting up the horses, and lighting the wood pile on fire. They tried to bust her up once too but she smacked the man's chubby cheeks red with her spoon and threatened to let loose her wolves on them. She didn't have any wolves, but the city boys from Ontario who were posted on their first tour to northern Alberta didn't know that. So instead of busting up Granny, they settled for busting up the barn dances.

*

That same night Uncle Jim went through the ice on the Amisk River on our ride back home. He was right pickled and somehow managed to fall out of the back of the wagon, off the bridge, and went all the way up to his neck in the muck and water even though the river's only about three feet deep in that spot and he's six foot plus. He kept screaming bloody murder about the beavers dragging him under the ice. Said he'd be back to "light them toothy fuckers up." My cousins and I threw him the rope, tied it off to the wagon. Granny got the horses going and we pulled him right out of his hole and over the ice to the bank. We got him out of his clothes and wrapped in a woolen blanket in the back of the straw-laden wagon. First thing he did was grab a bottle of hooch he must have stashed in the straw and took a big swig. Then he winked at me.

"You and me girl, it's just you and me," he said with a moonshine slur before he passed out. My cousins and I killed time on the rest of the ride home by putting straw up his nose. We tried to see how many pieces we could get up there before he would swat them out in his drunken stupor.

"Jim never could handle his hooch," Granny said as we unhitched the horses and headed into her cabin.

*

I moved into Granny's one-room shack shortly after my tenth birthday in 1942. Granny had just celebrated her birthday by shooting a two-year-old bull moose off her front porch right in between the eyes with her old lever-action rifle. All the family and neighbours came over to help butcher up the moose and celebrate Granny's good aim. It was at that party that my parents told me I wasn't coming back with them. My mother and father had just had their ninth child and there was no room in their own one bedroom cabin. It didn't bother me none. I liked the idea of having my own bed and not sharing it with four of my brothers and sisters. Uncle Jim had recently left Granny's to go and fight the Nazis over in Europe. My parents told me that Granny was going to need a hand around her cabin. I figured that meant chopping wood, getting water, and shooting the odd deer or bird, tasks I was well-suited to having done them for as long as I could remember. In reality it meant spending days doing all those tasks plus carrying the fifty-pound sacks of grain half a mile back into the woods to the old copper still. The trail to the still wasn't defined like the one that led back to my parents' house. It was rough, tough walking. You were continually dodging around the fallen birch and pine trees and old spruce boughs with all that grain or wheat or corn or barley or horse feed on your shoulders. Worst of it was covering your tracks on the way out. If even a little hint of a trail was showing, a footprint in the snow, a tree moved out of the way, even leaves crunched up, Granny would hammer on you with her wooden spoon.

"You going to lead dem mounties right to it," she'd yell. "Can't cover a track, walking around out there like a goddamn mooniyah."

*

At night, we'd sit around the wood-burning stove drinking spruce needle tea from the cast-iron pot permanently steeping on top of the stove. My night tasks were to make sure that pot was permanently full of water by melting snow in it and adding cups of spruce needles Granny had dried out during the summer. My other task was to place the beads on or thread Granny's beading needle. In the last few years, her hands had taken to shaking and she couldn't do either anymore. But once I got those on there for her, she'd be flying through the tanned moose hide creating elaborate flower designs. While she beaded, she'd tell stories of the land and all our relations that lived here with us. She told me about where mosquitoes come from, and why you should never trust a government official, a banker, or a mountie. She talked about long lean months in the winter when her, my mother and Uncle Jim wouldn't have anything to eat except for the donations from some of the neighbour families who were also on the verge of starving. How she would have to do the hunting since there wasn't a man around to go and get deer, birds, and moose. She talked about Jim, and how good of a shot he was with the rifle, how he learned to shoot animals in the head to ease their suffering and preserve more of the meat, how he had been doing that since he was six years old. Then she'd laugh and talk about how she pitied those Germans who got in the way of Jim's rifle.

*

Sometimes one of Granny's regular customers, usually one of the town folk from St. Lina or St. Paul, would make a special request for a fancy bottle. They'd show up with husked corn instead of the usual grain. Granny liked making corn moonshine. With the grain stuff, she would never bother checking it or caring what kind of proof it was. She would just bottle it up and send it off. With the corn mash moonshine, she would take extra time. She'd wait about a week after the mash first got cooking until the "dogs head" got going, watching for the large single bubbles coming up every twenty to thirty seconds. She'd slop it back, pouring it onto itself to kick out the cap. Then wait another three days until she really got shining. When she figured it was done, she'd fill half a jar from the still, take it in her right hand, and hit the wrinkled palm of her left hand with the jar three times. Not four times, not two times, but three times. She'd turn the jar onto the side and the shine would separate into three consistent pools if it had been done right.

"Hundothree proof, looking good." She'd take a little sip. She never drank the shine, would just sip a tablespoon's worth to check the flavouring. "She's good my boy, let's get this bottled up and out of here."

*

Granny and her husband were both little kids when the Canadian government dissolved the Papaschase First Nation. All the band members had been off hunting or at the Fort and they took advantage of that and declared the First Nation null and void. When they tried to go back to their home to get some supplies, the mounties were already there and the house was up in flames. They fled with their families to the bush north of St. Lina, Alberta. Eventually, they grew up and started having kids until Granny's husband up and died one day. My mother told me he died from heartbreak from being forced off the land he had loved, Uncle Jim told me it was TB. Either way, Granny never talked about her husband. And she never talked about the Papaschase land she had grown up on. But she loved woodpeckers. Anytime a woodpecker would be hanging around the cabin she would spend all day rolling hand-made cigarettes, drinking tea, and watching the bird work its way around a white poplar tree.

*

Uncle Jim showed up back at Granny's cabin a few days after I turned fifteen. He spent a year after the war "showing those Quebecois ladies how to really jig." Then he ran out of money and hopped a train back out to Alberta. When he first arrived, we'd sit around Granny's cabin night after night and listen to him tell stories about Europe and the war. Everyone who was anyone, plus a few others from the area, would be over at Granny's drinking 'shine and listening to Jim describe how the underwear looked on this lady from Trois Rivieres.

"You watch out she might be your cousin," Granny would yell, smiling, with a cigarette hanging out of her mouth as she ladled out drinks for the listeners. That summer was a real party. We went through more 'shine than we had in a long time, partly because of the nightly story session, partly because Jim drank it all day every day.

*

Even if Uncle Jim drank the still dry the night before, he would be up for the sunrise. Didn't matter if the sun was coming up at 8:30 in the winter or 4:30 in the summer, he would rise with it. I woke up every morning to the thwock of the axe splitting birch from the wood pile. The smell of tobacco trailed behind him as he walked past my bed carrying an armful of wood for the stove. I always tried to wait until the stove had the cabin roasting before I got out from underneath the wool blanket.

*

The morning after Jim fell through the ice on the Amisk River he was moving like a bear with an itch. After the stove got fired up, I could sense him standing right above me, but I refused to open my eyes, hoping he would get bored and wander off to check on the stills. He poked me in the gut with the barrel of the 30-30 lever action rifle we kept by the door.

"Hey girl, those beavers are probably dragging some kid under the ice right now." He poked me again with the barrel of the gun. "Might even be one of your brothers or sisters."

"Get out of here, you reek like booze you old bum." I turned over and pulled the woolen blanket over my head. "That thing better be unloaded."

"How would you feel about that?" Jim said.

"Don't really care."

He wasn't going to leave me alone. The stove had taken the frost out of the air in the cabin. Jim sat on the chair across from my bed and started rolling a cigarette.

"Roll me one of those and I'll help you out," I said.

Jim finished rolling a smoke and passed it to me. Then he started rolling another one for himself.

"I found the spot. Ain't no more beavers going to be dragging poor unsuspecting folk under the water any longer."

*

We saddled up the wagon horses. They both snorted and stomped their appreciation for going for just a little ride and not hauling the wagon around. Granny walked by us on her way down to the still. She nodded at us, the customary cigarette hanging out of her lips, unlit until she finished her walk. Granny never smoked while walking.

"If you see a moose, take that instead of the beavers. We could use the meat," she said.

Jim gave a faux salute and we set off through the bush. It was a good dozen miles or so to the spot on the river where Jim had gone through the ice. I settled into the saddle and lit the cigarette Jim had rolled for me. The sun had a warmth to it that we hadn't felt in months. All around us the land was waking up from its winter rest. Birds chirped and fought between the bare branches of the poplar and birch trees, squirrels chattered to announce our arrival as we passed underneath them on the trail, a couple coyotes howled in the distance. The worst of winter was behind us and everything in the bush was out in full celebration. Even Jim seemed to momentarily forget that he had a score to settle with some beavers.

The melting snow had left a series of cracks through the ice on the Amisk River, and you could clearly see the spot where Jim had fallen through after the party. There was a thin layer of ice over the hole and in the busted-up area where he had been dragged out. Whiskeyjacks swooped all around us checking out what we were doing in their area, their grey and black feathers bristling with the prospect of a free meal.

"Awas," Jim yelled at them, then muttered. "You're giving away our goddamn position. Damn beavers will know we're coming now."

"I think the yelling gave us away, not the whiskeyjacks," I said.

"No one cares what you think," Jim grumbled and pulled a jar of hooch out of his saddle bag. "Shouldn't be too shooken yah think?" He took a big swig.

"Not many beavers around here," I said.

"Oh they're coming, believe me, those toothy motherfuckers are coming."

Jim and I hopped down from our horses and tethered them to a couple birch trees. They immediately started pawing up the snow to get at the old grass underneath it. The horses both seemed more than content to bask in the sun and eat the grass while we figured out where the best place to watch for beavers was. Jim made sure to bring the hooch, rifle, and the rolling tobacco from his bag while I kicked snow out of the way to try and make a dry spot for us to sit. For the next couple hours, Jim and I sat beside the creek and he drank the first bottle of hooch, and then the second bottle of hooch, and then started to get into a third. At some point during the second bottle Jim started firing the 30-30 randomly at the ice.

"Think I got one there."

"Think the bullet ricocheted off the ice, Uncle."

"Yeah, ricocheted right into a beaver. Just like I was planning." He fired another one. "See, got another one."

"Don't know if you did, Uncle."

"How many men you ever shot kid? Huh? I think I know when I hit a beaver or not." Jim's dark brown eyes were rolling circles in his head. "Think that's enough killing for today. Let's head back and see what Granny's doing," he slurred.

I got the horses and saddled them up while Jim 'kept watch for beavers' while rolling smokes for the ride back. As soon as I helped Jim up on his horse, he lit one of the smokes and then immediately fell asleep. I grabbed the reins from his mare and hitched her up to my horse and we went down the trail. The animal noise and chatter had faded with the setting sun. The only sound now was the snorts and snores from Jim as he half dozed and half smoked from behind me on the trail. At one point he woke up from his drunk, looked at me and said, "You know any Cree?"

"Not much," I answered. "How about you?"

He had already fallen asleep before I finished asking. The smell of hooch on him was so strong it overpowered the mare's breath, which wasn't exactly mint fresh. All I could think of was getting him dropped off in a bed back at Granny's.

As we got closer to Granny's cabin, I noticed something was happening. I could hear shouts coming from inside. I stopped the horses, hopped down, and snuck up to the cabin. The shouts kept getting louder. It sounded like a couple of rough male voices with Granny's mixed in. As I got closer, I realized I should have grabbed the 30-30 from Jim. Then I decided that it might be some of the family from down the road getting into it after a few too many drinks. I eased up a bit with this thought and walked through the woods with a bold step. I was almost at the cabin when Granny came flying out the door, and not of her own free will; two mounties followed. Their pale cheeks red with rage. I ducked behind the wood pile and watched as the one hit Granny across the face, knocking her back down.

"Damn squaw, you're going to tell us where the still is or we're going to burn this all to the ground," the one who hit Granny yelled. The other mountie went and kicked her while she was on the ground.

I panicked. Granny swore at them in Cree and got up. The mounties kept pushing her back down. I gotta get Jim I decided, forgetting that he was wasted off his tree. The mounties, too obsessed with Granny, didn't notice me start running back towards where I had left the horses and passed-out Jim. The shouting from Granny and the mounties followed me. When I got there, I found the horses, but no Jim. Stupid drunk, probably passed out under a tree nearby, I thought. I had to figure out what to do about Granny and the mounties. I thought of riding to my parents' cabin and getting my father. It was only about fifteen to twenty minutes at a full gallop. In the distance the screaming continued. I was about to hop up on the horse when I heard the gunshot. And then another gunshot. And then another.

Back at Granny's cabin, I found Jim standing over the bodies of the two mounties pointing his 30-30 rifle at them, red blood splattered across the white snow. One had been shot in the arm and the leg, the other just in the arm. Their firearms had been thrown into a pile over by the cabin's steps. They stared at Jim with horror. Both young men from somewhere in Ontario, never guessing that they would be facing death in the northern Alberta bush. Jim held the rifle with the authority of someone who had killed before.

"Well now, why would you two go and beat up on an old lady for something as silly as moonshine?" Jim asked, his voice calm now, lacking the drunken stupor of earlier. Both the mounties stared at him, neither daring to answer. The one who had been shot twice started hyperventilating. "Alright, go on both of you back inside the cabin. We gotta get you bandaged up." Jim prodded them with his rifle. Neither of them could move on account that they had been shot up, so I took to dragging them inside on the sled we normally used for wood. They were both heavy boys, definitely had been eating well inside the depot back in St. Paul, and there was a good yellow piss stain on the snow mixed in with the blood under where the one guy had been laying. Inside Granny's cabin she had been prepping bandages and tourniquets and got to fixing up their bleeding. She wrapped them both in wool blankets and sat them down by the wood stove to help with the shock.

"Relax, no one's going to die tonight," Jim said. "But if either of you ever think of coming back to this area, well, that's going to be a different story." He lit a cigarette from where he sat in the chair with the 30-30 pointing at them. Granny finished fixing the mounties up and started pouring tea. I stood back in the corner trying to stay as close to the door or a window in case Jim changed his mind.

"After we finish this tea, thank you, Granny, by the way, you two boys are going to head back into town and tell the sergeant that you got in a fight with a couple of beavers out by the Amisk

River. Got it?" Both the mounties nodded their heads as fast as they could. "Or as we said in Quebec, a good old castor fight." Jim exhaled smoke in the faces of the two mounties. "Now you going to thank Granny for being so kind to make you tea?"

"Th-th-th-thanks," they both said.

"Now let's get you boys on those horses."

As the mounties set off on the horses towards St. Paul, Granny, Jim and I turned back to where the 30-30 cartridges sat in the snow surrounded by blood and piss stains.

"I think it's about time you headed back to your parents for a bit," Granny said to me. "At least until your goddamn trigger happy uncle figures out his place."

"They would have shot all three of us if I hadn't of stepped in," Jim said. "Should of known they would have been waiting until after we took off. Goddamn beavers."

"Mounties, Jim, mounties." Granny said. Her eyes were fixed on the blood. "Hooch is getting to that brain of yours."

"You know what, I think I'm going to go and fix those beavers up right now." Jim said. Without turning back to face us he walked over to where his horse was still standing saddled up from earlier that night. He hopped on the horse and headed back down the trail we had come from, the darkness quickly enveloped him.

"Should I go after him?" I asked Granny.

"Leave him be. Come on, let's get this cleaned up."

Jim didn't come back that night. Granny told me not to worry about him and to save my own skin and head back down to my parents. She figured the mounties would be coming back with everything they had. The next day, instead of heading in that direction, I went towards the river where I found Jim's horse tied up to the same birch tree that he and I had tethered up to the day before. A couple of empty hooch jars lay haphazardly in the snow beside a dozen cigarette butts that led in a trail towards a hole in the ice that hadn't quite frozen over yet.

MADAME FLORA'S

Camilla Grudova

Victoria's menses stopped. Her nanny looked through her old diaper bustles, the ones that hadn't been thrown away yet. It had not arrived when it was supposed to. Her nanny checked the diary she kept of Victoria's menses ('Light''Regular''Thick' 'An Odd Smell'). Each sentence was accompanied by a fingerprint of blood, from the moment little Victoria, aged thirteen, held up a bloody hand saying "Nanny I am dying," to which Nanny replied that the diaper bustle Victoria had always worn was in preparation for such bleeding and that the bleeding was best called blooming and the blood best called flowers by a young lady.

Ladies wore diaper bustles all the time so men wouldn't know exactly when they were menstruating, it was less obscene that way, the constant taffeta swish swish of the diapers that accompanied women's movements giving no indication of their cycle. They were large and scented, made out of cotton and plastic. Women past the age of menstruating still wore them, as did little girls, there was no sense of end or beginning. The bustles were reassuring: women would never leak. Women were like eggs made out of marble, not creatures made of meat.

Nanny told Victoria's mother who told Victoria's father that Victoria was dreadfully weakened. Victoria's father called the family doctor who hurried over, and without shock on hearing Victoria's period had stopped, handed Victoria's father a bottle of Madame Flora's saying he saw this affliction all the time in young ladies, it was nothing to worry about.

"It's such a horror, the idea of flowers from a woman's body. It seems a shame to bring it back when it has disappeared," Victoria's father said with the abstract disgust of a man who had never seen it before.

The doctor laughed. "It is indeed, but a necessity of life."

The bottle was made of milky green glass, opaque so the liquid inside wasn't visible.

They all knew of Madame Flora's. Her advertisements were everywhere, on billboards, and magazines, illustrations of fainted ladies contrasted with ones of ladies dancing, and carrying children. Ladies sitting on half-moons, laughing, bouquets of blossoming flowers. In many shopping arcades there was a mechanical wax girl in a glass box, eternally consuming Madame Flora's. When the bottle reached her mouth, a blush spread through her wax cheeks. Madame Flora's was "The Number One Cure for Weakness, Nervous Complaints, Fainting and Dizziness."

Victoria's father opened the bottle and took a strong sniff, then another. He stuck his finger in and pulled it out: Madame Flora's was a dense, dark brown syrup. The bottle label suggested mixing it with tonic water, or putting it in puddings or spreading it on toast with butter.

Victoria's nanny tried a spoonful herself. The doctor and Victoria's father looked away with slight disgust.

She spat it into her hand then wiped her hand on her apron. "Sir, it tastes of . . . bloo—"

"Nonsense. It's a one hundred percent herbal mixture, I have read the label and prescribed it to many patients. I would not expect you to know what blood tastes like," said the doctor.

"I only know sir, from the smell of it."

Victoria's father grabbed the bottle and looked for the ingredients, but they weren't listed.

In small letters on the bottom of the label it said, *For Extreme Cases, Please Consider a Vacation at Madame Flora's Hotel.*

The canopy curtains of Victoria's bed were closed. Nanny opened them. Victoria lay in bed, reading a book of nursery rhymes and smoking. Her long red hair was greasy-looking. Nanny grabbed her cigarette and put it out under her boot.

"Nanny!" Victoria cried.

The doctor and father's father chuckled.

Nanny prepared a glass of Madame Flora's in the bedroom kitchenette. Women weren't allowed in the main kitchens of houses, but the kitchenette was a place where they could prepare light meals—there was an electric tea kettle, and a tiny plastic oven, which used a light bulb and was decorated with flowers, that could warm toast and make little cakes but never burn anything. There were boxes of powders that could be turned into various porridges, tea, malt powder, and seaweed jelly powder, and always a fresh bottle of milk.

Victoria tried to spit out Madame Flora's but Nanny stopped her. She swallowed with a grimace. "Bring me a crumpet Nanny, and some milk, to chase it down, please Nanny."

"Be quiet, Victoria," said her father.

"Bring the child some milk," said the doctor. "The taste of Madame Flora's is not delicate."

Victoria was to be given Madame Flora's in the morning, at lunchtime, and before bed. She complained that Madame Flora's gave her fevers and constipation. She rinsed her mouth out after, and often went to the bathroom, sticking two of her fingers down her throat until she vomited it up. "I don't like iron," she said to herself. She did everything she could to get Madame Flora's out of her body. She didn't miss her menses, the gelatinous clots that reminded her of leeches, the fear of leaks even when she wore chafing rubber underwear under her bustle.

They tried the whole range of Madame Flora's products. In addition to the tonic, they sold pastilles, pills, powder, boullion squares for soup, and a line of chocolate-covered Madame Flora jelly that looked like Turkish delight but tasted like rust, sulphur and browned flowers.

Victoria poured Madame Flora's on the crotch of her diaper bustle hoping it would pass, but Nanny knew.

Victoria's father said he would send her to Madame Flora's hotel.

"Can't Nanny come with me to Madame Flora's?" Victoria asked

"No, she must look after your mother," her father said, and Victoria was secretly pleased, for she wanted to be away from Nanny.

*

They took the carriage. Victoria wore a green taffeta dress. Besides her trunk, she had a small black velvet purse. Inside were love letters from her father's butler and one of her father's friends. One contained a dried daisy, stuck to the page with horse glue.

Victoria's mother brought a large tin of wine gums along for the ride, keeping it on her lap. They were all she would eat. The black currant-flavoured ones in particular. Her father brought cold roast beef, a spiral sausage that resembled a round rag rug, and pâté along for himself. He didn't stop to eat it but let the smell fill up the whole carriage. "I feel so ill I want to die," Victoria said to herself. Women weren't allowed to eat meat. The smell of it was intolerably strong.

They had to stop twice, for forty minutes each time, so her father could go to the bathroom. There were men smoking and loitering about outside the men's public restrooms. On a bench by the bathroom door, there was a man with swollen-looking red legs, his trousers rolled up to reveal them. He was eating potted meat with his fingers and grinning. There was a smell around the place, like burnt mutton, her mother held a handkerchief to her face as they waited. "Why do men take ever so long to toilet," asked Victoria and her mother told her not to be vulgar, drooling as she spoke because of the wine gums.

Victoria knew the right amount she could piss in her bustle without it leaking or smelling. She did so. There weren't many public bathrooms for women.

Madame Flora's hotel overlooked the sea. It was a white building, like most in the town, a popular seaside resort. The words 'Madame Flora's' were written in gold, large letters and there was a billboard on the roof of the hotel with an image of Madame Flora's tonic surrounded by roses. The main doors were glass with golden bars. The veranda had no chairs, only large potted ferns.

The hotel foyer smelled of the bouquets of flowers placed everywhere, but it was overrun with suitcases, tennis rackets, and other sports equipment. In the centre of the foyer was an enormous, strong-looking young woman, wearing a fur coat, her dark hair in braided loops pinned to her head. In one hand she held a lacrosse stick. There was a vase knocked over in front of her, the water turning the red carpet a darker shade.

"I want my own room," the girl said loudly.

"If ladies are in a room together, their flowers will blossom together," a woman in a purple dress with red frills and a matching hat said.

"I don't understand what you're saying," replied the girl. "Where am I to put all my things."

"It is beneficial to becoming well again. It is our policy," the woman said and turned to Victoria and her family.

"A moment alone with the young lady, please," she said, taking Victoria's arm and bringing her behind the hotel counter into a small room.

The woman had a fob watch hanging down her skirt. She was Madame Flora. Her bustle was huge, an exaggeration of one. She looked like a dining room chair from the side. She wore a small glass vial on a necklace. She said it was full of Madame Flora's, from one of the first bottles she had made. The liquid looked dried, dark, and old.

There wasn't a desk in the room, but a matching set of patterned couches, a drink service on wheels with crystal glasses and tonic, and a few little side tables with more flowers on them and porcelain figurines and fruit made out of plaster. Madame Flora shut the door and told Victoria to sit down. The walls were covered in photographs and drawings of babies. "From former guests at Madame Flora's, once their flowers returned," she said. "Madame Flora's is available for anyone to purchase, but our hotel is reserved for the most exclusive of clientele. I take a personal interest in all the guests here. Madame Flora's is made in a factory in the north where the water is strong, but I prefer to be here, with the girls who need my help most, who need their flowers to return."

"I don't like it. It feels like a poison, I don't like it coming out of my body," said Victoria.

"And do you like taking your Madame Flora's?"

Victoria would've blushed, if she had the energy, but she knew her cheeks remained pale and slightly green.

"Well medicine is not supposed to be tasty, now is it?" Madame Flora said.

She poured a glass of her tonic and handed it to Victoria. Under her gaze, Victoria drank it.

"It is a policy here that girls share rooms, as you may have heard."

Victoria's mother handed her a wine gum wrapped in a tissue as they said goodbye.

The girl in the foyer was named Louise and she was the daughter of a baron. She was assigned the same room as Victoria.

They weren't allowed to take the stairs, only the lift. The stairs were gated off. Behind the gate the red-carpeted stairs were dusty. Victoria was afraid Louise would make the lift break with all her things. There were only three floors. The halls had dim lights and were stuffy.

Their room was on the top floor, filled with small but pretty beds, with rose-patterned bed sheets. There were lots of small mirrors, and nightstands with powders and Madame Flora's on them. There was a marble fireplace, lit, with a decorative brass fireguard in front of it, and potpourri in little china dishes. There was a small window looking out onto the sea, and a skylight. One wall had a mural of Mother Goose on it. A small pink door led to a bathroom. There was an indent with a curtain over it, which Louise pulled back, revealing another bed. There was a thin girl with pale blonde hair and a red scalp laying in it, holding a paper box to her chest. She wore a wrinkled cream-coloured nightgown.

"I was here first," the girl said quietly, not looking at her intruder.

When Madame Flora left, Louise pushed one of the beds under the skylight and, standing on it, tapped it with her lacrosse stick.

A few more girls came into the room through the door, carrying carpet bags, hats. One with black hair who took the bed beside Victoria was named Eliza, and a girl with curls was named Matilda. None of them had shared a room with so many girls before.

They wandered around their small room, touching things. In the fireplace there was a bit of a stocking and a burnt crumpet. On the wall, behind Victoria's metal bedframe, someone had scrawled "Mutton." There was a collage on the wall, of horses and dogs, badly cut out of newspapers. In the bathroom was a framed picture of a lady riding a rabbit.

Without looking at any of the girls in particular, Louise talked, taking off her coat. Her dress had a sailor's bib and a strange cut, with low hips, it wasn't suited to her bustle. The sleeves were short. On one arm she had a Union Jack tattoo which the other girls thought shocking until Louise said her father had it done to her when she was eight, which meant her father loved her very much.

"After this I'm going to Fairy Palace, in Wales, to fix my teeth. My Hugh had his teeth fixed there. Then we are getting married."

She suddenly looked at Victoria. "Are they going to send you somewhere to fix your nose next?"

Victoria covered her nose with one of her hands.

Louise continued talking "They've fixed my hymen twice now, both times it broke from riding horses. It has to be intact just before you're married so that a nurse hired by your fiancée can break it with a metal instrument. It's so he won't be put off by the sight of blood after the wedding. Your fiancée gets a certificate from the nurse saying it was done." Victoria didn't understand what a hymen was, perhaps a little male china doll? Victoria's dolls had never bled, though she often checked and made them diapers out of tissue.

Louise pointed to the collage of dogs and horses. "It's shaped like the Kingdom of Wales."

"No it isn't, I'm from Wales," said Eliza. Louise slapped her.

*

There was a diaper bustle dispensary: a tin box hung on the wall. Louise pulled out diaper bustles, throwing them into the room until they were called for dinner. The dining room was full of small round tables, only two or three girls could fit at each. There were many older women there who were married. The married women were in separate, individual rooms. It made Louise angry. "Bitches," she said. They spent most of their time playing cards in the parlour or writing long letters to their husbands and children.

There were large bottles of Madame Flora's surrounded by tiny bottles and oranges as table centrepieces. Oranges were said to help with the constipation that too much Madame Flora's could cause. They were served bowls of mashed potatoes with sugar and milk, or bowls of white bread with sugar and milk, cups of tea with sugar and cream, and more oranges, there were bowls of peeled oranges and orange jelly, crumpets, tiny pots of jam, cabbage and boiled carrots, rice pudding. Victoria sat with a pudgy girl with dark circles under her eyes who said, quietly, "I've not stopped my flowers for the same reason as everyone else. Have you ever been in love?"

Victoria thought of her father, her father's butler, and her father's friends, and said no. The girl ate too much cabbage and rice pudding and had gas. She told Victoria that she knew a girl whose flowers stopped after she saw a dead man in a ditch, but she was cured at Madame Flora's, and that she herself would never be cured, which she said with a little giggle Victoria didn't like.

After dinner, the girls were told to go to bed. Rest was the most important thing. Louise stuck a photo of Hugh, a real lock of his blonde hair glued to it like a toupee, in the middle of the dog and horse collage. "He has more dogs and horses then all that," she said.

Louise's hands were surprisingly dainty and pudgy, with expensive feminine rings, including her engagement ring from Hugh Orville. Her nails were polished, red and sharp like vole's teeth.

Hugh Orville turned up the next day. Madame Flora wouldn't let him visit, but he left gifts for Louise with her—a stuffed swan toy, a box of chocolates. He drove around the hotel in his motor car playing a popular song Louise loved called *Tinky Tinky Too Too,* a duet between a trumpet and a theremin. Louise moved from window to window, waving and dancing. Hugh was stunningly handsome. He wore a blue kerchief and a fur coat like Louise's, flashing his new teeth from Fairy Palace. Louise told everyone he was a duke.

Eliza had several black dresses, all velvet or silk, they all looked similar but she wore the same one every day until it smelled, as well as to bed, merely changing her stockings and bustle, discreetly in the morning. Matilda's dresses were exceptionally ugly, Louise told her. They were of calico, brown, mustard yellow, pink.

Each girl had her own way of taking Madame Flora's, of standing the nasty taste. Eliza liked to mix Madame Flora's with black tea, Matilda with tonic water, so it was weakened, she only put a drop or two in. Victoria copied her. The girl who slept behind the curtain and wouldn't say her name put it in milk, so that it was a pink colour. Many in the dining room put it in their porridge.

Louise took a straight teaspoon in the morning, with lunch and before bed, without complaining or grimacing.

She had an iron ball which she licked and threatened to throw at the other girls. Her nanny at home had given her the ball as an anemia cure and she was addicted to it, but Madame Flora took it away, saying it was bad for her, as were greens. "Spinach is poisonous. My tonic is the only safe source of iron for women."

Each evening, a maid came and took away their bustle diapers and dirty laundry in a cart, and examined the bed sheets and blankets for stains. It didn't feel as cruel as when Nanny did it, tuttering and sighing. There were so many girls at Madame Flora's. It wasn't personal.

Louise, who wore trouser pajamas to bed, talked into the night. There was nothing else to do, besides reading magazines.

"I saw a man eating a boiled egg, he grinned at me as he done so."

"I sniffed a rasher of bacon, once, in the kitchen at home."

"Hugh killed eight pheasants and a fox last spring."

There was a middle-aged woman who sat herself in the lift and wouldn't come out. Others squished buns through the brass grating, to make her eat, but she wouldn't let anyone pour any Madame Flora's in, she called it devil's juice. She wasn't married. Madame Flora put some of her concoction in a spray bottle and sprayed the woman with it but she turned around and crouched in a far corner of the lift. Madame told them to ignore her and look away when they passed. There were queues for the one elevator left. The woman screamed and shook the lift during the night and silently paced during the day. Louise spat orange pips at her whenever she passed by the lift.

One morning they came down and the lift was empty and clean again.

On his second visit, Hugh brought Louise a miniature golf set, which she set up in the parlour.

"Exercise is the enemy of your flowers, Louise," Madame Flora said, taking Louise's golf club as she took a swing. Louise was so despondent that Madame Flora made an effort to provide entertainment. Victoria couldn't see how Louise could be bored. There were so many ladies' magazines to read at Madame Flora's—*The Modern Priscilla, Dainty Day, News for Ladies*—in big stacks everywhere. Victoria's nanny had sent her some popular poems written out on card paper, she had written them herself in brown ink. Victoria ripped them up. She was scared of Nanny visiting Madame Flora's like Hugh did, of Nanny circling the hotel crying Victoria Victoria.

The town was full of hotels, shopping arcades, stalls selling postcards, seashell art ("Don't touch the seashells girls!" said Madame Flora) and novelty tea sets with the royal family on them. There were rides and other amusements. Madame Flora hired a long, covered rickshaw pulled by two cyclists to bring the girls around. The seats were very small, and metal, Louise struggled to fit in one, so she balanced herself on the back of the seat, her legs hanging down the arms. She harassed the cyclists, telling them to go faster, or slow down when she saw something that looked amusing, especially the butchers' shops which had striped curtains covering the windows and signs that said 'Gentleman Only'. "What do they sell eh?" She muttered, "Sausage. Eggs. Snouts."

Victoria half-covered her ears to make herself look good, but was intrigued by what Louise was saying. Louise could only be distracted from the butchers' shops by a carousel on one of the piers.

Madame Flora said yes to a ride on it, and made one of the maids run back to the hotel and get some soft paddings to put on the fake animals before the girls sat on them. "Sideways, girls, sideways, like you do properly on a horse."

She nodded to the carousel owner once she checked all the girls were rightly seated, but after it had gone round a few times, Louise changed positions on her zebra, so both legs hung down different sides. She had taken her bustle off and sent it flying. It resembled a swan as it fell into the seawater. Madame Flora shouted for the carousel to stop. By the time it did, Louise had wrapped her legs around the pole of the zebra, laughing wildly.

Madame Flora didn't let them go out anymore after that, saying it would use up the energy needed to restore their flowers. Someone came and gave a lecture on ferns, bringing samples in misty glass jars.

"I don't want my flowers again, ever, I just want out of here. I never want babies," muttered Matilda, touching one of the glass jars.

Madame Flora could tell at a glance the difference between menstrual blood and blood from a wound. When Matilda told the maids she had her flowers again, and held up her sheets, Madame Flora came in and pulled up Matilda's nightgown, exposing her diaper bustle. Her legs and stomach were covered in small cuts.

"How could you do this to yourself, sweetest of hearts? We just want to help you get better, don't we treat you well?" asked Madame Flora. They examined her for cuts each week. They put bandages over the ones she had and checked to make sure she didn't rip them off and reopen the wounds.

As Louise continued to act restless, Madame Flora hired two performers: a couple with their small dog, who wore fancy hats and sang and danced and were popular in all the seaside towns. Madame Flora placed a velvet railing to separate the girls from them. Louise made them sing "Tinky Tinky Too Too" twice, stomping her foot along so loudly the floor shook. Everyone was relieved to see Louise entertained, but the couple's dog went missing by the end of the show and they caused a fuss Madame Flora thought to be upsetting to her clients.

"Doggy, doggy!" they cried. "Where is our Doggy!" The man begged Madame Flora to let him carry around a piece of cheese to lure it out from wherever it was hiding. Madame Flora told them they were disgusting and made them leave without payment.

"Must have gotten out," said Louise. "Must have drowned in the sea."

Victoria thought once they were in their bedroom Louise would pull the dog out from under her dress, but she didn't. "I'm not interested in mutts," she said. Hugh had Bassett hounds, corgis, and Dutch partridge dogs he imported from the Netherlands despite the heavy taxation. They could hear the couple shouting outside the hotel. "Where is our doggy! Bitch, Bitch!"

A few days later the dog was found dead in one of the halls. Madame Flora was livid at the thought that there was now "meat" in her establishment, the hall was cordoned off, and the girls heard she burnt the dog in the kitchen oven. Victoria wondered if she was afraid to put it in the trash. The smell of burnt hairs and flesh wafted up through all the rooms, and Madame Flora filled her establishment with electric fans and more bowls of potpourri.

None of the girls told Madame Flora about the time, in the chaos of getting up and getting dressed, a sausage rolled out onto the floor of their bedroom. A first they thought it was a dried turd.

Louise picked it up and ate it before Madame Flora and one of the maids entered the room, having heard their screams.

No one knew who left the sausage, except it couldn't have been Louise because she would have eaten it beforehand. She ate things as soon as she received them because she knew she would always get more.

There was no change in Louise's pallor since eating the sausage, nor was she sick. All the girls that had been in the room watched her closely.

"What about girls who have too much," Victoria asked in the dark, in bed one night.

"Too much what?"

"You know, too many flowers."

No one replied, except for Louise who said, "You need a license stating you are male to buy meat, but I once heard about a woman who dressed up as a man and bought a rack of lamb and was arrested. Maybe the girls who had too many flowers were arrested too." Louise chuckled loudly, the sound filled the room like a horrid fart.

"Or died because they didn't have anything left in their bodies," said Matilda. "Maybe their hearts came out with their flowers."

After some silence, Eliza whispered.

"There was a boy Thomas, he loved me, he cut himself, on his arm, and let me drink the blood, he did it a number of times, on his legs and his arms, he said it doesn't count as meat, I started to get better but he died of infection from one of the cuts."

*

A week later, Louise was shouting "In here!" standing on a chair below the skylight. "Open the latch," she growled.

It was one of the rickshaw cyclists. Louise had sent him a message through one of the maids, perhaps.

He had put on cologne and it filled the room. He had sweat stains under the armpits of his beige suite, a fresh and red young face, and a little moustache that had been waxed and curled with care.

He took off his trousers and underpants but left on his jacket, shirt, bowtie, shoes and socks. He lay on his side on Eliza's bed, looking at them all and making kissing sounds. Eliza got up and sat beside Victoria, clutching her arm. "I want her to do it," he said, pointing to Eliza.

"Sit up," she said to him, and he did, spreading his legs wide. She went in-between.

He winced, but they couldn't see what was going on, her head was in the way. The man moaned.

"His thingie's in her ear," whispered Louise. Eliza turned around, blood on her lips. The man's thing was all sweaty and there was blood all over his thigh, where she had bitten. Louise went over but he said, "I'll come back tomorrow night," and zipped up his trousers, not thinking of the blood, as if he didn't know he was bitten.

There was a bandage over the bite when he returned.

"The other thigh," he said.

Louise didn't bite, but tried to use her nail scissors. The man screamed and said "No, use your lips and teeth." She did, but made a show of cleaning her face off with a hanky and perfume afterwards and all the other girls knew it was because he was working class.

The girl from behind the curtain came out and drank some too. Matilda and Victoria didn't.

"Bring a friend tomorrow then," Louise said to the man as he left.

The young man didn't come back the next night, but another came and knew what would happen, taking off his trousers too. After Eliza and Louise drank, Matilda took off her bustle, climbed up on the man, sitting on him, and moved around in an odd manner that made the man giggle and whelp.

"What are you doing," said Louise.

"I don't want any blood," said Matilda in a breathy voice. "I just want to keep doing what I'm doing."

Louise scowled and, grabbing one of the man's arms, made a cut in it and started drinking. He barely noticed. His other arm reached up and grabbed Matilda's breast, squeezing. It looked like it hurt to Victoria.

The next night, a different man came, and the same thing happened. Matilda sat on him while the other girls cut him and drank from him like a fountain in a garden. "But I don't want my flowers," said Victoria to herself, watching. The girl from behind the curtain copied Matilda and sat on the man too. Matilda said if you didn't have your flowers, you could do it all you wanted and you wouldn't have any children. All the other girls laughed, confused, except for Louise who said, "Hugh wants twenty children," in a serious voice. Later in the night, Victoria woke to the sound of Louise trying to do with a pillow what Matilda did with the men.

They accumulated left-behind socks, bowties, shirts, jackets, trousers, shoes, suspenders. One man left his underpants, which Louise used as a night cap. The girls tried them all on, taking turns, their bustles laying around the room like gigantic broken egg shells. How easy it was to become men.

"I could walk into a butcher's shop and buy myself a piece of ham," said Eliza.

One young man fainted after they drank his blood. Louise slapped him, and they poured Madame Flora's down his throat. He sputtered, and sat up, then vomited up the Madame Flora's all down the front of his suit.

"I'm bleeding again," the girl from behind her curtain said weakly one morning.

"Wonderful, delightful," said Madame Flora when she entered, looking at the bleeding girl. Her smile disappeared on closer inspection She called for one of the maids. Together, they carried the girl out of the room, blood dripping from her nightgown.

Hugh stopped by the hotel again to drop off a gigantic basket of fruit including a pineapple and three bananas. Louise ate too much and got diarrhea. She drank Madame Flora's straight from the bottle to stop it.

"I'll just have a small taste," said Victoria, next time a man came. Eliza was on one arm, Louise on the other, and Matilda was sitting on him. Victoria made a cut on his foot. Blood tasted like a fresh version of Madame Flora's, she thought.

At the end, they couldn't wake the man up from his faint. They poured Madame Flora's on his face but he didn't respond.

"He can sleep behind the curtain till he's better," said Victoria.

"He's dead," responded Louise. "He's meat now."

They put him in Louise's trunk.

All the blood from the man must have gone into Louise because her flowers started soon after. Wearing her stained pajamas, she ran down into the foyer to use the telephone box. Everyone in the hotel could hear her shouting into it,

"FLOWERS HUGH, FLOWERS." A few hours later a carriage from her parents' house arrived, followed by Hugh Orville in a motorcar.

Louise took the trunk with the man inside with her. "I'll take care of it," she said to the other girls.

Her wedding was in all the papers a few weeks later. She had new teeth too, they looked exactly the same as Hugh's. They both made sure to show the teeth off in the photos.

Eliza left soon after. She said she wished Thomas could see her flowers, which was a wicked thing to say even though he was dead. No one would ever now, unless she had to come back to Madame Flora's. She didn't have a nanny at home.

"Give me a spot of yours," Matilda begged Eliza. She didn't just spread it in her bustle, but inside herself and on her legs too. It tricked Madame Flora this time.

Victoria was left alone, except for the picture Hugh Louise had left behind.

I'll be in and out of here for the rest of my life, Victoria thought, I'll be stopping and starting my flowers, I'll be spitting up Madame Flora's, I can settle here forever with the parlour wives. There were left over Madame Flora bottles all over the room. She poured the contents of them into the toilet, without flushing, and giggled as she did so. She then sat on one of the beds, and opened a magazine. On the cover was a woman using a telephone, her spare hand sitting atop a bouquet of roses.

GOVERNMENT SLOTS

Omar El Akkad

Three brown dahlias, pressed and dried
A photograph of a meadow in spring
A compass

In the morning, just after we open, an old woman comes in. She stands in line—there's always a line, though never a long one—and passes through the metal detector without setting it off. It's Christmas Day and we are, as far as I can tell, the only state or federal building open. We're open every day. You never know.

The old woman makes her way past security and over to the ticket spitter. She takes a number and sits down on one of the grey plastic chairs bolted to the floor. She waits until a man at one of the inspection desks calls her number, then she stands, removes her paperwork from her handbag, and shuffles over. Without speaking, the man takes her papers—identification, social security, proof of ownership. He looks through them, disinterested. The old woman waits.

Finally, the inspector sets the papers aside. From a desk drawer he retrieves a blank deposit form.

All right, he says, let's see what you got.

The woman reaches into her purse and pulls out a small sandwich bag full of cloud-white fur. She slides it across the table.

The inspector picks up the bag, cautious, with the tips of his thumb and index finger. He stares at it as a jogger might stare at roadkill, repulsed but not repelled, curious about the insides of things.

A dog? the inspector asks.

Bichon frisé, the old woman replies.

That's a dog?

Yes.

The inspector starts to say something, then sighs and waves to one of his colleagues at the next desk. His colleague comes over, and he, too, picks up the bag, turns it over in his hand, holds it against the light.

Dog fur, the inspector says. His colleague nods, then shakes his head.

Not allowed, he says. Nothing perishable, nothing alive.

This isn't perishable, the old woman replies. This isn't alive.

Both inspectors look at each other, and when one shrugs and shakes his head again, the other does the same. Sorry, they both say, almost in unison.

This is usually the point where there'd be a fight, when the customer would demand to see a manager or start threatening lawsuits. Sometimes security gets involved. Sometimes things get undignified.

But the old woman does none of this. Carefully she puts the bag of fur back in her handbag and walks away.

Look, if you want you can go around to the office and ask for an exemption, one of the inspectors says to the old woman as she leaves. But she doesn't turn, doesn't acknowledge him. He looks ashamed and annoyed to feel ashamed, the way all men do when they're forced to look at the underside of their boots.

The old woman leaves. I watch her disappear into the blue December light. Then I go back to mopping. It's important we keep the floors clean at the government slots. People get upset if the floors aren't clean.

*

An endorsement letter, signed by a cardinal
A miniature compendium of prayers for the dead
A pack of condoms

You're taught in school that it was an oil speculator who found it. Somewhere out in southwest Arizona, where now they've got a museum and a gift shop but you can't get within ten miles of the mine itself without written permission and an armed escort. In winter the wrens swirl around the place, little black dollops of life against the endless flush-red land.

It was an accident. The speculator was busy tearing the ground open with dynamite and pressure pumps. One day the dust clears and what he sees at the bottom of the crater is this purple-grey metal, shards of it everywhere. It's softer than it looks, but not malleable by hand. It's light but not too light.

He doesn't know what to make of it, what value it might have. He takes a sample to a friend of his, a physicist and metallurgical engineer. He leaves it with her for a few days and when he comes back she's still staring at it, dumbfounded. He asks her what it's made of and she says nothing anyone's ever seen before. It's a new square on the periodic table, the insides of its atoms at once indecipherable and coherent.

For years there's great excitement, mostly in academic circles. There's a naming ceremony, a slew of papers published in *Nature* and *Science*. But what the speculator wants is a commercial use, and for a long time there is none. Save for its novelty it offers nothing. Slowly interest fades, even among researchers, and eventually it's only the metallurgical engineer who still dedicates herself to studying the metal.

For the most part, her work comes to nothing. But one experiment yields unexpected results. The metal's fundamental physical properties change when it's made to form an enclosure, a closed space. From this finding, the engineer develops a theory about containment. She posits that a space enclosed by this metal has properties of superposition, and in this way there's a place to which anything enclosed this way might travel—a distant but interlocked point on the other side of the universe perhaps, or another universe altogether. She builds a small airtight box and as an homage to her favourite physicist she places a cat's collar inside. At first she checks on it hourly, then daily, then once a month. She tries running a current through it, tries raising and lowering the temperature. She tests the metal's reaction to organic matter; she smears it with drops of her own blood. She subjects the thing to pressure, stress, violence. She almost burns her lab to the ground, trying.

Eventually, within certain academic circles, the engineer becomes a laughingstock of sorts, her name a shorthand for futility. She retreats from the world. The cat's collar sits in the box for years, untouched.

Decades later, on her deathbed, she exhales for a last time and in that moment the friends and family assembled by her side hear a loud crumpling from her hallway closet, a sound like a hundred bones snapping at once. When they check the closet they find the box, collapsed in on itself. They pry it open and find it empty.

Hearing of this, the speculator remembers his friend's old theory about the metal as a conduit of passage. He is by now nearing death himself, a prosperous but strangely unfulfilling life behind him. He commissions the building of a similar box for himself and all the staff at his mining company. He marks his with a drop of blood, asks his staff to do the same. Some do. Many refuse. He places a pocket Bible in his box. He keeps it by his bedside, and at the moment of his death, there comes the same crumpling. The Bible inside disappears.

From such smallness a universe is formed.

*

Three chocolate chip cookies, smuggled
A small plush unicorn, its horn half-severed
A photo album titled: Your Grandchildren

What you get, by law, is a box the size of a fist. Everyone who can prove citizenship gets one, no different than a passport or the right to vote. Out here at the North Coast station we cover most residents in the 707 area code. They haven't split it up yet, and that makes us one of the biggest stations in the state, maybe the country. You can see it from miles away on the turnpike, this huge grey building that looks like a row of office towers laid on their sides. The bureaucracy sits in the building out front, a couple of offices where you can get your power-of-attorney forms approved or appeal an inspector's decision or get on a waitlist as soon as a doctor signs a Probable Viable Pregnancy form. Otherwise, it's just the afterboxes. Hallways and hallways, rows upon rows—a storehouse of all the things people believe will follow them into the next life.

You can see the building from space, they say. It looks like fingers, like a hand reaching out.

*

A tiny vial of blood, smuggled
A Swiss Army Knife
Twelve gold coins

Out in the hills there's a billionaire with a box the size of a dozen airplane hangars. Inside he's been building a facsimile of the neighbourhood he grew up in and a facsimile of the estate he lives on now. He's building a grain silo and a water tower, a seed vault and a gun locker, a bunker and a stockpile of antibiotics. By law the doors of the box must stay open while there are workers inside.

*

A yearbook page

Not far from the original mine in Arizona the cops found a cult commune, its members all gone but one. In a small cabin at the centre of the ranch the spiritual leader's assistant sat next to the leader's body, whispering a small chant of gratitude. On the other side of the property, outside a sealed, shack-sized box, they found a fading mandala in the sand and a hundred pairs of shoes.

*

A recipe for bundt cake

If you drive a few miles south of here, into the Bay Area proper, you'll find the Green Hospice, where people go to die altruistically. Years ago, a technology baron donated money to build a box the size of a single-family home, and at all times the box is filled with refuse—landfill trash, nuclear waste, contaminated material from the Superfund sites. Every time a resident of the Green Hospice is on the verge of dying, the box is marked with a sample of their hair or blood, and in dying they rid the world of a small piece of its ugliness. The hospice is run by Orthodox Ascensionists. They believe the next world to be a place of infinite space and infinite grace, and so believe it a sin not to use one's death this way, as a cleansing rite. They post pictures of every deceased, along with a picture of the garbage they take with them, and a small note of thanks. Should everyone choose to die this way, they say, the world would be made significantly cleaner.

*

Underwear

Last Christmas the Supreme Court ruled against the assisted-dying facility in Burlington. In the year since, all fifty-four petitioners in that case have died. Only not together, and not without pain.

*

A bottle of aspirin
A Purple Heart
War and Peace *in miniature print*

Around noon, a woman and her son walk in. The boy is maybe six years old and too thin. There's a strange device strapped to his arm; it looks like a clear phone case and there's some kind of liquid inside. A tube snakes from the case to a needle in the crook of the boy's arm. It appears painful and he can't bend his arm, but he looks happy.

It must be the case that sets off the metal detector, but the security guard waves the woman and the boy through anyway. The woman takes a number, but she doesn't get two steps toward the chairs before an inspector calls her ahead of everyone else, and if anyone in the waiting area thinks this is unfair, they don't say it.

The woman has all kinds of paperwork, but the inspector doesn't look at it. He smiles at the boy instead and asks him what he's got there in his hand. A Transformer, the boy says. That's so cool, the inspector replies.

The inspector leads the woman and her son down a hallway. I follow them, keeping my distance. I watch.

The inspector opens an empty slot. Each slot sits atop a scale, and every time the weight of the slot drops for an instant to almost nothing, a little light on the slot's lid turns from red to amber to green. The inspector takes a gloved hand and makes a small show of pulling a single hair from the boy's head, pretends it's a magic trick of sorts. The boy laughs. The inspector places the hair in a tiny compartment within the slot's lid and on the lid's digital screen a checkmark appears.

I've seen this before. This isn't how it's supposed to be done. There are rules, procedures.

It's all yours, the inspector says. He pushes the slot inwards and it pops out, revealing the inner compartment. The boy gently tries to places his toy inside, but it won't fit. The inspector's face drops but the boy says, Hold on. Awkwardly with one hand he manipulates the toy, turns it from robot to car, and as a car it just barely fits.

The inspector says Yay, and the boy says Yay, and as the slot slides closed the boy's mother breaks down crying.

*

A scented candle
A wristwatch
A Taser

There are protestors in the parking lot. It's a bigger crowd than usual. Usually we get them on Sundays and on Christmas Day and today happens to be both. On one side of the lot the Second Amendment people are demonstrating against the handgun ban. It's said the standard box size for government slots was chosen specifically to be too small for guns, and I don't know if there's any truth to that, but in the years since, they've come up with smaller guns, so now there's a ban. It's not universal. None of the rules are. In New York State you can't store anything that could conceivably be used as a weapon; some folks have been turned away with their grandmother's sewing kit. In Delaware, you can put a grenade in if it fits. But here in California you can't store guns, and every Sunday someone's out in the parking lot protesting.

On the other side of the lot is an assortment of the outraged devout. Every religion, it seems, has a branch or denomination that considers what goes on here heretical. They stop people on their way in, the same way members of the Forward Club do, but instead of trying to convince people to put the latest gadgets in their slots so as to keep the next life as advanced as this one, they try to convince them not to use the slots at all. If God exists, do you think these things will help you, they ask. And if God *doesn't* exist, do you think these things will help you then?

Some people stop and listen. Most don't. It's hard to uppercase God in a place like this.

Otherwise it's quiet. The most excitement we get for the rest of the day is when a detective and a plainclothes show up with a warrant. I shuffle over to the hallway where the slot they're looking for is. I watch the guy from the law enforcement liaison's office turn the master key. The detective looks inside. It's empty.

When did it clear? the detective asks.

The liaison officer checks the paperwork. It never did, he says. It's always been empty.

The detective curses. He hands the slot back to the liaison officer and walks off, the plainclothes following.

Most people would never guess it, but almost all the government slots are empty. People rush to get on waiting lists for them, rush to stake their claim as soon as their children are born, sometimes even before their children are born. But they hardly ever get around to putting anything inside. There are books you can buy, seminars you can attend, a whole industry of advice on what to bring with you. But people just don't follow through. They die in car crashes and house fires and of sudden failures of the heart and of the blood and they never believe such things are coming and even if they did, it would make no difference. We weren't built to think this way, to imagine the else-space of our lives. We don't know how not to know. Here, and I'd bet at every other centre, most of the government slots are taken and most of the government slots are empty.

*

A memory stick full of movies and songs
A small jar of sand
A resumé

We close early on Christmas Day. The inspectors and the security guards and the other janitors go home, a day's worth of time-and-a-half pocketed. I stay to do the overnight clean. It's quiet at night. I like it when it's quiet.

They make a sound, the boxes. It's a soft thing, like breathing, and hardly anybody notices it. During the day it hides behind the background noise of the place, the sound of people arguing, the beep of the metal detector and the squeak of soles against the linoleum. But at night you can hear it.

It's the sound of air rushing in. When a box empties it empties completely, and were it not for a small pneumatic hose attached to the bottom of each one, the slots would crumple in on themselves every time. The hose pumps air in, and the air wards off collapse. It's a sound like a sharp breath through the nostrils, a whispered leavetaking.

A little after midnight a young woman starts slamming her hands on the front doors. The sound is loud enough that I hear it from one of the hallways. She's yelling to be let in.

I walk to the lobby to see what's going on and I make the mistake of letting her see me. They come to the centre after hours sometimes and we're never supposed to let them in. We're supposed to ignore them and if they get too violent, we're supposed to call the overnight guard.

But I make the mistake of letting her see me and once she does she starts begging me to come closer, to just listen.

I know it's a bad idea but I walk toward her, until I'm standing on the other side of the locked door. The evening sleet has made a mess of her. She waves papers at me, waves a key.

He doesn't have time, she says. Please.

I can't help you, I reply. I hold my mop up to her, as though it proves something.

Then she screams at me. Not words, just a sound, an emptying. I don't know what to do. I take my key out; I open the door.

She pushes past me, and as she does she shoves a few sheets of paper at my chest. It's the usual stuff—photocopies of drivers' licenses, a power of attorney, the Expedited Processing form any doctor will fill out for a couple hundred bucks. She runs down one of the hallways. I follow, watching.

She stumbles, gets the wrong box at first, then the right one. I can tell it's pointless before she even turns the key. The light has already changed from green to amber. But I don't tell her. I watch her open the box, and I watch her look inside. I watch her fall to the floor.

What's human about us is a burden, I think.

I walk to where she is. The sound of the mop-bucket's wheels against the ground seems for the first time obscene to me. I lift the bucket slightly, and within the walls the whispered rush of nothings is once again audible. I set the bucket back down. I let the wheels squeak.

She sits there, vacant. She holds a chocolate cupcake, half-mashed in her hand. The inspectors would have never allowed it.

I want to ask her a question, but I think I already know the answer. People die a long time before they're dead. So instead I tell her the same trite thing I've heard a million times, the thing the counsellors say to people who show up too late, people who waited too long, people who just didn't see it coming.

You know, they have no proof, I say. It could just as easily be these things go nowhere. It could be they just disappear. Nobody really knows.

She looks up at me and I think she's going to slap me. Instead she laughs. You see that a lot, too, people laughing. She smears the cupcake against the floor, the way a smoker puts a cigarette out. She stands up and walks past me. She doesn't bother taking back her forms.

Another thing you notice, working here—they don't walk out the same way they walk in. If they show up confident, purposeful, they walk out looking at the floor. If they show up broken, they walk out with their heads held high. Something about this place does that to people. It inverts them.

I dip the mop. I clean the mess she's left behind. There's a window at the end of each hallway, but the sleet has turned heavy and I can't see much outside.

DAUGHTER OF CUPS

Kristyn Dunnion

"You know what to do," he says. "Pretty girl like you."

It's like a baby eel in her hand, skin as smooth but hot, dry. Ohio lets go and it bounces against his beer belly. She laughs.

Don takes hold of her wrist. "Like this," he says, pressing. His *Live to Ride* belt buckle jingles when her hand pumps. He breathes louder through his nose, a high-pitched whinny on the exhale. Ohio wants to give him a Kleenex but she doesn't have one. She stares at the tattoos covering his forearms and biceps and peeking out the sleeves of his black T-shirt. Don's face is tan and wrinkled, his stubble silver. His eyes crinkle shut.

Ohio closes hers, too. The curl and crush of waves smacking the sandy shore lulls her. Now she is Melanie Williams—blonde, popular, stacked—and Don is Kevin Moody, the cutest boy at school.

After, Don drives off and leaves her sitting at the end of the Lake Erie pier. She squints across to Sandusky. She can swim, but how far? She can dive, sink to the weedy muck and disintegrate surrounded by treasure and ballast from long-ago shipwrecks, succumb to the naiads, handmaids to the lake queen, as per campfire lore when she was a kid. Or she can walk back to town, north on the main road. Ohio hoists herself up and walks. She can keep going to the highway and hitch the hell out of here, or she can turn left at the only stoplight. She stands in the heart of town, eying the fingernail sliver of moon in the still-bright summer sky.

Eeny meany miney moe.

Friday night. The bank clock says eight-thirty. A car drives by and Darryl Hicks chucks a crushed beer can out the window.

Ohio turns left, toward home.

At the convenience store she scours magazines until Mr. Cooper yells, "Gotta be eighteen!" She buys Fun Dip. There's a crisp twenty-dollar bill in her pocket, but she doesn't break it, not for candy. Across the street the Bingo is packed—cars zigzag on the grass and sidewalk. She jumps on the gas station hose to ring the service bell, so Tommy Knight will have to get off his lazy ass. She keeps walking. The closer she gets, the stronger it smells: dirty chicken grease blowing from the KFC. The Colonel's secret spice is her homing device. She sits on the KFC stoop. Stares at the empty road, eats Fun Dip. Dips the candy stick into the grape powder and licks. Dips and licks.

Her mom yells out the upstairs apartment window, "Ohio, where you been?"

"Nowhere!"

The window slams shut.

Ohio waits for something to fall from the sky.

Don had said, "What kind of name is that, anyway?"

He'd gotten it wrong, twice.

"That's me," she'd said, pointing over the lake.

"Erie?"

"Ohio."

"Wiyot—I knew a girl called that," he said.

"Not Wiyot. *Ohio*. Like the state."

"Some kind of Indian name?"

"That's where my mom had me."

"Oh," he'd said. "Used to work the car plant over in Sandusky. Good union job. 'Til I got jumped in with the boys."

Full truth: she was named Ohio because that's where her mom met the man and fell in love and that's where her mom got knocked up and where she gave birth, on the side of the road, right where the man left her. Her mom says they're never going back. Says she hid her baby girl up in her sweater and brought her across Lake Erie in a bartered boat. Swears a monster, the fabled queen of the lake, emerged from the depths, demanding a toll. No word of a lie. In exchange for safe passage, her mother sheared the matted ropes of her hair with a knife, dropped them overboard with her maidenhead, sacrificing her womanly powers. The waters quieted, and she paddled all the way back to her hometown. Been here ever since.

"Whatcha doin'?"

It's Mary Louise, who lives in a run-down bungalow on the other side of the KFC. She pushes her glasses up her nose. A piece of tape holds the broken arm in place. Mary Louise's mom cuts her hair using a mixing bowl as guide, which makes her look like a medieval clown. Mary Louise is twelve, two grades behind Ohio. Her parents regularly kick her out so they can party all night.

"Oh-*hi*-Oh," she says, "Can I have some?"

Ohio gives her the last bit of powder. Mary Louise jams her finger in the corners of the packet and sucks back and forth until it's gone. Her mouth and finger are purple. Ohio wipes her face hard on her sleeve.

Motorcycles.

The girls lean forward at the first faraway rumble. Reverberating bass fattens with grinding gears that choke and pop, that spit like gunfire. Sky begins to shake. Like a funnel cloud ripping from the west, gathering strength, flattening an unrepentant path in its wake, the hogs' engines detonate a primal roar in Ohio's cranium: her mouth waters, belly pools to nausea. A red sun hangs low in the sky; its light explodes off chrome, blinding. Motorcycles fill the road, two across. Ohio shields her eyes with sugar-stained fingers. Her molars vibrate, her braids dance. Ribs rattle, thighs too. The girlfriends sit tight behind the men, long hair slapping vests as they zoom past. There's darkness in the leather. Boots clamp silver stirrups.

Ohio can't breathe; her mouth is full of metal, her nose of gasoline.

Mary Louise claps like a headcase. "Two, four, six, nine—thirteen!"

Don, the last biker, rides alone. As he passes, Don winks and pops a wheelie.

Ohio sits taller on the stoop. A secret flush dapples her skin, heats the bill in her back pocket. Earlier that afternoon, Don had thrust forward with a gurgled shout, releasing himself in long arcs on the sand. One gush had landed wet on her leg and dried like snot. He'd zipped himself, smaller and softer, back into his jeans. *That's a good girl.*

Mary Louise looks at Ohio, mouth open.

An engine backfires somewhere down the road.

"You *know* him?"

Ohio shrugs. Why didn't he stop, put her on the back? Take her away from this place?

Later, Mary Louise says, "Why don't they ride their own bikes?"

"Who?"

Ohio is shrinking. Pieces of her dull life fall back into place now that Don and the bikes have vanished.

"The girls."

"Those things are really heavy, Dork."

"I guess."

If Ohio's mom had had her own motorcycle, maybe she wouldn't have been such a mess when the man dumped her ass. Might have fixed him good, stone-pillar punishment. Wouldn't have severed her own Goddess head and dumped it in the lake, defeated. When she was a kid, Ohio had a green two-wheeler she pedalled everywhere—banana seat and tall, rusted handles with streamers like seaweed. That was joy, the kind of freedom she'd never have traded.

"Even my dad can't fix his," says Mary Louise, hopping from one foot to the other. "It's been in pieces all over the garage since I was born."

Ohio climbs on top of the KFC garbage can. Says, "Your dad's a dick. No offense."

"It's getting dark," says Mary Louise. "I'm going home."

*

"Move it, Ohio."

Saturday morning.

Ohio sprawls on the bed. Her mom pulls the faded seahorse-print sheets out from under her, spilling Ohio this way and that as she yanks them off the mattress. Her mom's stubby ponytail shivers with every tug. Her hair is greasy and there are dandruff flecks near the roots. She stuffs the sheets into a basket of dirty clothes.

Ohio flattens face down, arms and legs a starfish. "I never get to do anything," she says into the mattress.

"You get to do the laundry any minute."

"No!" Ohio curls like a sea urchin and transports herself to Atlantis. She's a mossy-haired beast with venom-tipped fangs.

Her mom sits on the edge of the bed, and her weight sags the mattress. Ohio rolls into her, unbidden. Her mom wears stretch pants, a too-tight Club Med T-shirt, and the pink-sparkle flip-flops Ohio gave her for Christmas. The waistband at the back of her pants is frayed. Ohio can see the large mole a couple inches above her crack through the thin, grey fabric.

"Ohio."

Ohio grunts.

"I'm doing the groceries."

"You're changing, right?" says Ohio.

"What's your problem?"

Ohio chokes on the memory of her mom wearing these same pants while bending into other people's trash for empties, to get the deposit.

Waste not. Want not.

Ohio says, "I hate this town."

Her mom sighs and her shoulders droop.

"It's not the worst place in the world."

She heaves off the bed and the mattress plumps back up. Sets the laundry basket on an old skateboard they found at the beach and rolls the towering pile to the door. Ohio is supposed to push it all the way through town like that.

"No wonder I don't have a boyfriend," says Ohio.

"Oh, you *think* you want a man," says her mother. "Divide your money and multiply your sorrow. I was a bit older than you when I started working summers at the factory."

"Right."

"I was bored, so I quit."

"I get it."

"Had some adventure. Met your smooth-talking snake of a father. Haven't been bored since."

"*You're* the one who liked him," says Ohio.

"Loved." She hands over some quarters and the box of detergent. "I'm on afternoons. Be home late."

Ohio kicks open the door and lets it slam behind her. Mary Louise is curled in the stairwell. "Morning, Oh-*hi*-oh!" Her hair sprongs in all directions and she's got the same shirt on as yesterday, only dirtier.

"You can't go downtown like that," says Ohio, and goes back inside to grab a clean shirt from her dresser. She tosses it to Mary Louise and slams the door again.

"Put yours in the basket."

"Okay."

Ohio hauls the basket down the steps. Mary Louise gets the skateboard. They push the laundry up to the stoplight. It's hard work, even with both of them. South one block to the Coin-o-

Matic. Penny Middleton's sister is inside with two dirty kids. One of them doesn't even have pants on, just a filthy T-shirt and bare bum, tiny bobbing penis. Penny Middleton's sister's big belly pushes out from her T-shirt and joggers. The hard knot of her bellybutton stares: kid number three! Ohio picks the farthest away washer and loads it, measures out soap. Mary Louise jams in the quarters. The machine shudders. Water spits onto the clothes and the girls can't help it, they thrust their hands inside to cup the rush, let it soak their thirsty skin. When the machine is filled, Ohio slams the lid. It's hot, so they sit outside on the plastic chairs.

Kevin Moody walks by with his peach-fuzz moustache and his blond hair parted down the middle, a perfect flip on each side. His tight jeans are ripped at one knee and bunched at his puffy white sneakers.

Ohio tosses her braids and wishes they were blonde. She puckers up, as if readying for a kiss. She read all about how to get your lips noticed in *Teen Beat Magazine*. Kevin Moody stands in front of her, obviously noticing her lips.

He says, "Is that your sister?"

Ohio turns. Mary Louise has one finger up her nose.

"What is she, retarded?"

"Fart off," says Mary Louise. She flicks a goober at him.

"You girls are the ugliest chicks in town, you know that?" Kevin shakes his head and keeps walking.

"After your mama," shouts Mary Louise.

Ohio slugs Mary Louise on the arm, hard. "No one picks their nose in front of Kevin Moody."

"Who cares," says Mary Louise. "He's a burnout."

*

Saturday night, TV is broken. Melanie Wilson, also going into grade nine, is having a party, but Ohio isn't invited. Lying on the linoleum, she fingers the Great Lakes on the most worn page of their atlas. Voices like tiny cracked bells whisper:

join us. There's an X pencilled north of Put-In-Bay, where her mother saw the beast. A zigzag line traces their journey along the chain of cormorant- and gull-infested islands—Rattlesnake, Sugar, the Sisters—where they stopped to rest. It took days. The crap motor conked out and her mom had to row. "This is how you got here," she says, showing her biceps. And, "You're lucky to grow up in Canada. We got health care." Another X on Pelee Island, where a local took pity and drove them to the ferry dock. Ohio was just a newborn, but sometimes memories surge: the slosh of waves against a rusty bow, the thud and creak of oars in the outriggers, the smell of fish and gasoline, and the fearsome sound of her mother by turns swearing, weeping, beseeching the gods, all the way across the lake. "All for you," her mother likes to say.

In the atlas, Ohio finger-trails a shoal of minnows against the current, leaves Lake Erie, enters Lake Ontario, floats down the adjoining canal. Watersogged, she beaches on the Manhattan shore. With her eyes closed, she can be anyone. A runaway in New York City. A waitress. A drug lord boss baby. Madonna sings *Papa Don't Preach* on the kitchen radio and Ohio gets up to prance in the kitchen. She's all slippery legs and dark eyes; an empty belly, hands open, begging.

At the back of the freezer, hidden behind the fish sticks, is a small bottle of vodka. Ohio takes a swig. It burns her throat. The heat fades to a warm glow. She gulps again. She puts on her mom's make-up using the kitchen mirror: coral lips, sea-foam lids, tangled green lashes. Ohio's thick hair is natty, coiled with life, like her mom's used to be. She has her mother's eyes—stony black, damning—but her skin is darker, more like the man's.

Ohio undoes her buttoned shirt and ties it above her waist. She's as flat as the Erie pier, but it looks good with tight shorts. Especially when she puts on her mom's cork-heeled sandals. She peels the forbidden leather vest off the final hanger at the back of her mom's closet. It smells like mildew and stale tobacco, like something wild and not quite dead in a ditch. Its weight is armor across her shoulders. It gapes under the arms, in the chest, where her mom's notorious rack stretched it out, once upon a time, that summer she ran with the gang.

"You look like a hooker."

"Thanks."

Mary Louise turns down the music and sits on a stool at the kitchen counter. "You left the door open. I could hear the radio outside."

"So?"

"So, you're lucky it's only *me* who came up."

"Am I ever."

Ohio pouts and blots her lips with toilet paper. Pieces of it cling to the lipstick. She swaggers to the freezer, pulls again from the bottle.

Mary Louise pushes her glasses up her nose. "Alcoholic," she says, blinking.

"As if."

"You're gonna do this all night? Boring."

Ohio says, "You're right. Let's go downtown."

It takes longer walking in the shoes. As she goes uphill, Ohio's feet slide backwards with each step. She tries to buy smokes at the convenience store. Mr. Cooper says, "Nice try, Ohio. Mom working tonight?"

Mary Louise steals Pop Rocks and they sit in the parking lot, letting the tiny pink crumbs explode in their mouths: stinging sugar pings. Bingo is rammed, cars everywhere, motorized wheelchairs parked in a crooked line down the block.

"Look." Mary Louise points to the gas station. It's Don filling his Harley. She waves wildly until he nods back.

"Come on," she says, trotting over.

Ohio follows, nearly wiping out on the curb.

"Ladies," he says, staring at Ohio.

Ohio cringes, tugs the vest. Should she button it or leave it loose to show her bellyskin? Her mom wore it over a studded bra the summer she was seventeen, waitressing the biker bar in Ohio. That and a pair of cut-offs showing the smiles of her ass. Says they queened her, over in America. Says she made great tips, mostly. Then she met the man.

Don's eyes peel away the make-up, the shorts, the slutty shoes. They linger on the leather, on a silver pin above her right nipple—entwined adders, tongues flicking one another.

He says, "Where'd you get that?"

"Yard sale," she lies.

"You're flagging colours, Sweetheart."

Don opens her vest, fiddles with the pin and removes the backing, pulls it free from the leather. He reattaches the backing and tucks the pin into the tiny vest pocket with a fat finger. "Gang stuff. Never wear what you don't know," he says.

"My dad has a motorcycle but it's broke," says Mary Louise. She points to Don's large belt buckle. "R-ride to live—"

"Live to ride," he finishes. "Know what that means?"

She shakes her head, no.

"Means there's nothing better on this earth. Wanna?"

Don sets his helmet on Mary Louise's head and carefully tightens the strap. Ohio is stabbed by a jealous fork, seeing the way Don tucks strands of flyaway hair into the helmet. He lifts and settles Mary Louise in front. Last time he gave her a ride, Don helped Ohio onto the wide leather seat, but today she scrambles up on her own. She wears the girlfriend helmet. The motorcycle leans to one side when Don kicks the stand away and the muffler burns Ohio above her ankle. She clenches her mom's shoes at an angle so she won't get burned again.

Don revs the engine. Mary Louise squeals. Ohio is pancaked on his back just like the biker girls. Don smells like gasoline, sweat, and cigarettes. He says something Ohio can't hear, not with the helmet on, not with the hot motor running between her legs, vibrating everything.

They hit the street with a lurch. Wind rushes Ohio's face. Aphids swarm her open mouth like tiny fish. They turn south at the stoplight and she's sure she'll fall, but she doesn't. They cruise past the Coin-o-Matic, they're coming up to the Legion, the only bar, where a bunch of kids are smoking out front. Don opens her up, gets the lead out, and they speed the rest of the way to the pier.

Take that, Ohio thinks, squeezing tightly.

At the lake, Don turns off the motor and kicks the stand. He lifts Mary Louise and sets her down, takes the helmet off her head. Her lunatic grin is contagious.

"Live to ride, ride to live," she chants.

Don doesn't offer to help Ohio, so she slides off the leather seat, puts her weight onto one wobbly shoe, and lifts her other leg over the back of the bike. She sets it, trembling, onto the ground. She removes the helmet and shakes her braids. Don and Ohio walk across the sand and sit on a large, flat rock. Mary Louise twirls around, sugar high, leaps to the water's edge. She skips flat stones, throws driftwood spears at waves, draws in the sand with a stick.

The red glow of the setting sun lights up one side of the lake like a fairy tale. The rest of the sky begins to darken. Ohio wonders what a real girlfriend would say. Don lights a home-rolled cigarette. He inhales, holds it in, slowly exhales. Stinky blue smoke hangs in the air. He passes it, and she copies him. It pinches her throat worse than the vodka. Makes her choke. Is she smoking pot?

"Why'd you dress like that?"

"Dunno." Ohio looks down at the skin folds bunching on her stomach. She sits up and they disappear.

"How old are you, sixteen? Seventeen?"

Ohio takes another puff so she doesn't have to lie, or worse, tell the truth. She'll be fifteen next spring. Her mouth is dry. She reaches under the vest and unties her shirt, smoothing the fabric. She does up the buttons. After Don flicks the dead butt away, he puts his oil-stained hand on Ohio's thigh. He has a silver serpent ring and hairy knuckles. Ohio's heart beats so fast she might barf. Thoughts stutter in her mind: *Will I ever get boobs? Did I say that out loud? Did I already think that?*

"Get your friend," he says, pointing to the crest of a large wave.

Ohio hops off the rock. She runs, leaps. Her body feels strong; her arms slice through time and space, windmilling the warm air. She laughs. Slaps bare feet on wet sand, then into the cold lake. Water rushes her toes, freezes her ankles and higher up her calves, splashes her thighs. Shadows twist and reach from inside the curled wave. Somewhere in that murk a clam-crowned princess is living a life meant for Ohio, magic and free. Hair tangled and billowing with tide, skin pale and tantalizing as a trout belly, arms undulating hypnotically. Ohio dreams her almost every night: that tinkling ghost wail and the beckoning fingertips. Mary Louise flops closer and clasps Ohio's hand. They jump whitecaps, leaning their bodies to take the hit. Ohio knows there are no cowards underwater, only the softened, gnawed-upon bones of sailors, fishermen, and rum runners, cradled in ritual piles in the lake's darkest, coldest crook.

Under the surface all men want.

Under the surface all men love.

Don slides one hand around Ohio, the other around Mary Louise. An old man with two dripping girls shivering on a rock. "Let's show her what we did the other night." Don works the hand that had been on Ohio's leg inside her wet shorts, into the crotch.

That's not what we did, thinks Ohio.

Don's fingers push her goose-fleshed thighs apart. They press and flick a lightning rush of heat.

"Uh," she says.

Someone is walking a dog down the beach, so far away the dog is a leaping smudge on the horizon, the person a short stick.

"Don't worry, they can't see us," he says.

Ohio feels good, like something might happen next.

Don's other hand is busy with Mary Louise. Mary Louise leans forward. "Bor-ring."

Don says, "We do other things, too." Don pulls his hand from Ohio's shorts. His left hand resurfaces and rests on Mary Louise's leg.

"Like what?" says Mary Louise.

Don smiles at Mary Louise until she tilts her head and really sees him, until she starts smiling, too.

Ohio's tingling crotch spot is forgotten. Tossed over the gunwales with fish guts, net trash. Upstaged by a twelve-year-old with a crappy haircut. Ohio rubs off her lipstick with the collar of her shirt, smearing the cotton pink. "I'll show her."

Don turns back to Ohio. Her skinny legs swing from the knee, feet wet with grit. She wriggles her toes.

"Look at you," he says.

Ohio tugs on the buckle of his thick belt. When she stands she feels woozy, so she leans against the rock. She rubs him the way he showed her. Mary Louise quietly slides down and runs back to the water. Don frowns. They watch Mary Louise jump into foamy waves that purr onto the hard-packed sand.

"She okay out there?" he says.

"Of course. This is *our* lake." Ohio squeezes until Don faces her again.

"Careful," he says.

This time Ohio keeps her eyes open. Three stubbled chins bob in time with her hand. She can see right up Don's wide nostrils, see the grey hairs inside. His breath comes in hot blasts. White fluid shoots into her fist, drips from her fingers.

"Taste it," he says.

It is sea salty, the runny part of an undercooked egg, and when she swallows, the acid trails her throat.

"Like it?" he says.

Ohio falters, smiles.

"That's a good girl."

Don gives himself an extra shake and zips up. He lights a smoke and leans on the rock. A mosquito bites Ohio's temple. She swats, scratches, and a drop from her hand gets in her eye, stinging. She rubs it, making it worse. Don says something about a club meeting, says he'll see her around soon, he hopes. He leaves a crisp twenty-dollar bill on the rock beside her, "For a little treat, for you girls," and walks toward his bike.

Ohio's eye burns and waters. She slips the bill into her pocket.

The further Don gets on the darkening beach, the less Ohio sees. His head is a blur. His clothes blend with the night. A few more strides and he disappears.

Mary Louise jogs up from the water's edge. "Now you see him, now you don't. Like his thing." She cracks up.

Ohio says, "That's not funny." But it is, and she laughs, too.

Mary Louise yanks Ohio's arm. "His Thing," she shouts.

Ohio stumbles, tugs Mary Louise back, spinning her in the sand.

They shriek, "Thing Thing Thing!"

They spin like fireflies, whipping each other in circles until they collapse in a gritty pile, panting, hysterical.

Don's engine turns over once, twice; it roars. His headlight clefts the beach and lights up a circle of churning water.

"Look!" says Mary Louise, pointing.

"What? Where?"

Ohio hears it first: a tidal suck, the shrieking gale, the whizz and pop of meteorites. The hissing of a thousand jagged voices. Finally, Ohio sees her in the bike's spotlight—the legendary lake mother, bare-breasted with weedy swirls of hair. Suckling fish cloak her in open-mouthed kisses, flit at the swell of her barnacle-spackled hips. She dives. Dorsal fin splashes. A shimmering ripple—an iridescent web binding her legs, slick captives in silver scales. Here, the levy queen: she who exacts a toll for safe crossing. She who lures the friendless and the forsaken.

"Take him," says Ohio.

Ohio could feed him limb by limb to the surf; Mary Louise would help. Together, they can do anything. But Don's headlamp is already cutting an arc, lighting the pier, pointing toward the road. The dark settles. Just the motor whining quieter and the red brake light growing smaller, smaller.

THE DRAIN

Lynn Coady

She wasn't worth killing, that was the problem. Because Marietta was not liked. Fans joked online about wanting to shoot themselves, or someone else, the moment she entered a scene. It wasn't the actor's fault. Well, it was, kind of. But it was Annie's fault in conjunction with everyone else—the show, the collective Us. In some mysterious whim of TV alchemy, Annie's energy ended up not gibing with ours. She'd been great on her last series—a supporting role on a show about nurses. She'd been an audience favourite, was cute yet tough yet vulnerable—everything you'd want in a TV nurse. I hadn't watched it, but the clips had been good. And she auditioned well and did a sizzling chemistry read with both our male and female leads—which was important because Marietta was going to be our show's first bisexual about which the network was, initially, very excited indeed. But both the chemistry and the excitement sputtered when she came up opposite the show itself. The suffocating Us-ness of it all. Annie had arrived beaming and freckled, with buckets of charisma, and somehow our show had tipped those buckets over, dribbling all that charm away.

We tried changing her hair. Switched her styling from buttoned-up/sexy to masculine/sleek to (and this was pure desperation) flouncy/bohemian. God help us, we gave her a motorcycle. Then we decided we'd been focusing too much on her appearance. We had drunk the network Kool-Aid, we scolded ourselves. We had to get back to what made the show great—the writing! Depth of character, that was the ticket. What Marietta needed was a meaty backstory. And so we spent a full week in fevered discussion of her tragic early life—her abusive mother, her subsequent drug use, her beloved high school bestie, carried away by opioid addiction. We rolled this out in a Very Special B Story. Which the audience hated. The next week, we tried changing her hair again. The failure was relentless. With every episode, every Marietta scene, the audience cringed, and—worse. They laughed. They didn't even know *why* they were laughing, they confided to one another in their social feeds and forums, festooning their posts with tearful, hee-hawing emojis. She was just so *bad*. No one could explain it. They didn't want to explain it. It was a mysterious, ineffable phenomenon that at this point they almost enjoyed.

It was my job to get all this across to Liz (who barely used the internet, who dismissed any conversation taking place on social media as "not real," who still referred to Google as "The Google") in my helpful, non-confrontational, just-asking kind of way. And to do it without using words like "cringe," or "laugh," or "hate her." But how do you kill a character who is a joke, without making her death feel like the biggest joke of all? I also took care not to say "joke." But lately it was the word that rang in my ears each weekday morning ever since we started breaking Episode Nine.

Because the thing was, Liz was under it. We were all under it. We were a month away from prep and *Marietta Dies, Finally* (as I called it in my head) was the penultimate episode and we didn't even have an outline yet—just a few scattered beats on a terrifyingly white whiteboard. Liz wanted to give her a big send off, to devote the entire episode to Marietta. Marietta, she'd announced, would be the A story.

Bad idea, I thought at once. Leaving audience antipathy aside, Marietta was the supporting-est of supporting characters, she'd only just been introduced midway through last season, she wasn't worthy. "Great idea," I said. The other people in the room gulped their agreement.

Liz looked around at us—her beloved, supportive team. Besides me there was Ellen, Riva, and two men in their twenties, one black and straight and one white and gay, both named Bruce. Bruces aside, we were a roomful of crones compared to most, because that's how Liz liked it. Every time I looked at the Bruces I remembered she once told me that a woman-led writers room can only tolerate two men at a time, and those two men must always be young, timid, junior to all the women, and ideally neither straight nor white, otherwise they take over. You couldn't mess with that balance, she said.

She knew this from dire experience. On her last show, she'd installed her usual two, one of whom she had assumed was gay but who it turned out was not. Then she made the mistake of allowing a third into the room—an intern who was also straight—and one morning she arrived to find all three with their feet up on the table, firing a mini basketball into a toy net they'd secured above the whiteboard. And the Act Three she'd spent the previous day breaking was erased and replaced by, as one of them described it, "something a little more spicy."

And, the hitherto-timid young man who made this announcement? Liz told me that as he spoke, he'd been sitting there idly combing his *beard* with a plastic *fork*.

But our current, timid Bruces mostly stayed in line, as was their job. As was all of our jobs in this business—be there for the showrunner. Support the showrunner. Help make the showrunner's occasionally dubious, defective vision somehow take flight. I knew this better than anyone, having worked with Liz the longest without getting fired even once. (Liz was notorious for firing you on Friday then calling you up Monday morning to ask where the hell you were.) In short, I was considered the Liz-whisperer, so the room took its cue from me in that moment—nodding and gulping in agreement after I told Liz what a great idea it was to devote an entire episode to one of the most reviled characters on the network.

"But," I continued, nodding vigorously to convey to Liz how much I agreed with her, "it occurs to me the last time we gave over an episode to Marietta it didn't go over so well."

"That was a B story," said Liz. "And this is different. This is her farewell."

"Right, yes," I said, nodding harder.

"It's just that I feel like Marietta never got her due, not really," explained Liz.

"No, no, she hasn't really," I murmured, we all murmured.

"If it was up to me," Liz went on, "I'd give her another season, really dig into that backstory, give her a brand new arc—like maybe the abusive mother shows up."

We all nodded some more because Liz had been saying this ever since the Very Special B Story, after which the network had made it clear that a Season Three order of our female-forward spy-fi kick-ass odyssey was heavily contingent on whether or not we persisted in trying to jam this repellent character down the throats of our devoted yet increasingly exasperated viewers.

"She has so much potential that hasn't even been realized," insisted Liz. "We haven't even begun to explore the possibilities. So that's why having to do this makes me so sad."

I looked up at Liz, grimacing. I didn't want her to be sad. I'd been working for her for so long, was so psychologically and financially dependant on her good will and approval, that I couldn't tell the difference between Liz's happiness and my own anymore. If giving an entire episode over to Marietta was what it would take to dispose of her—if that's how we make Liz feel less sad and our show less cancelled—we would all just have to get on board. And I would have to get the room on board, convince them that together we could make *Marietta Dies, Praise Jesus and Pass the Biscuits* an episode of television worthy of the splendid, nuanced, endlessly fascinating character Liz seemed to be carrying around in her head. This was the job.

But that was when I noticed Liz had sprung a leak.

I glanced around to see if anyone else had noticed. *Everyone* had noticed. I could tell, because they were all studiously looking away. Riva was staring into her laptop as if at some urgent anti-virus notification. The Bruces had both picked up their phones. And Ellen was looking at me, eyebrows up.

"Liz," I said. She turned to me and widened her eyes—her go-to "I welcome your input" expression. I pointed at my neck. Then I pointed at her neck. Her neck was actually spurting, which alarmed me, slightly.

I'd seen people leak, but never spurt. My mom had issues with leaking all her life—especially during menopause, as with a lot of women. But my mom would merely *teem* for the most part, or sometimes drip discreetly when she'd been standing at the stove awhile, not even knowing she was doing it half the time, gradually soaking her clothes, leaving damp spots on the floor here and there. It was hard to say where the leaks were coming from at any given time because she'd only feel the moisture after it pooled, and cooled. With Mom it seemed to come from mostly her lower back and upper arms—never her buttocks, which of course is always the fear when it comes to leaks. In her later years she lived in dread of leaving a puddle on the seat of someone's chair, having them think the worst.

Liz brought her hand up to her neck, and it got spurted on. "Oh, wow," said Liz, looking at her hand. She wiped it on her jeans and stood up. I reached for a bunch of napkins left over from lunch but Riva was ahead of me—she had lurched for the box of Kleenex in the middle of the table and now she offered a handful to Liz.

"Thanks," said Liz. "Sorry about this, guys." The Bruces had put away their phones and now just sat with eyes downcast, either being squeamish or respectful. I've noticed that on the rare conspicuous occasions that men leak, they'll laugh and josh each other, like when one of them gets a bad haircut. But when women do it, men become sombre and awkward.

Liz excused herself to go to the bathroom. After a respectful few moments I went to check on her. She was standing in front of a mirror, holding a towel-wad against the leak.

"There she is," I said. "The human sprinkler." This was a lame joke, but jokes—lame or otherwise—were part of my job. When I was hired, the producers spoke privately to me in my capacity as Liz-whisperer. They took me to lunch, so I knew whatever they were about to say was something I could not dismiss. We *love* Liz, they kept saying over and over again. But she can get bogged down. Things can get *heavy* very quickly with Liz. She cares about her characters so much! And that's why her shows are such hits! But sometimes, as you know, she goes *dark*. Of course we want that Liz sensibility, that aesthetic—that's what we love about Liz! But at the same time—

Light, not dark, I interrupted, nodding. Light, not heavy. Bright, light. I am the light-bringer. Got it. Everyone smiled. They were so happy not to have to say anything else that might be construed as critical of Liz.

"This is just what I need," said Liz, looking into the mirror and meeting the reflection of my eyes. "Three weeks to prep and I start dribbling everywhere."

I threw my hands into the air, as if in celebration. "Womanhood!"

"I don't have time," said Liz.

"Has it been happening a lot?"

"Started on the weekend. Almost short-circuited my computer."

"Maybe you should try one of those spas," I suggested. Although I knew the spas were bullshit. They gave you treatments that were supposed to promote leaking *exudation*, as the spas called it—so that you could get it over with if you had a big meeting or a hot date coming up and wanted to avoid any awkward puddles. All sorts of physical and psychological benefits supposedly followed—your skin cleared up, your chakras aligned and so forth. But I'd read an article in the *New York Times* months ago debunking exudation therapy and I was pretty sure Liz had read the same one. The article said there was no scientific evidence whatsoever that exudation therapy actually gave rise to exudation. Leaking is neither healthy nor unhealthy, the article scoffed. It's just one of those pointless, annoying things our bodies do, like foot cramps or sneezing five times in a row for no good reason.

"The spas are bullshit," said Liz.

"I know," I admitted.

We stood there for a while staring into the mirror at the reflection of Liz's soaked wad of paper towel being held against the reflection of Liz's neck.

"Why is it always just one thing after another?" said Liz.

*

We went in circles, in the room, for days. Our other scripts were more or less ready, but Episode Nine was getting nowhere. I kept thinking that if it had been up to me, I would have written Marietta into gentle oblivion right around the time we gave her the motorcycle. The motorcycle was the perfect opportunity. Such thoughts were mutinous, considering Liz was my captain, so I tamped them down. My job, after all, was to help facilitate her vision. While bringing light. The problem was, Liz's vision was divorced from reality—the reality of the girl-power fantasy that was our show. The reality of that fantasy, whether Liz could see it or not, was that Marietta did not fit and the audience needed her to die. They did not want a big send off. They did not want long, poignant scenes showcasing Annie's Shakespeare-trained talent for reciting massive blocks of dialogue. They did not want lingering close ups on her pale, suffering, face. They wanted her to stop showing up.

But Liz, her ears being permanently shut to the clamour of social media, could not hear this. So she'd come to work and plunk her coffee on the table and say things like: "Last night I was thinking that Marietta might actually be one of the most complex characters I've ever created. I was looking over my notes. I filled *notebooks* on that girl! More than I filled for Tamlyn, even!" Tamlyn being our beloved, mysterious spy-ninja female lead.

"It could be that's the problem?" suggested Riva, whose thing in the room was to make all her statements sound like questions.

"*What's* the problem?" said Liz, turning to her. Riva didn't understand that there were ways of expressing such thoughts without using a word like "problem."

"Could it be we've overthought Marietta?" queried Riva. "Somewhat? I mean given her secondary status? On the show?"

"I honestly don't know how you can overthink *character*," said Liz.

"Right," said Riva, nodding. "But—?"

I would've kicked Riva under the table if my legs had reached that far. Riva's uptalk had turned Liz frosty. What saved Riva in that moment was Wanda, popping her distracted, bird-like head in through a crack in the door. "Liz? Got a sec?" She'd been doing this with more and more frequency lately, popping in, blinking rapidly, the tendons in her neck straining, both wanting and not wanting to speak to Liz about the latest network concern or looming production disaster.

The sound of Wanda's voice, however, was anything but bird-like. Even after she and Liz stepped out into the hallway, closing the door behind them, we could hear her rasping indistinctly through the walls. Her voice had a grinding, aggressive quality that seemed to achieve a higher register, I'd noticed, with every passing week. Lately the sound of it made my eyes water, as if Wanda's head in the doorway brought with it a waft of pepper spray.

I took advantage of the Liz-free moment to glower around at everyone. "Guys," I said, "this is happening. We're not going to talk her out of it at this point."

Riva went limp and turned into the person she became when Liz wasn't in the room. "Fucking fuck," she said.

"No more questioning it. We just need to be fully on board at this point."

"But if we're going to make it work," said Ellen slowly.

"—We need to talk about why Marietta sucks so much!" finished Riva. Ellen was the most reflective person in the room, and it could be frustrating, because people like Riva were always jumping into her reflective gaps and cutting her off.

"Well let's do that when Liz is out of the room, if we feel the need to do that," I said. "Because right now it's just getting on her tits."

"She hired us to be straight with her," said Ellen. Every once in awhile Ellen would bowl me over with a statement like this—a statement that would make you think she'd just wandered into the studio with a sprig of hay between her teeth as opposed to a decade's worth of TV experience under her belt.

"It doesn't matter why Marietta sucks," I said, pretending Ellen hadn't spoken. "And Liz doesn't need to hear that from us. She's been hearing it all year from the entire world."

"She *hasn't* been hearing it, that's the problem," muttered one of the Bruces. I didn't bother looking over to see which one.

"The problem is," said Riva, "she hears it secondhand, from the execs. They think they're bolstering their case by talking about the backlash online, but as soon as she hears the word *Twitter,* she dismisses it. They might as well be telling her the criticism's coming from Narnia."

"It doesn't matter," I repeated. "Did you guys not see Wanda? She's a human forehead vein—because we're running out of time. I know Liz, guys—she's not going to come around on this. We need to just forget about the Marietta that sucks. And believe in the awesome Marietta Liz believes in."

"I guess it's like faith," considered Ellen. "Religious fai—."

"More like believing in fairies," said Riva. "So Marietta's basically Tinkerbell. Asshole Tinkerbell." One of the Bruces snorted at this and Riva looked gratified.

Then Liz returned, looking beleaguered, as she often did post-Wanda. She dropped into her chair like a sack of rocks.

"Long story short," she said, "we need to figure out Nine today. No more fucking around. Let's go."

We began, but got sidetracked when Liz started talking about the network's notes and how they could be "invasive" like weeds in a garden, or fungus. Then someone made a joke about slime molds, but a Bruce took exception to that, claiming slime molds did not actually qualify as fungi. It had something to do with the way slime molds took in nourishment, apparently. Then Riva had to look this up to confirm if it was true (it was). Then the other Bruce pulled up some online clips for us to watch. They were fascinating and repulsive—time lapse videos of a seething, toxic mucus expanding in all directions, taking over the landscape, eating everything in its path.

"Well—let's take lunch," said Liz. "We'll nail it down this afternoon."

The whiteboard glared. I went outside and bought a green smoothie because solid food wasn't doing me any favours these days. Plus, my metabolism was operating at the speed of a particularly indolent slime mold as the result of sitting motionless in a room for seven hours every day. I speed-walked around the block, sucking up my smoothie, the colour and consistency of which also reminded me of the slime molds. I couldn't taste it. I meditated on Marietta. I needed to get on the same page as Liz. As Liz-whisperer, I had always prided myself on being able to anticipate my boss's creative flights of fancy before they could even take wing, but this Marietta thing had completely blindsided me. It made me anxious, off my game. *I love Marietta*, I tried telling myself. *Slime mold*, my self replied. *Listen*, I said. *Just try and feel this, ok? I love her. I love Marietta so much.*

I hated her, however. Why did I hate her? Why did *anyone* hate her, was the question. She was *good*. She wasn't TV-generic. You couldn't call her bland—Annie had a lopsided and bashful smile that recalled a young Renée Zellweger.

I mentally addressed the viewing audience—*Why do you hate her?*

Because you want me to love her, the viewing audience replied. *You want it so badly. You think you can throw anything at me and because it's you, I'll get on board.* My internal viewing audience seemed to be addressing Liz, so I replied as Liz.

That's not going to stop, said Liz. *I've always done that and it's always been fine.*

Things change, said the viewing audience. *You've changed. And you don't even know it.*

But I thought we were on the same side, fretted Liz. *We always got along so well.*

We liked what you did. We enjoyed it for a while. But we owe you nothing. Don't start acting like we owe you something. We will hate you for it. We will punish you for it.

Shaken, I ducked into a Starbucks and ordered a grande cold brew to take back to work. I figured more caffeine couldn't hurt, even though this thing had been happening to me at night where, as soon as I tried to sleep, my heart would start thrashing around in my chest like a creature in a panic to be released.

*

The following Monday Liz was an hour late, because, she confided to me in the ladies' room, she was *streaming* water from between her breasts all morning. She had come out of the shower with water rolling off her and, she said, it just kept rolling. After checking the stalls to make sure we were alone, Liz lifted her shirt to show me how she had stuffed a maxi-pad down the middle of her bra to soak up the leak. She seemed pretty proud of this ingenuity. As I watched, she yanked the wet maxi-pad—an old-school, industrial-strength cotton slab—out of her bra and replaced it with dry one from her purse. Then she wrung the used one out into the sink to show me how full of liquid it had been.

"Kee-rist," I said.

"Just call me Yellowstone," said Liz.

"Have you talked to a doctor?"

"When would I do that? Anyway—it's a natural process right? You always hear it ramps up around menopause."

"How've you been feeling?" I laughed as I asked this because of course Liz had to be feeling like me, like the rest of us—desperate, frantic, under the gun.

"I feel fine," said Liz. "Really good, actually. I'm really happy with the work we're doing on Marietta."

I laughed again, figuring this could only be irony.

"It's so satisfying," said Liz, patting her fresh maxi-pad and pulling her down her shirt. "To be giving all this time to her—to be really digging in on her character and what she means to the show. You know, as pissed off as everyone is about it, I'm feeling very clear that it's the right thing to do."

I followed Liz back to the room in silence because what was there to say after *I'm feeling very clear that it's the right thing to do?*

In the room, Liz explained that Wanda was shrieking at us all the time because she, Wanda, had lost sight of "what the show is" and "how the show works." "This work we're doing," said Liz, "is fundamental. When you've got a TV show up and running and you're into the third season, people tend to forget about the deep, foundational work that's so essential. We can't scrimp on this work, guys—we can't just blow through it because it's hard, because everyone's behind schedule and the network hates us and Wanda hates us and the director hates us and the crew hates us. Everyone out there? They exist to serve us. Our vision. They think the kindest thing we can do for them right now is to hurry up—no. The kindest thing we can do—the only thing we can do, as storytellers, is to honour the truth of the story and go where that takes us."

There was nothing to say to that either.

"So," said Liz, leaning back in her chair. "Does the Syndicate murder Marietta because she's been one of them this whole time and is about to blow the whistle? Or is it simply a matter of throwing herself in front of Tamlyn when the gun goes off kind of thing? One gives us a juicy reveal, but I like the potential emotional fallout of the latter. I feel like it's important her death feel like a sacrifice—a completely selfless moment."

So, this was easy. We just had to pick one. I suggested the room take a vote and we move forward on whatever option carried. But Liz looked over at me as if I had placed a finger over one nostril and exhaled the contents of my nose across the table.

"Slow down," said Liz. "We shouldn't rush this. I wanna pin down this idea of sacrifice first."

And that's how we spent the entire morning, pinning down Liz's idea of sacrifice. I could see, by the movement of Ellen's shoulders, that she was taking long, deliberate breaths throughout the entire conversation. Whereas Riva looked ready to shatter her computer over someone's head.

The week went on like that. We would pitch ideas and Liz would tell us to slow down. *Slow down.* And consider every possible implication. One after the other. By Thursday we had still accomplished next to nothing and I could feel my stomach lining disintegrating within me. The problem wasn't that we couldn't decide about Marietta. We were so ready to decide. We *yearned* to decide. The problem was that Liz wouldn't let us.

Over lunch on Friday, as I was rounding the block sipping another slime mold special, I received a call from Mackie. She and a couple other execs would love it, she said, if I would meet them for breakfast bright and early Monday morning—before work.

*

"We love Liz," said Mackie.

"I know," I enthused, "I love Liz too." This exchange of pro-Liz enthusiasm was, I observed, turning into a kind of ritualized greeting between myself and the execs whenever we met, like Japanese business types bowing excessively and exchanging cards.

"She's the best," said Mackie.

"Totally," I said. "I always feel so lucky to be working with her."

"And we feel so lucky too," said Mackie.

"Oh my god, *so* lucky," chimed someone else further down the table, whose name I hadn't caught.

"She's an extraordinary talent," said Armelle, and I stiffened a bit, because I wasn't used to being in Armelle's presence. I hadn't known or expected Armelle would be at this meeting. Armelle attended almost no meetings as far as I could tell. Armelle's thing was that sometimes she would have dinner one-on-one with Liz. They would go somewhere with white tablecloths and have long, warm, sisterly conversations and drink a great deal of wine. They would talk about their husbands (or, dog in the case of Liz, who adopted a bullmastiff named Roger not long after her divorce). Then move on to their kids, the schools they'd applied to, the pros and cons of each. Hug and kiss goodbye. And then, presumably, Armelle would tell Mackie and the rest of her colleagues the best way to do their jobs vis-à-vis Liz and Liz would come to work and tell us all about how supportive and on our side the network was. That was always the relationship as I had understood it.

But now Armelle asked me, "How do you think Liz is *doing*?"

"Well, she's leaking quite a bit," I said. Armelle blinked at this a great many times but her face didn't change.

This was pure panic on my part. This was me desperate to get across the trouble we were in without betraying or undermining Liz's leadership. So instead I had betrayed her confidence. I was flailing, stuck there like a pinned butterfly under Armelle's gaze. I had always been the Liz-whisperer. I was the go-between, the interpreter, the unruffler of feathers on both sides. I *got* Liz—that was my value, to both her and the execs. But I did not get this. I did not get Marietta. And so, what was my role here? What exactly was the point of me?

I couldn't say, *She's making bad decisions*, or, *She's holding everything up with a kind of insane obsession with a minor character*, or, *Everyone in the room is starting to feel like a hostage.* I couldn't say, *Help, oh please help!* So I told them about the leaks.

"Leaking," repeated Mackie. "You mean exudation?"

"Ugh, I hate that word, but yes."

"Apparently it ramps up during menopause for some women," reflected Armelle.

"Right," I said. "Well—it's just—giving her some trouble these days."

I couldn't look up from my plate. I'd blathered Liz's business and now I had all the executives thinking about her *body*, her *exudations*, as if this was the problem, as if it could have anything to do with her talent, or ability to pull off another season of the wildly successful show that had made the careers of everyone at this table. I felt sick with the shame of disloyalty.

"Stress can be a factor, too," said Mackie.

"I don't think that's true," I said. "I think the *Times* debunked that last year." I wasn't sure it had, but I just wanted to shut this entire avenue of conversation down. "Look, look, look," I said. "It's not even an issue. I shouldn't have mentioned it. It's just one more thing she has to deal with lately."

Armelle cocked her head. "Do you feel Liz might be overwhelmed?"

"She's just extremely focused," I said, "on getting the final two episodes right."

"But if she's being distracted by all this leaking—"

"She's not," I insisted loudly. "She's totally rolling with it. She's improvising. She's sticking maxi-pads down her bra. It's amazing."

The table went silent.

"You *know* Liz," I said, my voice becoming even louder in an effort to dispel the image I'd just planted in the minds of the execs, not to mention the busboy who was currently pouring our water. "She's an innovator! She thrives on stress! She gets shit done no matter what!"

"We would like to know," said Armelle, "if there's something we can be doing on our end. To help things along."

"Production should've had those scripts weeks ago," said Mackie.

"I'm very curious to see them myself," murmured Armelle.

Ridiculous, unhelpful directives rose up in my mind. *Pray for her*, I wanted to say. *Light a candle. Sacrifice a goat.*

Armelle took an unhurried sip of coffee. "What do you feel the hold up is exactly? Is there some kind of roadblock? I've asked Liz if she'd like to bounce any ideas off me, but she's keeping mum."

Armelle shouldn't have told me that last part, because I had been all set, eager even, to answer her question. *Killing Marietta. The hold up is killing Marietta.* Armelle was Liz's bestie, after all—or so I thought. If anyone could nudge Liz around this mental roadblock—the thing that was preventing her, preventing all of us, from imagining an honourable death for Marietta—it was Armelle. But if Liz had "kept mum," if Armelle had been nosing around previous to this, making her delicate inquiries, and getting nothing, getting shut down, getting stonewalled to the point where Armelle had to resort to a breakfast with me, then it was clear Armelle's opinion on the Marietta question was not remotely something Liz was interested in. Tears of frustration blurred my eyes. It would've been so good to unburden myself to Armelle, and Mackie, and whoever the hell these other blinking, smiling people I was having breakfast with were. But I couldn't without betraying Liz more than I already had.

I felt handcuffed. I couldn't tell them about Liz's Marietta hang-up because I didn't understand it. And because I didn't understand it, I could not explain it. And if I could not explain it, telling the execs about it would make Liz seem irrational. And if I, Liz's lieutenant going back a decade, were to make my captain sound irrational, well then, questions would arise, wouldn't they? Questions and insinuations—of the cold-blooded, show-business variety, when everybody turns their minds from the glorious nobility of the story-telling impulse to exactly how much money is at stake. There'd be no need to say an ugly thing like "washed up," but key people would wonder innocently to each other if Liz hadn't been doing this job a little too long.

So I blinked the tears back into my head and repeated to Armelle, "She just really wants to get those episodes right."

Armelle sighed. "Look at the time," she said after a moment—but she was looking at me. Not her watch, or her phone. *Look at this pile of garbage sitting in a chair like a person*, she might as well have said. Beside her, Mackie dutifully waved her tanned, toned arms at our server, bracelets a-jangle, a human alarm bell.

*

Liz showed up wearing thin running gloves with bulges in the palms where she had stuffed them full of tissues.

"It's like stigmata this morning," she told me as we stood at the coffee machine. "Spurting palms."

"Pretty soon we'll just wrap you in gauze head to toe, like a mummy," I said. "And you can just . . . seep into your gauze all day long and not have to worry about it."

"That sounds cozy," said Liz. "I think I'd be okay with that."

It struck me I'd be okay with that too. To be swaddled, secure. Free to seep.

*

I contemplated her as we settled around the table, opening our computers, silencing our phones. Her face was poreless and glowing, which made me reconsider all the claims I'd dismissed about exudation being good for the skin. The glow of her face complemented her expression, which was serene. She looked faintly holy, like a lady saint in a renaissance painting.

I couldn't figure it out. Was Liz being a trooper? Putting on a brave face for us, her team, but secretly miserable? Was just she bravely sucking it up every day—the intolerable professional stress in combination with the sodden inconvenience of her body—then going home and sobbing into the neck of Roger the bullmastiff for the rest of the night? As a tiny lake took shape around her? I didn't think so. I knew I would be, but Liz seemed fine. Which was craziest of all, in its way. She was practically melting in front of us but she sat at the head of the table shoving tissues into her gloves with nonchalance.

The word *cozy* came back to me as I watched her tucking tissues away.

"I think the best thing we can do today," said Liz. "Is talk about what Marietta's death is going to mean to the rest of the ensemble individually. Let's go through them one by one. We need to think about how they'll be situated with respect to—"

"WE NEED TO KILL HER," said a loud male voice I'd never heard before.

It was the white Bruce, speaking above a mutter for the first time any of us had ever heard. Liz raised her eyebrows at him. All of us did. Except for the other Bruce, who looked away as if to distance himself, even though they sat, as usual, side by side.

"We *are* killing her," said Liz, not in the frosty tone I was expecting. She spoke to the Bruce almost soothingly, as if to a spikey-furred cat. "This is the process we're engaged in, Bruce. At this very moment. We're killing her as we speak. It may not feel like it, because we're being mindful. And loving. But killing Marietta is very much what we are doing."

I could see Riva vibrating in her chair and I knew the Bruce's outburst had emboldened her.

"But Liz, we need to figure out the basic beats. How she dies. What actually *happens* in the episode. We only have a couple days left." I was astounded. Riva wasn't even using uptalk. On the opposite side of the table, Ellen started nodding. Uh-oh, I thought.

"Guys," said Liz. "I know the process is arduous. But this is a woman's life. Okay? This is someone's daughter. Someone's sister. Someone's mother. A fully realized ... human ... child of this earth. Seen, felt, and beloved by the people she's encountered along the way."

"Wait," I said. "Marietta has a *kid*?"

Liz nodded and stuffed some more tissue into one of her gloves. "It occurred to me last week. When she was seventeen. She had to give him up for adoption. She's never gotten over it. Her mother told her she—"

"IT DOESN'T MATTER," said the insurgent Bruce in his new voice. "IT DOESN'T FUCKING MATTER THAT SHE HAD A BABY."

Liz blinked at Bruce for what felt like a good half hour. But she wasn't angry. She looked stymied, and sad. Let down. If Liz ever looked at me like that, I felt I would've hurled myself out the nearest window. But all the Bruce did was look down at his keyboard.

Ellen leaned forward, "I think what Bruce means to say is that the time for delving into character is past. What we need to do now—" here Ellen made the fatal mistake of slowing down to consider her words, so Riva jumped in.

"—What we need to do now is break the episodes. We just gotta break 'em, Liz. Now. We don't have any time left."

"We still have the weekend." Liz turned to me. "How long will you need to write Episode Nine?"

I'd been avoiding thinking about the fact that whenever—*if* ever—we finished breaking the Marietta episode, I was the one appointed to go off and actually write it. Me, with my non-functioning digestive system, my recent flirtation with cardiac dysrhythmia and my three hours (on a good night) of sleep. I closed my eyes as if to think, saw a creeping river of bright, pulsating slime-green mold, felt like vomiting, and opened them again.

"However long you want to give me," I told her. "You need it in two days? I can do it in two days."

"YOU ARE JUST ENABLING HER," said white Bruce. "THAT IS ALL YOU DO IN THIS ROOM."

"AND YOU NEED TO SHUT UP, WHITE BRUCE," I said. At which point both Bruces reared back in their chairs.

"I apologize," I said in my normal voice. I realized I was standing, so sat back down. "I apologize to both of you for that." But really I was apologizing to the Bruce who was black and I tried to make sure with my eyes that he knew it. But that Bruce wasn't meeting my eyes.

"Guys," said Liz again, in a voice so calm it was madness. "I'm begging you to have faith in this process."

With that, white Bruce got up and left. After he shut the door we all sat there.

"Well I guess we know where that Bruce stands," said Liz.

Then the other Bruce got up and left too.

"We've lost both Bruces," I announced in a daze. "We're Bruce-less!" Somehow I was still trying to make jokes and bring light, as I had been hired to do. I kept thinking, as I had been so uselessly all along, *I just have to do my job. I am here to do a job and I just have to do my job.*

That's when Riva, chin wobbling, got up and left too.

Liz leaned forward in her chair and extended a hand each toward Ellen and I. We were seated directly across from one other—me to Liz's right and Ellen to her left. I took Liz's hand immediately. After a moment, Ellen did too. Liz squeezed. Ellen and I looked at each other.

The gloves were soaked completely through.

*

At some point, Liz said *fuck it* and went online and ordered multiple plush terry-cloth robes that she could change in and out of throughout the day. This struck me as ingenious—much better than my mummy-wrapped gauze idea. The robes even had hoods for when she was spurting from her cranium—on those occasions, Liz would take a belt from one of the surplus robes and wrap it around her head, sheik-like, to keep the hood secure against it. She had all sorts of little strategies now.

And speaking of strategies, that's what we were supposedly doing—strategizing. For the first month of our unemployment, I'd show up at Liz's a couple of afternoons a week and Liz would lounge, be-robed, on her ottoman, as we discussed how to get her show back. There was no real point to this exercise, but it made us both feel better—we were used to seeing each other every day, after all, talking things over, solving problems. We defaulted to the process we knew best, the process that had always worked for us in the past, even though it did nothing anymore but give us comfort.

Liz would gaze out the window at her boat launch—feet up, robe on, looking like a woman in a day-spa ad except for the occasional trickles of water meandering from various parts of her body. Over the first week, she spent much of our time together just marveling at Armelle's betrayal. "I mean, I should have expected it," said Liz. "I've been in this business long enough. But honestly, I thought it would be different with us. I thought that now that we were finally running things, we'd do it right. That's what we always talked about, Armelle and I, in the early days. We'd banish the cynicism, the knives in the back. The bottom-line mentality. We'd support one another. We'd give each other the space to . . . self-express." Liz flicked a hand at the phrase "self-express" and a couple of tiny droplets flew from her fingers and landed on my glasses. I realized that by "us" Liz wasn't just talking about herself and Armelle. She meant *us*—our entire side of the human equation. It seemed naive but at the same time, didn't we all nurture that hope back when it seemed so impossible? The impossibility of it made it safe for us to dream crazily like that—to be innocent in our imaginings, open-hearted, bursting with moronic faith in one another.

Liz had at some point forgotten to close that door in her heart, it struck me. She'd been closing it throughout her career, every time it blew open, like any smart, professional woman would. But then one day along came Marietta. And Marietta, for no reason in particular that I had been able to discern, was where Liz finally drew the line.

When I finally did ask about Marietta point blank, Liz's response didn't offer much illumination. "It just felt like time," she shrugged, dabbing at her face with the sleeve of her robe. "After all the years I spent doing this job. It just felt like time for me to—" And here she interrupted herself with a sigh. "Stand firm."

Eventually we abandoned the pretense of strategizing and just drank and lounged like ladies of leisure. For me, those were glorious, peaceful afternoons, not to mention a wonderful way to be unemployed—imbibing good wine in the splendidly appointed home of a wet, well-to-do woman. Liz would stroke Roger's massive, snoring head, and we'd sip and gripe, gazing out over the lake. When the weather got warmer, Liz told me to bring a bathing suit and we could swim. We both knew there was nothing to be done, not really. The final episodes were in production, and who knew what they entailed, what kind of ignominious end had been devised for Marietta—certainly no one was telling Liz, or me. Ellen would sometimes text me minor updates with the eye-rolling emoji, but I never shared them with Liz. They mostly had to do with Riva and how much she sucked as a leader. Riva had been given the helm, something Ellen would not soon forget. It should have been Ellen, but Ellen's slow way of talking had made everyone nervous, made her seem (as Mackie had explained apologetically) "too thinky"—*eye-roll emoji*—which was not "what is needed right now."

Liz told me her final meeting with Armelle was not like any of their previous meetings. It did not take place at a restaurant, or at a catered soirée, but in Armelle's actual office—for it turned out Armelle had an office. It was a beautiful office, of course, with an expansive sitting area, fresh flowers on every surface, practically. And there was coffee and dainty, expensive pastries served. But the point is, it was undeniably a *meeting*. In an *office*. An affront that Liz had trouble getting over to this day.

Liz had walked in wearing a billowing smock that concealed a thick towel she had tucked around her middle that morning. At a one point in the conversation, the point at which she'd decided she had had enough, Liz reached up under that smock, yanked out the towel like a magician revealing a bouquet, and slapped it, sopping, onto the coffee table, displacing the dainty arrangements of pastries Armelle's assistant had laid out.

I made her describe that splattering moment to me over and over. I marveled and cackled every time. "Did you have a feeling," I asked her, "like, *this is the end*? This is the end, so fuck it, I'm going out with a bang?"

She looked at me, surprised. "Not at all! I just thought: this is my moment! *Finally*, they'll hear me! Finally I'll make my feelings known! And once it's out in the open—it'll be great! We can all move forward together!"

This struck me as tragic. I stopped cackling and Liz looked up at me—saw it on my face.

"No, no, no," she said. "I wasn't wrong. I wasn't wrong."

She leaned forward and held my gaze. Something big was coming now—a big *reveal*, we would've called it back in the writers' room. Her face was like a gleeful child's.

"*Marietta is still dying*," she told me. "I haven't stopped. I've been working on her this whole time."

And then Liz laughed, as happy as I'd ever seen her. A large droplet that had formed on her chin shimmered from the laughter and plopped down onto Roger's closed eyelid. The dog raised his head, snuffling but otherwise was too content in Liz's lap to budge. After a moment, he noticed a rivulet streaming down his mistress's forearm and lapped it up with total reverence.

BENEATH THE RUINS

Maxime Raymond Bock

Translated by Pablo Strauss

The heat wave was all over the news and the city smelled like a backed-up sewer. When the traffic ground to a halt, a wheezing from under the hood of Xavier's old Civic made him worry it might be overheating, and he turned off the engine. It was so hot the figurine left on the dash by his niece had melted into a puddle of plastic from which only the tip of a witch's broom poked out. With the windows rolled down and no air conditioning, Xavier too was roasting under the punishing rays of the midday sun. Not one micron of air moved. Fanning himself with the torn flap of a cardboard box salvaged from the junkyard on his car floor only made it worse, hitting his face with excruciating drafts of heat and pungent wafts of whatever lay rotting between the seats—the now flapless box held fried-chicken scraps, the dregs of a latte sprouted fungal growths that stretched fingers toward the light, and a plastic bag left by his niece last week oozed with the sludge of what had once been grapes. Moving his arm made Xavier sweat more, in drops that trickled from his armpits down along his ribs. He had unbuckled his seatbelt when the Turcot

Interchange turned into a parking lot that morning, and could sense that this day would be an ordeal. A band of sweat ran diagonally along his chest. His T-shirt was soaked. He opened the door, less to get the air circulating, as he was well aware the air would do no such thing, than to foster the illusion that he was not trapped in this sauna. What a moron he'd been to paint this old beater black. He could have kept it powder blue. The rust had only returned to claim its due. And, anyway, who even cared about the colour of their car?

To his right, in an immaculate white 4x4 with its windows rolled up, a small family consisting of a husky guy with Oakleys on his forehead, a pony-tailed blonde, and two kids bent over their respective screens, was waiting to get back to the safety of their South Shore suburban home. From time to time Xavier stole a glance in the rear-view at the car behind him, and more specifically at its driver, whom he imagined was pretty, and his age, based on nothing more substantial than her sunglasses. They were similar to his own knock-off Ray Ban aviators. Hers might be real, he guessed, but she didn't look like she could afford them, so he was betting fakes. Her car, like his, was a heap of scrap metal held together by a few coats of paint. The hood wasn't the same colour as the body, and an accident had left her car with a broken left headlight and dented bumper. She gathered her hair up into a loose bun and blew away the strand that fell onto her nose. Behind her, Mount Royal shimmered in the heat. In front of Xavier's Civic, four young people emerged from a red sedan whose back window was almost completely obstructed by luggage, smoking cigarettes to mask the smell of the joint they were sharing. All around, drivers and exhausted passengers were killing time, spilling out of their cars, chatting and cursing the orange cone mafia. The owners of an RV had taken out chairs and a folding table and sat playing cards in the shade of an unrolled awning. Traffic had been rerouted into the wrong lane. To the left lay the shoulder, the parapet and, beyond, the city skyscrapers. Every half hour a helicopter hovered over the gridlock a while, and then flew off in search of other stories. A convoy of three police motorcycles, sirens off but red and blue lights flashing, rolled slowly between Xavier's car and the parapet, and then weaved its way through the cars, indifferent to the smell of weed.

Xavier had been on his way to do some hiking in the Montérégie mountains, though he hadn't decided which one yet, and he'd been planning on pitching his tent in the Eastern Townships. But he'd lost interest, macerating in this traffic jam as his exasperation moved past anger into weary resignation. Why pick the Turcot? When traffic finally got moving again, he'd take the first off-ramp and head back through the city to Rosemont. To pass the time he occasionally turned the key a notch and listened to some music on the radio, his sole option since his niece broke his CD player by jamming coins into the slot. The ads were as inane as ever, the traffic reports weren't improving; nobody was moving, and no one, not even the Ministry of Transportation, could say when they might get moving again, or whether they had been immobilized by a fatal accident or a bridge shedding chunks of concrete. Xavier turned off the radio, determined not to turn it on again, put his key in his pocket, and got out of his car, just to move his legs a little.

He did some stretches, rotated his torso to crack his vertebrae, and tried sitting on the hood, but the metal was too hot. He looked straight ahead, then behind, and even stared off into the interchange's lower reaches where countless flashes of sunlight refracted off the windows of immobilized cars whose passengers had dispersed. Some had gathered next to trucks or buses, to enjoy what little shade these tall vehicles cast as the sun reached a few points beyond its zenith. He couldn't see the cause of the gridlock. They were stuck here under a cloudless sky. There were no ambulances, no firemen, no road crews.

The woman in the car with the broken headlight got out and went over to the parapet to stare out at the city. Over the past couple hours he'd caught glimpses of her in his rear-view—standing behind her car looking for something in the trunk, or talking on her phone or to the people in the car behind her—but this time she was right there, just a few metres away from him. They did have the same glasses. Like him, she had hair so soaked with sweat it looked like she'd just climbed out of a pool. He couldn't even have said what colour it was.

Under normal circumstances Xavier wouldn't have approached her, but these weren't normal circumstances. Thousands of people were stranded in this non-place where none had stopped before, and this unaccustomed density rendered visible things that were concealed at full speed—cracks in the concrete, a plastic bag buried in warm, gooey asphalt, a shoe smashed and crushed a hundred and fifty times a day under flowing traffic, a strip of rubber hanging like a snake's skin from the steel rod connecting two sections of parapet set dangerously far apart. While children ran between the cars and strangers flirted through lowered windows, a group of men off in an especially tight knot of cars began to raise their voices a little, and the helicopter hovered motionless above them like a dragonfly over water, waiting for the next mosquito to leap. Xavier walked over to the woman, so he too could look at the skyscrapers. When they'd been standing in silence so long he thought he'd be better off retreating to his car just to escape the awkwardness, she spoke.

"We'll be stuck here a while. They don't know. They said it on the radio."

Xavier searched for something to say. The metropolis sprawled out in suspended animation, and while it was possible to imagine a hive of activity, from Xavier's vantage point it lay still and empty. A nauseating, organic stench rose up on the roadside, stronger even than the backdrafts from the city sewers. Xavier imagined that once this heat wave dried up the waters of the Lachine Canal, all that it normally concealed beneath its surface would be revealed, from fish carcasses half-buried in the festering silt to bikes, grocery carts, and tires. The police might turn up clues to open investigations. He edged toward the parapet and leaned over to look out below, his face scrunched up against the reek. Twenty metres below, in the deserted worksite, the dump trucks and diggers poised atop their mounds of rubble seemed tiny. The arm of an excavator was resting on the top of a wall, one of a series of staggered quadrilaterals that looked like disinterred foundations. Rusty pipes ran through the heaps of stones and concrete blocks pierced with drainage wells. The girl had also come forward to look. Xavier was still looking for something to say. She beat him to it.

"Know what they're doing down there? It's an archeological dig. Really old stuff, from back before the English came. And they're paving over it all for a new highway. It's kind of our last chance to see what's down there. We should take a look. I'm Sarah, by the way."

Xavier looked at her for a few seconds, startled by her boldness. It never would have crossed his mind to do anything but wait for traffic to start moving. He gazed out at the side of the highway, in search of a way down. To the north, the length they were standing on extended in a gentle curve, then descended by a few degrees under the cloverleaf. Perhaps a couple kilometres to the south, though it was hard to say for sure from this distance, the next off-ramp emerged like an outgrowth covered in stopped vehicles, before tucking back under the deck, only to fold back into the interlaced ramifications further on. A roaring helicopter hovered overhead.

"How are we going get down there? You just said we were stuck here till next week."

She pointed into the distance, beyond the parapet.

"See that, over at the base of the pillars. Some of them have little doors."

"Like an emergency exit?"

"Could be. I don't know. A little closet, maybe an electrical room. I had a look, to see if there was a door up there, or some kind of access, a platform, something.... Not too far off, there's a manhole. I could see rungs through the grid. It might all be connected. Want to check it out?"

Xavier took another look down. Orange cones were scattered around the worksite, which was bordered to the east by a row of porta-potties. Further off in the distance, heavy trucks sat parked. The site was deserted: no workers, no one scoping out the materials, no protesters demonstrating to save the heritage site. A flock of seagulls flew under the highway. He watched them until they broke formation somewhere over Little Burgundy.

"What were you going to do? Before you got stuck here?" asked Xavier.

"Meet some friends and go climbing. In Saint-Hilaire. But now it's too late, I'm not going."

Up to that point, Xavier had done his best not to check her out too closely. Now he noticed her muscular shoulders and prominent triceps. Another strand of hair had slipped out of her bun and was clinging to her neck, wending its way down to her black tank top.

"We don't know each other. You have no idea who I am, or if I'm dangerous. And in the middle of the traffic jam of the century you're asking me to follow you down into a twenty-metre cement pillar. To go see some rocks. From back before the English came."

"You look pretty harmless."

"What if it's locked?"

"We'll come back. Sit here all week till the traffic gets moving."

"Okay. Let's do it. I'm Xavier."

Their clammy palms slipped so the handshake was little more than a clumsy finger grasp. Under normal circumstances, Xavier's pride would have made him do the shake over. Clearly, these weren't normal circumstances. They both laughed at their own awkwardness, and then kissed on the cheeks to conclude introductions. Feeling that this was a moment to embrace the unexpected, coincidence, and maybe even magic, Xavier was already on his way back to his car to close and lock the doors, and rummage through his camping gear in the trunk for his flashlight, needle-nose pliers, multi-head screwdriver, and Swiss army knife. While he was at it he finally did the thing he'd been dreaming of for hours: changed out of his soaked T-shirt and into a technical hiking top, which involved twisting his body to ease the cotton shirt loose from his sticky skin and get it over his head, with his back to Sarah, so she wouldn't see his chest. He wasn't in his best shape since he'd stopped working as a garbage man a few years ago, when the city privatized the service. It was demanding work, requiring stamina and the ability to stomach the stench of trash, but of all the blue collar jobs he'd held, it was his favourite. He'd never been in such good shape.

As he put his T-shirt in the trunk, he noticed the bag of emergency food he always kept, and remembered that, in with the first aid kit, candles, waterproof matches, sardines, and crackers, he would find two litres of water. He asked Sarah if she'd like a drink, then and there. The water was the temperature of warm tea; it was the most refreshing drink of their lives. Then he with his small climbing pack of tools and half-empty water bottle, and she with her rope around her shoulder, powder bag, and a couple of carabiners clipped to her harness, set off together in search of a path to the ruins.

The grill over the manhole Sarah had spotted earlier, maybe 30 cars behind them, wouldn't budge, and Xavier's little tools were no help, but they found another not far from the Civic, a few metres in front of the pot smokers' red sedan. It lifted off easily.

A series of rungs ran down a curved wall, deep into the foundation pit, until they receded into darkness beyond the flashlight's range. The heat in this shaft was even more intense than outside, concentrated like a chimney's blast, and it carried with it an altogether different smell—watery yet sharp, with a hint of rot. Rank, really. Curious onlookers had gathered around them. Xavier took a coin from his pocket and dropped it down the hole.

A few seconds passed before they heard the tinkling of metal—the coin must have hit a rung—followed by the irregular sounds of it hitting the walls. Two drops of sweat fell from Xavier's chin and down in a straight line, without making a plop.

"That smell," he said. "There must be a dead animal down there."

"You chicken?"

Sarah was already clipping her sunglasses to her tank top, tying her rope around a carabiner, kneeling down to clip it to the first rung, adjusting her headlamp, and powdering her hands. She disappeared down the hole. Xavier followed, after attaching his own sunglasses to his collar and doing his best to secure the rope she'd lent him around his waist. He carried his small flashlight between his teeth, which made him drool, and clung fast to the rungs where Sarah had left traces of powder, endeavouring to avoid the spinning rope that interfered with his descent. The view above changed, and Xavier looked up to see a few backlit heads blocking off the circle of blue. Their yells were audible, but so distorted by the tubular concrete chamber that he couldn't understand what they were saying. He was finding it hard to breathe with his headlight between his teeth and his saliva dribbling onto his chin, and so he took a moment to put the light in his back pocket, then continued his descent by feel, sweeping each step in search of the best hold, and then stretching his foot out into the emptiness until it found purchase, which he gingerly tested before transferring his weight. It was getting hotter and hotter in this chimney. The smell was changing: it was now so thick it felt like they were actually climbing down into it, and he kept drooling even though his mouth no longer held his flashlight, an atavistic secretion reflex caused by the fetid air that made him choke and want to vomit. He was starting to feel trapped, the tunnel so narrow he could rest his back against the wall behind him. Responses kicked in that he thought he'd outgrown. The claustrophobia that hadn't bothered him since adolescence made him feel like he might not survive this arduous expedition. He had no idea whether he should turn back or follow it through to the end. He began to worry he might slip. He was soaked down to his socks, and now each rung was covered by the paste formed by his sweat and the powder from Sarah's hands. Xavier wiped his own hands on his damp shorts, on his shirt, and on the concrete wall. He stopped a moment, trying to figure out what it would take to climb back up to the surface right now, when a yell from below—"There's a door down here!"—helped him get ahold of himself.

Xavier's climbing skills couldn't rival Sarah's, and it took a few minutes to reach the alcove she was illuminating with her headlamp. It looked like a cell, one so tiny any prisoner would be sure to go mad. Yet with his feet back on the ground, Xavier felt suddenly free. He undid the knot at his waist and pulled the flashlight from his back pocket and the water bottle from his bag. They did their best not to finish it in two gulps. They'd be baked alive if they didn't get out soon. He looked up. At the end of the tunnel, high above, a small white point. Sarah, headlamp in hand, was examining a strange metal door, a thick hatch out of a science fiction movie. The door harboured a sticker with an indecipherable message and a fleur-de-lys, suggesting the Quebec government, and it looked heavy enough to challenge even the strongest garbage man. Under their footsteps they could hear concrete chips and other unidentifiable debris that must have fallen through the grill over time.

In the centre of the room, on the ground, was another grill, a drain for rainwater, and in the corner there was, indeed, a desiccated animal carcass. The relief of its skeleton could be seen through its ruffled, patchy coat flecked with garbage and dust. The creature had found the entrance, but not the exit. Judging by how its huge scaly tail had been flattened like a Ping-Pong paddle, it looked like this massive rodent had been run over on the highway above and then, like them, come down through the open grill. Sarah, squatting on the ground, examined the mummy by adjusting the angle of her lamp.

"How long have beavers have been extinct around here, you think? Centuries, right?" she asked.

The smell engulfing them was turning acidic, stinging their eyes. Next to the corpse, Xavier saw a coin, and leaned over to pick it up. He thought he'd tossed a quarter. It was a dollar. He picked it up, turned the doorknob, and pushed the door. It opened with no resistance. Light flooded into the alcove. He smiled at Sarah; she smiled back.

"My lucky day," he said, and walked through the door while she undid her harness. The door shut behind him.

In his ten minutes in the shaft he'd grown so accustomed to the gloom that the sunlight hit him like the lash of a whip. He pressed his eyes shut as hard as he could and covered them with his hands. He could feel the heat on his face. The smell had changed. As before, it was pungent, but it now stripped his throat raw, dashing any hope that it might be less concentrated once he got out into the open. The humidity was unbearable, far worse down here than up above. He walked blindly forward, giving Sarah room to open the door, but she didn't seem to be coming. Slowly, he unclenched his hand, and when his sight returned, he noticed that he wasn't in the open air, as expected. Sunlight poured in through a large window in the wall, on the second floor of a sprawling wooden warehouse.

It was hard to believe he could have missed this building from the parapet. He figured the door must lead to a space under the overpass, and the warehouse could be used to store excavating equipment. But in this recess of the warehouse all he could see was an arched entryway over a dirt floor. There was no machinery. His view to the right was blocked by an outcropping of wooden planks, and behind this blind corner men shouted curt instructions that lay somewhere between encouragement and orders. The fear of getting caught gripped Xavier. Site access was surely reserved for the demolition company and civil servants with clipboards and checklists. He nonetheless managed to take a few steps out of the sunbeam to see what lay beyond.

Five metres off, a few men were bent over wooden vats dug into the ground. They stirred the contents with poles and used long metal pincers to pull out what looked to Xavier like wet hides, saturated sheets which were then piled in heaps on a wooden wheelbarrow dripping with a viscous white liquid. The men's dress—billowy blouses with rolled-up sleeves that had once been white, pants held up with suspenders, and crude boots—was both peculiar and too loose for their work, and their splattered, shiny leather aprons were clearly unequal to their task, as they were soaked. The men worked like dogs wrangling the revolting hides. When the youngest, slightest member of the crew, no older than thirteen, lost his grip on the tongs and dropped one of the hides onto the clay beside the wheelbarrow, a brute with abscess-covered arms and neck cursed and shoved him to the ground. Another few centimetres would have sent the youth into the tub. Xavier's reflex to step forward was idiotic—he would have never dared try to reason with these men—but at that moment a cart came in, drawn slowly by a horse swarmed by flies, pulling a load of verdigris hides stacked like blankets and hanging with clumps of fur and chunks of bloody fat, tails, ears, and horned scalps. Two burly men left the tanks to receive it.

What a horse pulling a cart of cattle hides was doing in these ruins in Saint-Henri, Xavier couldn't say, but his gut told him he had no business in this humid warehouse redolent with rotting carcasses, and that he'd made a mistake, and he should have just waited up above in his old car until traffic got moving again, so he turned back toward the heavy wooden door he had come in through, and when he yanked it toward him he found not Sarah but a rough tool shed with shelves full of unfamiliar implements reminiscent of medieval instruments of torture: pincers, curved-blade shears of black iron, bungs, knives, clamps, combs with outsized teeth, and mallets; the whole thing stank atrociously and made him salivate once more. He closed the door and opened it again, but nothing on the other side had changed. He went looking for the metal hatch with the fleur-de-lys, but everything he saw was made of wood. In a panic, he backed out of the corner, stood still, and saw that the cart had reached the part of the warehouse where the hides were unloaded onto trestles to be sheared of ears and tails by two Black men. Then they were tossed into a pile, while other men transported the trimmed hides in little wheelbarrows to a stream that flowed right through the warehouse. At the water's edge, men with long double-sided cutlasses gathered up ever more skins, spread out onto easels to drain off thick, lumpy ooze which pooled onto the ground. A child came by with a scraper and pushed this molasses-like mixture back into the stream.

The husky man who had thrown the boy down earlier noticed Xavier and yelled out.

"Right, Étienne! About time! What's you doing in that gear? In your togs now! We've got to fill the lime bath before Barsalou gets back from town."

The man hesitated, slowed a little. Then he moved faster, and his voice rose a third.

"Mother of—that's not Étienne—who are you, now?"

Xavier took off toward the open double doors the cart had come through. Outside there were no ruins, or piles of gravel or heavy machines, but a dirt road lined by rows of country cottages and pastureland dotted with grazing cattle; above there were no concrete pillars or interchange or helicopters, but a cloudless sky and pounding sun, and Xavier ran with no clear sense of direction, his knockoff Ray Bans tucked into his collar.

After trying to open the door, knocking, yelling, and just waiting for him to open, Sarah had given up. She was now halfway back up the ladder, hurling abuse at Xavier specifically and his entire generation in general. It's not like things were better before. She didn't give a shit about empty gestures of gallantry. But she'd always thought only true degenerates didn't bother holding the door open for the ones who come after.

METCALF-ROOKE AWARD 2020

I am pleased to resume my sponsorship of the Metcalf-Rooke Award for the best Canadian short story in English after a hiatus of some years, and to present my cheque for this year's winner, the unanimous choice of the judges, Kristyn Dunnion's "Daughter of Cups." It is a tough, disturbing, pitch perfect story of life in the slow lane on the shore of Lake Erie. My congratulations to Ms Dunnion.

— Steven Temple, Steven Temple Books

In the tradition of *Comments of the Judges*:

Hey Leon, hey, Leon. Have you had a chance to read through that *Best 2020* stuff yet?

Mmm-hmm. How ya doin'?

Fine.

That neck—thing?

And your knee?

So who...?

Well, there's nothing to talk about, is there?

Right, precisely. That is precisely what I thought.

We are talking about the same story?

That Ohio girl.

She's the one. Live to ride, ride to live.

— John Metcalf and Leon Rooke

CONTRIBUTORS' BIOGRAPHIES

Maxime Raymond Bock was born in Montreal, Quebec, Canada, in 1981. After pursuing studies in sports, music, and literature, he published four books of fiction, of which two, *Atavismes* (Atavisms, Dalkey Archive, 2015), and *Des lames de pierre* (Baloney, Coach House, 2016), were translated into English by Pablo Strauss. His latest collection of short fiction, *Les noyades secondaires*, was published with Cheval d'août éditeur (Montreal) in 2017.

Lynn Coady is the critically acclaimed and award-winning author of six books of fiction, including *Hellgoing*, which won the Scotiabank Giller Prize, was a finalist for the Rogers Writers' Trust Fiction Prize, and was an Amazon.ca and *Globe and Mail* Best Book. She is also the author of *The Antagonist*, winner of the Georges Bugnet Award for Fiction and a finalist for the Scotiabank Giller Prize. Her books have been published in the United Kingdom, United States, Holland, France, and Germany. Coady lives in Toronto and writes for television.

Kristyn Dunnion has published six books, including *Stoop City* and *Tarry This Night*. Dunnion earned a BA from McGill

University and an MA from the University of Guelph. She has worked as a housing advocate to combat homelessness in marginalized communities. A queer punk performance artist and heavy metal bassist, Dunnion was raised in Essex County and now resides in Toronto. www.kristyndunnion.com

Omar El Akkad is an author and journalist. His debut novel, *American War*, has been translated into more than thirteen languages and was selected by the BBC as one of the 100 novels that changed our world.

Camilla Grudova lives in Edinburgh, Scotland, where she works at a cinema. Her first book *The Doll's Alphabet* was published in 2017.

Conor Kerr is a Métis writer, descended from the Fort des Prairies and Lac Ste. Anne communities. He grew up in Buffalo Pound Lake, Saskatchewan, and currently lives in Edmonton, where he works as a part-time magpie interpreter, labrador retriever wrestler, harvester, and educator.

Alex Leslie has published two collections of short fiction, *People Who Disappear* (Freehand), shortlisted for a 2013 Lambda Award for debut fiction, and *We All Need to Eat* (Book*hug), shortlisted for a 2019 BC Book Prize for fiction and the Kobzar Prize. Alex has also published two collections of poetry, *The things I heard about you* (Nightwood), shortlisted for the 2014 Robert Kroetsch Award for innovative poetry, and *Vancouver for Beginners* (Book*hug). Alex's writing has been published in *Granta*, the Journey Prize anthology, and many journals throughout Canada. Alex is writing a novel.

Thea Lim is the author of *An Ocean of Minutes*, which was shortlisted for the 2018 Scotiabank Giller Prize. Her writing has been published by *Granta*, *The Paris Review*, *Globe and*

Mail, and others. She grew up in Singapore and now lives with her family in Toronto, where she is a professor of creative writing.

Madeleine Maillet is a writer, translator, and French Canadian. Her stories have been published in *PRISM international*, *THIS Magazine*, *No Tokens*, *Joyland*, *Matrix*, and anthologized in *The Journey Prize Stories 27* (McClelland & Stewart).

Cassidy McFadzean was born in Regina, graduated from the Iowa Writers' Workshop, and currently lives in Toronto. She is the author of two books of poetry: *Hacker Packer* (McClelland & Stewart 2015) and *Drolleries* (M&S 2019). Her story "Victory Day" was runner up in *PRISM international*'s Jacob Zilber Prize for Short Fiction.

Michael Melgaard is the author of the short story collection *Pallbearing* (House of Anansi, 2020). His fiction has appeared in *Joyland*, *The Puritan*, and *Bad Nudes*. He lives in Toronto.

Jeff Noh, a writer based in Montreal, was born in Seoul and grew up in New Jersey, New York, and Southern Alberta. He is an inaugural UNESCO City of Literature writer in residence in Bucheon, South Korea, where he is completing work on a novel in progress.

Casey Plett is the author of the novel *Little Fish* and the story collection *A Safe Girl to Love*, and co-editor of the anthology *Meanwhile, Elsewhere: Science Fiction and Fantasy From Transgender Writers*. A winner of the Amazon First Novel Award, the Stonewall Book Award, the Firecracker Award for Fiction, and a two-time winner of the Lambda Literary Award, she has written for multiple publications including the *New York Times*, *McSweeney's Internet Tendency*, *The Walrus*, *them.*, *Plenitude*, and others.

Eden Robinson's latest novels are *Son of a Trickster* and *Trickster Drift*. The final novel in the Trickster series, *Return of the Trickster*, is forthcoming spring 2021.

Naben Ruthnum is the author of *Curry: Eating, Reading and Race*, and, as Nathan Ripley, of the thrillers *Find You In the Dark* and *Your Life is Mine*. Ruthnum has won the Journey Prize and a National Magazine Award for his short stories.

Pablo Strauss has translated many works of fiction from Quebec, including Maxime Raymond Bock's *Atavisms* (2015) and *Baloney* (2016). He grew up in Victoria, BC, and makes his home in Quebec City.

Souvankham Thammavongsa's first story collection is *How to Pronounce Knife* (McClelland & Stewart, 2020). Her stories have won an O. Henry Award and appeared in *Harper's Magazine*, *The Atlantic*, *Granta*, *The Paris Review*, and other places.

NOTABLE STORIES OF 2019

Senaa Ahmad, "The Women, Before and After" (*PRISM international*)

Lisa Alward, "Wise Men Say" (*The New Quarterly*)

Kris Bertin, "Mon Semblable" (*Halloween Review*)

Shashi Bhat, "Good Enough Never Is" (*The Malahat Review*)

Jowita Bydlowska, "Penelope" (*The Fiddlehead*)

Steven Heighton, "Notes towards a new theory of tears" (*PRISM international*)

Ben Ladouceur, "Man and His World" (*The Puritan*)

Allison LaSorda, "Satellites" (*The New Quarterly*)

Sadi Muktadir, "Quadruple Bypass" (*Joyland*)

Téa Mutonji, "Property of Neil" (*Joyland*)

Kira Procter, "Mucho Mucho Fun" (*New England Review*)

Eliza Robertson, "The Aquanauts" (*Carte Blanche*)

Natalie Southworth, "The Realtor" (*The New Quarterly*)

John Elizabeth Stintzi, "Coven Covets Boy" (*The Puritan*)

Anne Stone / Wayde Compton, "Antiquing in Vermont" (*PRISM international*)

Kasia van Schaik, "Evening Mood at Schlachtensee" (*Cosmonauts Avenue*)

Martha Wilson, "Binoculars" (*EVENT*)

PUBLICATIONS CONSULTED

For the 2020 edition of *Best Canadian Stories*, the following publications were consulted:

Adda, Bad Nudes, Border Crossings, Brick, Broken Pencil, Canadian Notes & Queries, Carte Blanche, Cosmonauts Avenue, The Dalhousie Review, Electric Literature, EVENT, The Fiddlehead, filling Station, Geist, Grain Magazine, Granta, Halloween Review, Joyland, Maisonneuve, Malahat Review, Minola Review, The Nashville Review, The New England Review, The New Quarterly, Orca, The Paris Review, Plentitude, Prairie Fire, PRISM international, The Puritan, Queen's Quarterly, Ricepaper Magazine, Riddle Fence, Room, 2019 Short Story Advent Calendar, *subTerrain, Taddle Creek, The /tmz/ Review, THIS Magazine, Trinity Review, The Walrus.*

ACKNOWLEDGEMENTS

"Government Slots" by Omar El Akkad first appeared in the 2019 Short Story Advent Calendar (Hingston & Olsen Publishing, 2019).

"The Drain" by Lynn Coady first appeared in *Electric Lit.*

"Daughter of Cups" by Kristyn Dunnion first appeared in *Orca: A Literary Journal.*

"Madame Flora's" by Camilla Grudova first appeared in *The Puritan.*

"The Last Big Dance" by Conor Kerr first appeared in *The Malahat Review.*

"Phoenix" by Alex Leslie first appeared in *Cosmonauts Avenue.*

"If You Start Breathing" by Thea Lim first appeared in *Granta.*

"Victory Day" by Cassidy McFadzean first appared in *PRISM international.*

"Drago" by Michael Melgaard first appeared in *Bad Nudes.* From *Pallbearing* copyright © 2020 by Michael Melgaard. Reproduced with permission from House of Anansi Press Inc., Toronto. www.houseofanansi.com

"Jikji" by Jeff Noh first appeared in *Carte Blanche*.

"Hazel & Christopher" by Casey Plett first appeared in the 2019 Short Story Advent Calendar (Hingston & Olsen Publishing, 2019).

"Your Random Spirit Guide" by Eden Robinson first appeared in *The Fiddlehead*.

"Common Whipping" by Naben Ruthnum first appeared in *Granta*.

"The Gas Station" by Souvankham Thammavongsa first appeared in *The Paris Review*. "The Gas Station" from *How To Pronounce Knife: Stories* by Souvankham Thammavongsa, Copyright © 2020 Souvankham Thammavongsa. Reprinted by permission of McClelland & Stewart, a division of Penguin Random House Canada Limited; Bloomsbury Circus, an imprint of Bloomsbury Publishing Plc; and Little, Brown and Company, an imprint of Hachette Book Group, Inc. All rights reserved. Any third party use of this material, outside of this publication, is prohibited. Interested parties must apply directly to Penguin Random House Canada Limited for permission.

ABOUT THE EDITOR

Paige Cooper's debut collection of short stories, *Zolitude*, won the 2018 Concordia University First Book Prize, and was nominated for the Scotiabank Giller Prize, the Governor General's Literary Award for Fiction, the Paragraphe Hugh MacLennan Prize for Fiction, and the Danuta Gleed Award. CBC, *Toronto Star, The Walrus, Globe and Mail, The Puritan,* and *Quill & Quire* all listed it among their best books of 2018.

ABOUT THE EDITOR